BLACK MONDAY

BLACK MONDAY

A STAN TURNER MYSTERY

by

William Manchee

Top Publications, Ltd.
Dallas, Texas

Black Monday
A Stan Turner Mystery
Volume 6
A Top Publications Paperback Edition

Top Publications, Ltd.

ISBN: 1-932475-08-7

To Lisa Korth
We shared a dream that might yet become reality.

INDEX

1

Collapse

If there was a day of the week I could skip it would be Monday. Clients had too much time to think and worry over a long weekend and by Monday they were often riddled with fear and anxiety. Nearly half of my week's telephone calls from clients came on Monday. But today it wasn't just a few clients who had succumbed to their fears, but the entire population. I got a frantic call from my old client Tex Weller late Monday afternoon. The stock market had taken a nosedive dropping 22.6 percent since the opening bell. Tex was an active trader and often traded on margin. I had advised him against it more than once, but he often ignored my advice.

The press quickly dubbed October 19, 1987 as Black Monday. The market collapse shouldn't have been such a shock as many experts had warned that, after five consecutive years of economic growth, stocks were way overpriced. Unfortunately, most investors were caught up in the glitter and euphoria of the long bull market and didn't think it would ever end. Tex Weller was one of them. Fortunately, I wasn't a stock trader. Not that I wouldn't have liked to invest in the market, but with four kids I spent ever nickel I earned.

If the stock crash wasn't bad enough, banks and

savings and loans were failing left and right—184 banks and 17 savings and loans nationwide. Of course, Texas had the most failures of any state in the union. I blamed President Ronald Reagan for the derailed economy. During his campaign, he had promised big tax cuts and an overhaul of the tax system. A year earlier he had finally delivered on his promise and pushed a tax relief package through congress. The new law lowered individual tax rates dramatically but it also eliminated most tax deductions. In theory it made sense and, in the long run, probably made our tax laws more equitable, but in the short run it totally upset the economy and nearly destroyed the banking and savings and loan industry.

"Can you believe it, 508 points?" Tex moaned. "Jesus Christ, what a disaster!"

"How much did you lose?"

"I don't know—a hundred grand easy."

"Well, the market will come back," I said, trying to sound upbeat. "Don't panic."

"Yeah, but the problem is, I pledged that stock on the Metroplex note. Tomorrow morning I'm going to be getting a call from Fred, my loan officer. He's gonna want some more collateral."

Metroplex Savings and Loan was a local thrift owned by millionaire Donald T. Baker. Baker owned a large construction company that managed to land almost every state highway project in North Texas. Baker was known to have close connections with Congressman Horace Manning and John Potts, Speaker of the Texas House. Several years earlier he had purchased Metroplex Savings and Loan, a local thrift with several branch offices. Speaker Potts and

Congressman Manning were rumored to be part owners.

When Tex decided to invest in a string of nutrition centers, he went to Metroplex Savings & Loan for the funding. They agreed to give him the loan but insisted on some rather onerous conditions. Above and beyond the loan at 3.5% above prime, they wanted a consulting contract whereby Tex's company would pay $3,000 a month to a vice-president at Metroplex Savings and Loan. This was a way around Texas' stringent usury laws, although I doubted it would stand up in court. I advised Tex against the deal but he really wanted the loan and, once again, ignored my advice.

"Wonderful," I said. "Do you have anything to give him?"

"Not really. Everything's tied up."

"Maybe they'll give you some time to come up with some more collateral."

"I hope so. If not, I'm screwed. The assholes will probably call my note. You know what a bunch of greedy bastards they are."

"Maybe not. Why don't you take a few days off and get away from here? That should buy you some time. Hell, the market may bounce back in a couple days."

"Oh God, Stan. What if it doesn't? I curse the day I met Don Baker."

Tex told me how they had met at Baker's daughter's wedding. During casual conversation Baker invited Tex to come visit him if he ever needed a loan. Tex figured he'd get a good deal since he knew Baker, but that's not exactly what happened.

"Well, if you know him, don't you think if you talked to

him he might cut you some slack?"

He shrugged, "Maybe."

Although I tried to be optimistic with Tex, I was sick inside. I didn't have any ready solution for his problem. If the savings and loan called his note, he would be expected to pay the full balance within thirty days. That would be pretty much impossible and mean he'd lose everything. The only other option he'd have would be a chapter 11, but that would be a monumental undertaking with only a slim chance of success.

While I was contemplating Tex's predicament, Jodie buzzed in and said that Derek Donner was there to see me. Derek Donner was my casualty insurance agent. We referred each other business from time to time. Derek was Pakistani but had grown up in South Africa. Consequently, he had developed a slight British accent which the ladies loved. When he called to make the appointment, he had mentioned something about a probate case. I asked Jodie to send him in. She did, and we exchanged greetings and talked a bit before getting down to business.

"I think I'm going to be needing your services," he began. "Remember doing that will for Lottie West?"

"Lottie West. . . . It kinda rings a bell."

"She's the one who was afraid to leave her house. You had to meet me out at her place so she could sign the bloody thing."

"Oh, right. The lady with all the dogs."

"Yes. Why anyone needs thirteen dogs, I'll never understand."

I shook my head. "That wasn't a pleasant afternoon as I recall."

Lottie West lived in an old rundown house on Cole Avenue in Dallas. Even though I loved dogs I felt very uncomfortable at her house. She seemed to be living with a pack of wolves. The place stunk and the dogs leered at us as we walked through the living room to the kitchen table where we were going to execute the will. One of the dogs barked incessantly making it nearly impossible to think, let alone explain the complexities of a last will and testament.

Derek continued, "I went out to collect her premium on a health insurance policy the other day but when I knocked on her door she didn't answer. That concerned me because, as you know, she never leaves her house."

"Right."

"So, I walked around the back yard and it was awfully quiet. I couldn't understand why the dogs weren't barking. When I looked in her back window, I noticed the place was a mess—furniture knocked over, lamps broken, and debris everywhere. I didn't know what to do, so I went next door and asked the lady who lives there if she had seen Lottie lately. She said no and that it had been unusually quiet over there for a couple of days, so we decided to call the police."

"Hmm."

"When the police got there, they forced open the front door and went in. The place was in shambles— drawers pulled out and the contents dumped, cupboards emptied onto the floor, and the place had a god-awful smell. They found Lottie in the hall amongst a dozen dead canines—apparently all victims of a natural gas leak. The coroner said they'd been dead for twelve hours or more."

"Oh, my God," I said. "She was such a nice old lady."

Derek shrugged. "I know. I was really fond of her too."

"Where was the gas leak?"

"I don't know. They hadn't found its source by the time I left. They said it was a wonder the whole place hadn't blown up."

"So, who's the executor of the will?" I asked.

"You are?"

I frowned. "I am?"

"Yes, don't you remember she didn't have anyone to be her executor, so she asked you to do it?"

I took a deep breath. "Gee. She must have caught me in a weak moment. I don't usually take fiduciary assignments."

Some attorneys loved to be appointed the executor of their clients' estates. That meant they could charge both an executor fee and attorney's fees. Sometimes estates were literally plundered by these attorneys. I considered it unethical, a conflict of interest, and would only agree to it if there was no other alternative. And if I did agree to it, it would be understood that I would only charge for my time spent and expenses incurred. Even under these circumstances it was still a bad idea. I had no particular expertise in business or finance nor the time to give it the attention that would be expected.

"As I recall you weren't thrilled with the idea and suggested a relative or bank, but Lottie said she didn't trust banks and had no relatives, so you agreed to do it."

"Wonderful," I said. "So, did she have any property other than her home?"

"There's fifty thousand dollars in insurance proceeds, so you won't have to work for nothing," Derek replied. "I don't know if she had any other assets."

"Thank God for small favors. . . .Well, the first thing we need to do is get some security for the house. There are a lot of thieves who work the obituaries. While the family is at the funeral, they clean out the house."

"Speaking of funerals, where do you want them to take the body after the autopsy?" Derek asked.

"What? Doesn't the family take care of that?" I asked.

"Usually, but in this case, there is no family."

"You gotta be kidding. I can't believe she doesn't have a single relative," I said.

"Apparently not. She made the SPCA the sole beneficiary of her estate and made you put in all those provisions to provide for the care of her dogs if she died?"

"Right. I vaguely remember that now. Who would have figured they'd all die together."

"I know. What were the odds of that?"

"Will you help me inventory the place after the funeral?" I asked.

"Sure. No problem."

After Derek had left, I looked at my calendar and saw I had one last appointment for the day. It was with a Robert Huntington and was scheduled for later in the day at 4:00 p.m. I buzzed Jodie and asked her who he was. She said she didn't know but that Mo had referred him. That aroused my curiosity as Mo was with the CIA. Several years earlier he had disclosed that startling information to me after I had completed his bankruptcy. He indicated the Agency would be sending me other agents who needed their credit card debt discharged, but that I wouldn't know who they were. I wondered why this time he had alerted me to the fact that he had referred Mr. Huntington to me. It had to mean that this was a special case.

At 4:00 p.m. Jodie brought Mr. Huntington into my office. He was a tall, lean, somber-looking man, with wire-rimmed glasses, and a short military type haircut. Jodie offered him a cup of coffee but he looked like he needed a drink.

"So how do you know Mo?" I asked.

"Mo? Oh, well, my company does a lot of exporting, so you've got to have connections in the government to be successful."

"Oh, really? I didn't know that."

"Yes," he nodded, "to export to some countries you have to . . . you know . . . pay off certain people. The Agency helps us out in that regard."

I frowned. "Really? How do . . . I mean, what do they do, tell you who to pay off?"

"Right. Who, how much, delivery—that sort of thing."

I shook my head. "That's amazing. I never realized our government provided that kind of service."

Huntington shrugged and gazed out the window. There was an awkward moment while we sized each other up. Finally, I took a deep breath and said, "So, what can I do for you?"

"I need to retain you to deal with a little situation I have."

"Really. What's that?"

"The IRS has garnished one of my bank accounts. I've got to have the money released by Friday, so I can wire transfer $150,000 to our . . . our Beijing office. If I don't wire transfer it by Friday, my partner—" Huntington swallowed hard, then looked away again apparently struggling to control his emotions.

"Your partner will what?"

"Be arrested—maybe killed."

I just looked at him for a brief moment bewildered at what I was hearing. His hands were shaking.

"Why would he be arrested?"

"I can't be more specific . . . you know . . . for security reasons. The less you know the better."

"I see. . . . Okay, why will—what's your partner's name?"

"Luther Palmer."

"Why will Mr. Palmer be arrested? And why would you be *sending* money if you're the one *selling*—what do you sell anyway?"

"Grapefruit mostly."

"Grapefruit?"

"I can't tell you anymore, unless you agree to represent me and I can depend on the attorney-client privilege."

He was right. Unless he retained me, there was no attorney-client privilege. I assumed by the remark that I had passed his scrutiny and he was prepared to hire me. The question was, did I want to represent him? It would definitely be an intriguing case, but I had no idea if I could even help him. I needed more information. I wasn't good at turning down work anyway, since I was by nature an optimistic person and wanted to help whoever walked through my door. But this attitude had got me in trouble in the past and I had vowed to be more careful. In the end, I succumbed to my inherent weakness and said, "Okay, but you'll have to sign a fee agreement. I guess you know lawyers are expensive."

"Yes, I know. You're not the first lawyer I've had to hire."

"Good. I charge $150 an hour and I usually require a retainer. Is that agreeable?"

"Sure, but with all my money being tied up in this garnishment, I can't give you a retainer right now."

I took a deep breath and replied, "Well, okay. You can write me a check for the retainer and I'll cash it when we get your money freed up—although I can't guarantee that we'll be able to do that. If we're unsuccessful, you'll have to figure out another way to pay me anyway. I don't do contingencies."

"I understand. I'll pay you somehow. Don't worry. But I have to try to get the account released. I don't have any other choice."

I pulled out my standard fee agreement, filled in the blanks and handed it to Huntington. He signed it immediately without reading it and handed it back to me. Then he wrote out a check and gave it to me.

"Okay. It would be a lot easier if I knew more about your business. I don't do much international law, so I'm not sure exactly how the export business works."

"Like I said, I'm not at liberty to go into any details. It's not relevant anyway."

"But now I'm your attorney. You can tell me everything."

"Not really. This is a matter of national security. You don't have the proper clearance."

I just stared at Huntington. I hated working in the dark but I figured it was too late to back out now. Huntington's rigid expression didn't change. He looked like a man you didn't want to cross. I wondered what had I got myself into?

"Right. Well, I'll talk to the Revenue Officer and see if I can convince him to drop the garnishment. What kind of taxes do you owe?"

"They say my corporation owes $1.5 million in income taxes."

"Whoa! That's a lot."

Huntington shrugged.

"They sent me a bill for $1.5 million but it's not right. The company didn't make any money. In fact, we lost money on the deal."

"What deal?"

Huntington looked around suspiciously. "Okay, I'll tell you this much. The money I have to wire is off the radar. I've been paid for the grapefruit and now I have to wire $150,000 back to a certain government official. If I don't, he will have Luther arrested and probably kill him. I had to leave Luther back at our offices as collateral."

A chill darted through me. This was some serious business Mr. Huntington had gotten himself into. Although it was a fascinating case, I felt a little overwhelmed and didn't really know what to do. Reversing an IRS garnishment wouldn't be easy and there was so little time—not to mention the whole question as to the legality of what Mr. Huntington was doing.

"It's not easy to get a garnishment released. It normally takes weeks or months to even get a hearing. I'm not sure I can help you."

"The IRS thinks I'm evading taxes. If we can somehow let them know that I'm working for the CIA this whole thing might go away."

"Why can't you talk to your friends at the CIA and have them get the word to the IRS?"

"The CIA has disavowed any knowledge of what I'm doing?"

"I don't understand," I said. "Why would they do that?"

"There were other things besides grapefruit in the shipment."

I just stared again at Huntington. "Listen. This may be out of my league. I don't practice international law and I can't be involved in anything illegal."

"Listen, Mr. Turner. You're my last hope. I don't have time to get another attorney. Mo said you could handle this. Just contact David Barton, the Revenue Officer responsible for the garnishment, and tell him he's interfering with a CIA operation."

"I'll do that," I replied, "but he's not going to take my word for it, nor would that necessarily make any difference anyway."

"Don't worry about that. I've got a person he can call to verify my story."

This was blowing my mind. I hated things going on that I didn't understand and Mr. Huntington was a complete enigma. What were the CIA and he up to and was he really telling me the truth?

"I thought the CIA was disavowing any knowledge of what you were doing." I asked.

"The person I'm referring to is not with the CIA. He's a politician. That's all I can tell you."

My neck was beginning to stiffen and I felt the onset of a headache. My instinct was to stand up, thank Mr.

Huntington, and respectfully decline the employment. But Mo had sent him and I presumed the CIA was working for the good of the country. I wondered if I should just go along with what they apparently wanted me to do. . . . The thought also occurred to me that if I refused, there could be repercussions as well.

"Who's the politician the IRS can call?" I asked.

"Horace Manning?"

"The congressman?"

"Yes, he's a friend. He'll verify that I've been working behind the scenes for the government."

Huntington gave me the garnishment papers and left. I looked at the check he'd written to the firm. It was drawn on Metroplex Savings & Loan. How ironic, I thought. I fell back into my chair angered that I hadn't been strong enough to turn down the case. As I was thinking, my partner Paula Waters walked in excitedly.

"Did you hear the news?"

"Yeah, the stock market crashed."

"No, not that. Donald Baker and his girlfriend Amanda Black were murdered?"

"Donald Baker?"

"Yeah—like in Metroplex Savings & Loan."

"You're kidding," I said. "Tex and I were just talking about him."

"They haven't arrested anyone yet, but I talked to Bart and speculation is that his son-in-law, Jimmy Bennett, did it."

Bart was an assistant DA at the Collin County District Attorney's office. Paula had worked with Bart in the past and they were friends as well as occasional lovers. She routinely called him for inside information.

"What makes them think that Jimmy did it?"

"He worked at his father's construction company. Apparently, they've been feuding lately and Saturday morning, Donald threatened to fire him for the fourth or fifth time. They almost got into a fist fight right then on the spot."

"Sounds like Donald Baker finally got what he deserved."

"What do you mean?" Paula asked.

"I didn't know him personally, but Tex has told me a few interesting things about him."

"Like what?"

I told her about the consulting contract Tex was forced to sign.

"I'm sure his lawyers drafted it so it was technically legal."

"Maybe so, but I've also heard he lends a lot of money to his friends and they don't have to sign consulting contracts or put up collateral for their loans."

"Well, it's all about *who* you know, right?" Paula said.

"How were they killed?" I asked.

"They were found in bed together early this morning with their throats slit."

"Where did they find them?"

"In the company condo. Baker and his girlfriend were seen dining at Sal's Italian Grille on Greenville earlier in the evening. I guess Amanda lives in the condo and they retired there for the evening. They think the murder took place Monday between 12:00 and 1:00 a.m."

"Hmm. . . . So, who's defending Jimmy?"

Paula looked at me and winked. I instantly knew the answer to my question. *She* wanted to defend Jimmy

Bennett and now she expected me to make it happen since I knew Tex and Tex knew Jimmy. Technically it was unethical to solicit business, but this particular canon of legal ethics was under attack as being in violation of federal antitrust laws and wasn't strictly enforced by the State Bar.

"Okay. I'll give Tex a call. Maybe he can make it happen."

A broad smile came over Paula's face. She said, "I knew I could count on you. Thanks, Stan." Then she turned and went back into her office.

Later that afternoon I called Tex about Jimmy Bennett. He said he'd just got off the phone with Jimmy's brother and that Jimmy hadn't retained an attorney as yet. I told him, if he got a chance, to drop Paula's name as a possible choice. He said he would.

After hanging up I started working on a real estate contract. The next time I looked up it was five-thirty. I quickly packed up my briefcase and headed home. Rebekah was putting supper on the table when I strolled in. She looked up and smiled.

"Oh, just in time. Dinner is ready."

"Good, I'm starved. Just give me a minute to get out of this suit. I'll call the kids."

Rebekah nodded and I continued on to the base of the stairway. I could hear the kids talking upstairs.

"Come on down! Chow time," I yelled.

"Daddy, daddy," Marcia yelled and came bounding down the stair. She jumped into my arms and gave me a big hug. Mark and Reggie followed her close behind.

"Where is Peter? " I asked.

"On the computer," Reggi said.

I had given the kids an old Apple IIe to play with and it was hard to pry them away from it, even for dinner. I yelled up to Peter again and he finally came running down the stairs.

"Hi, dad," he said.

I said, "Supper is ready."

After I had changed into a T-shirt and a pair of jeans, I joined everyone at the kitchen table. The Six O'clock News was in progress on the kitchen TV and the reporters were talking about the stock market crash.

"Did you hear about the stock market?" Rebekah asked.

"Yeah, I did. Tex called and told me about it. He lost $150,000."

"Oh, my God!" Rebekah exclaimed.

"Did you lose any money, Dad?" Reggi asked.

Rebekah laughed.

"No, I don't invest in the stock market."

"Why not?"

"Because you kids cost me so much money. I'm always broke."

"Mark got an "A" on his science project," Rebekah said.

I looked at Mark and smiled. "That's great. What did you write it on?"

"Acid rain," Mark replied.

"Hmm. Interesting. I'll have to read it," I said.

"It's on the coffee table in the living room," Rebekah said. "There's a letter from Father Bob too. They need money for the new women's shelter. If they don't raise $100,000 from the parish they'll lose their matching funds and have to scrap the project."

"Well, write him a check?" I said.

Rebekah smiled. "I don't think a hot check will do them much good."

"It's the thought that counts, right?"

"No, I think they want hard cash."

After dinner, the kids went upstairs and Rebekah and I settled down on the living room sofa for a night of leisure. I was telling Rebekah about Lottie West's death when my attention was drawn to the television where the Six O'clock News was in progress.

"First Lady Nancy Reagan is reportedly doing well after undergoing surgery for breast cancer earlier in the week. Doctors are optimistic about her chances of a full recovery. She is expected to go home to the White House on Thursday.

"On Capitol Hill democrats pledged today to continue to push the investigation into accusations that President Reagan authorized the illegal diversion of proceeds from arms sales to Iran to the Contra Rebels fighting Nicaragua's Marxist government. This action was taken despite denials by Colonel Oliver North and Rear Admiral John M. Poindexter of any knowledge or involvement by the President.

"In related news, the U.S. Navy today attacked an Iranian oil platform reportedly being used to launch missiles against U.S. ships in the area."

Rebekah said, "There was a plane flying over town today pulling a sign that read, 'We Love You Ollie.'"

I laughed. "Oh, really? Huh. Well, this is Collin County one of the most conservative counties in the country. I'd imagine old Ollie would have a lot of supporters here."

"I'm glad you're not in the Marines any more."

"You and me both. Can you imagine serving your country for fifteen years and then suddenly having to take a fall to protect the President?"

Rebekah shook her head and said, "His poor wife. She must be so humiliated."

I nodded. "I had another interesting case come in today,"

"Really. A busy day, huh?"

I nodded and started telling Rebekah about Robert Huntington and his frozen bank account. She couldn't believe it.

"Couldn't his partner go to the American Embassy for protection?"

"I don't know.   They probably have him under surveillance and if he tried to get there, they'd stop him."

"What are you going to do?"

"I have to get the IRS to release the account. There's no other way."

I told her about Horace Manning who was supposed to put the fear of God into the IRS.

"I've heard about him," Rebekah said. "He's a congressman, isn't he?"

"Right, from East Texas, but I doubt he'll be able to get the money released. Congressional interventions take time."

Rebekah gave me a sympathetic look. I forced a smile. How I could possibly get the account released in such a short time I didn't know, but with someone's life at stake it was a time for some creative thinking and lots of prayer.

2

The Plan

After Stan and I successfully defended Dusty Thomas, we were the talk of the town and I was quickly inundated with work. Dusty Thomas had been accused of murdering an IRS agent and looked guilty since he had been found standing over the agent's body with his shotgun in hand. It had seemed like an impossible case and we probably shouldn't have taken it on, but Dusty had been a long-time client, so Stan didn't feel he could abandon him. Since Dusty, years earlier, had been a tax protester, organizations like the CDC and the Texas Militia got involved in the case ensuring lots of media attention. Needless to say, the government aggressively prosecuted the case to protect its primary revenue source. They even attacked Stan and I and called us traitors! But somehow it all worked out and Dusty was acquitted. Unfortunately most of the cases coming in now were routine DWI's, possession charges, and domestic violence cases—nothing very challenging. That's why I was so excited about the Baker murder. That was the kind of case I wanted and since Stan had a connection to the prime suspect through Tex, why not go after it.

My plan worked like a charm. Around 8:30 a.m. on Tuesday I got a call from Jimmy Bennett's brother, John Bennett. He told me Jimmy had been arrested and that he wanted me and Stan to represent him.

On the news the previous night, I had learned that Jimmy Bennett was the construction superintendent for Baker Construction Company and had pretty much run the company since Don Baker bought Metroplex Savings and Loan several years earlier. The two men had been very close since Jimmy married Don's daughter, Betty. None of the TV stations knew what the argument was about, but they all agreed Don had threatened to fire Jimmy.

The double murder had gone nationwide due to the fact that a CEO of a major thrift was involved. I asked John if he knew of his brother's whereabouts on the night of the murder. He indicated he didn't have a clue.

The Dallas County Courthouse was surrounded by media trucks when I arrived. I avoided them by parking underground and entering the building from the underground tunnel. When I got out of the elevator, several reporters spotted me and rushed over.

"Miss Waters. What are you doing here? Have you been retained by Mr. Bennett?" the first reporter asked.

"Yes, I have. That's why I'm here," I replied.

"Why do you think he killed them?" another reporter asked.

"I'm sorry. I have no comment at this time. I haven't even met with him yet," I said as I pushed my way past the reporters and into the small waiting room. I approached the deputy at the desk who I knew very well from my days working for the DA's office.

"Hey, Joe," I said.

"Hi, Paula. Who are you here to see?"

"Jimmy Bennett."

Joe raised his eyebrows. "Well, I can't let you see him quite yet. He's still being processed."

"Listen, Joe. I've been retained by the Bennett family to represent him and I want to see him now. I don't want anyone interviewing him without me being present."

"I'm sorry, Paula, but I was given strict instructions—no visitors until after 10:30 a.m."

"How long have you had him in here?" I asked.

"He checked in about 8:45 a.m."

"Then you've had enough time to book him and process him into the jail. Who's been assigned the case?"

"Rob Wilkerson."

The name sent a chill down my spine. Although I had never met him, he had a reputation as being a male chauvinist and a first-class asshole. I had heard stories about him often demeaning and berating the female assistant DA's that he was forced to work with, so I could just image how he was going to treat me, his adversary.

"Call him and tell him I'm here and I'm pissed off. I want to see my client now!"

"Okay, don't get your panties in a wad. I'll call him."

"Thanks," I said forcing a cheery smile.

Fifteen minutes later Joe informed me that Jimmy Bennett was in booth number three. I found it, opened the heavy door, and took a seat. Jimmy sat across from me separated by a thick glass window. He was a tall, slim man of about thirty-five years. He had dark hair, blue eyes, and a handsome face. We communicated via a telephone and, even though we were less than two feet apart, the connection was terrible.

"Jimmy. I'm Paula Waters. Your brother hired me to represent you."

He nodded.

"They say you killed your father-in-law and his girlfriend Amanda Black."

"Amanda's dead too?" he said sinking back in his chair and rubbing his forehead. He looked genuinely shocked. "Jesus. I can't believe it."

"You obviously didn't do it, then?" I said.

"No. Of course not. I may have been pissed off at Don but I wouldn't kill him. And I liked Amanda. She was a good friend." His voice broke. "I had no reason to kill her."

"Good. Where were you last night between ten and daybreak?"

He took a deep breath trying to regain his composure. "Out driving."

"Driving? . . . Alone?"

"Yes, alone. I didn't feel much like company. When I'm upset I usually just take off and drive. The open road calms me down."

"Did you see anybody or talk to anybody during the night?"

"No, I stopped at a convenience store in Gainesville. The clerk might remember me. I bought a cup of coffee and some cigarettes. . . . You don't have a cigarette, do you?"

"No, sorry. . . . Did you use a credit card?"

"No. Cash."

"Too bad," I said. "Do you know the clerk's name?"

"No, but she was there alone, so you can find out her name from the owner of the store. She was from India or Pakistan—a young girl—not a day over 25."

"I'll check it out."

"Good. If I had known Don was gonna get his throat slashed, I'd of made sure I had an alibi," Jimmy said with a grim face.

"Right. Has anyone interrogated you yet?"

"Yes Detective John Perkins did about an hour ago. What a prick."

I nodded. "What did you tell him?"

"Pretty much what I told you—I just got in my car and headed for Oklahoma City."

"Why Oklahoma City?"

"No reason. When I take off, I just start driving and end up wherever I end up."

"Where were you arrested?"

"At my house. The police were waiting for me when I drove in the driveway."

"Well, at least they didn't get you on your way out of state. That could have made it difficult for you to get bond."

Jimmy shrugged. "I didn't do anything, so I had no reason to run. When I saw the police, I got scared. I thought something had happened to Betty."

"They must have some other evidence. They wouldn't arrest you unless they did. Are you sure you didn't go by the condo last night?"

He glared at me. "Yes, I told you I went to Oklahoma City."

"Okay. Do you have any idea who might have killed Don and Amanda?"

He shrugged. "Don, sure—Amanda, no. I'm sure she was killed simply because she was there and would have been a witness."

"So, who do you think did it?"

"Oh, God. It would take a week to compile a list."

"Right. Well, I'll need you to do that just as soon as you get out of here."

"Sure, no problem. Just get me out of here and bring some damn cigarettes when you come next time. I'm dying in here."

"I'll do that. . . . Okay, then. Your arraignment is at 11:00 a.m. Hopefully the judge won't set your bond too high. Don't talk to anybody from now on, okay?"

"No, ma'am."

"Your brother is doing the paperwork for your bond right now, so we should be able to get you out of here pretty quick."

"Good. This isn't a very healthy place to hang out."

"Yes, I know. Just be patient. It won't be long now."

The deputy told me Judge Wingate had been assigned to the case. He was a large man with a wide curly mustache. Some of the attorney's called him "the Walrus" which he resembled when he walked. The Walrus was known for his generally calm, deliberate disposition, and everybody I knew liked him. But he occasionally got mad and when that happened everyone just prayed they weren't the subject of his displeasure.

I called John Bennett and told him to meet me in the courtroom at 10:30 a.m. with the bondsman and character witnesses we had lined up. I assumed the bond would be ready with the exception of filling in the amount. By eleven o'clock the courtroom was packed with spectators and the press.

Rob Wilkerson and his assistant were at the prosecution table. It was the first time I had seen Wilkerson, so I gave him a hard look. He was medium height, had dark hair, and was impeccably dressed. If I hadn't known him by reputation, I'd have probably thought he was an attractive man. I figured that was how the jury was going to see him. He would be a formidable adversary. At two minutes past eleven the bailiff brought in Jimmy. When Judge Wingate entered everyone rose.

"Be seated," he said and then began sorting through a stack of files. Finally he looked up. "Okay, Mr. Wilkerson, what do you have for me?"

"Well, Your Honor. We have Jimmy Roger Bennett accused of two counts of capital murder. The victims were his father-in-law, Don Thompson Baker, and a lady friend, Amanda Black. The victims were asleep when their throats were slashed."

The judge nodded and then looked at me. "Miss Waters. How does your client plead?"

"Your Honor. Mr. Bennett pleads *not guilty* and we respectfully request a reasonable bond. We have several witnesses ready to testify that Mr. Bennett is a respected member of the community, a family man, property owner, and that there is absolutely no flight risk."

"Absolutely no flight risk?" the judge said. "There's always a flight risk Miss Waters—particularly in a murder case. I'll set bond at $250,000 and Mr. Bennett will need to surrender his passport."

"Thank you, Your Honor," Wilkerson said. He looked

over at me and grinned. I forced a smile and turned to Jimmy.

"Okay, we've got the bond arranged. We'll be over in a few minutes to get you out. Jimmy nodded and the bailiff took him away.

Thirty minutes later we escorted Jimmy out of the jail and drove him back to our office to talk strategy. Stan and Jimmy's wife Betty joined us in the conference room. Jodie got everybody coffee or a cold drink before we got started.

I began. "I know it's been a difficult day but we need to take care of a few formalities right away and work up a game plan for the future. These types of cases move pretty fast so we don't have any time to waste."

Stan went over the firm's fee agreement and asked for a $50,000 retainer. Betty opened her purse and pulled out a checkbook. She wrote the check, gave it to Stan, and then everyone signed the agreement. With that out of the way we discussed strategy.

I said, "Obviously, our task for the next few months is to try to find out who killed Don and Amanda. We do that and Jimmy is off the hook. Have you had a chance to work on that list of persons who you think might have wanted to see Don dead?"

"No, not yet."

"I'm going to need it soon."

"Okay, I'll get it to you."

I continued. "If we can't prove someone else killed them, then we at least have to create reasonable doubt. I think you are all probably familiar with that concept if you watch much television or go to the movies."

Betty nodded and said, "What do you think Jimmy's

chances are?"

I shrugged and said, "We can't give you odds. There are too many variables and I don't have enough information yet."

Stan added, "If he's innocent and doesn't have to lie about anything, then his chances should be pretty good. Our system of justice isn't perfect but it usually works pretty well."

"What Stan and I are going to have to do over the next few months," I said, "is to thoroughly investigate Don Baker, Amanda Black, Baker Construction, and Metroplex Savings and Loan. In order to do that we'll need to talk to each of you in depth and interview all your employees, friends, and business associates. It's going to be a tremendous undertaking and will be extremely time consuming and tedious. Before you leave, Jodie will schedule an appointment for each of you with Stan or me over the next two weeks."

"What about the funeral? Can I go with Betty?" Jimmy asked.

I looked at Stan. He shrugged. "Sure, you're presumed innocent until proven guilty, so you have every right to be at Don's funeral. Some family members may not like it, but that's too bad."

"We'll all be at the funeral," I said. "The killer will most likely be there too, so I want everyone to be very observant and report any strangers you might see, all right?"

Everyone nodded.

"Then that's all for now unless anyone has a question," I said.

Betty lifted her hand. "What about the press?"

"Keep your mouth shut for now," I replied. "No interviews and do not discuss the case with anyone."

"Especially you, Jimmy," Stan added. "Don't discuss the case with anybody because whatever you say, even in private, may be used against you in court."

He nodded. "Right."

After the meeting Stan and I got a cup of coffee and went back into the conference room to map out our investigation plan. We both knew it was going to be very difficult to defend Jimmy since he had an obvious motive to kill Don and no alibi.

"Well, are you happy with your new case?" Stan asked.

I smiled and nodded. "Yes, as a matter of fact I am. I'm really looking forward to digging into it."

"I wish I felt that way. I feel like someone just strapped a giant boulder on my back."

I shook my head. "Stan, come on. You're an old pro at this."

Stan laughed. "Right. . . . So, do you really think Jimmy is innocent?"

"Yes, I do. He seems very honest and straightforward about everything."

"Well, I hope you're right," Stan said.

"Me too. I'd hate to lose."

"So, are we going to hire a private investigator or investigate this ourselves," Stan asked.

"Let's just do it ourselves for now," I replied. "Later on we might need some help, but for now I'd like to personally talk to each witness."

"Okay," Stan said. "Why don't you let me handle

Metroplex Savings and the Bakers and you can concentrate on Baker Construction and the Bennett family."

"That's fine," I said. "We can compare notes every few days."

When we were done brainstorming about Jimmy Bennett, Stan briefed me on his meeting with Robert Huntington. He told me he'd been referred by his CIA friend Mo and that Huntington had been very secretive about his company, Continental Exporters. Stan was fearful that Continental Exporters might be involved in something unlawful.

"Well, he has a right to hire an attorney to represent him before the IRS. As long as you don't know of any continuing illegal activity you should be okay."

"I don't know squat. That's what's bothering me."

"Just do your job and don't ask questions. I have to do that all the time when I represent some of my lowlife criminal clients."

"I know. It just bothers me being someone's pawn."

I shrugged. "So, did you call the Revenue Officer?"

"Yes, I did, but he hasn't called me back. You know how hard it is to make contact with them. He could be on vacation or off somewhere on temporary assignment. I only have a couple days to get the garnishment released or Luther's partner will be arrested or maybe even murdered."

"So, what are you going to do?" I asked.

"If I don't get a call back soon, I'll have to talk to his supervisor, but he's not going to be familiar with the case at all. If I only had more time."

"Can you file something in federal court?" I asked.

"Sure, but it would take weeks to get a case filed and

get a hearing."

"Hmm. I don't know what to tell you, Stan. I guess you'll just have to keep trying to get in touch with the agent."

"I guess so."

3

Garnishment

David Barton at the IRS didn't return my call on Tuesday, so at eight a.m. on Wednesday I called him again. The message on his answering service said he was in town but was tied up and would get back to me shortly. I couldn't wait any longer so I called the number for the supervisor in charge for that day. His name was Anthony Perez.

"I have an urgent matter to discuss with Mr. Barton. Will he be in today?"

"I think so. He's out in the field right now but he should be back later this afternoon," Perez advised.

"I don't have much time. I've got to talk to him today."

"What's the urgency?"

"You've garnished my client's account and captured a sizeable amount of money. He has to have $150,000 tomorrow or face dire consequences."

"Well, once we capture funds we don't give them back."

"I know that may be standard policy but there are unusual circumstances here."

"Maybe so, but you'll need to talk to David about that. I can't do anything without talking to him first and finding out his position on the issue."

"Well, have him call me the minute he gets back in,

would you?"

"I'll put a note on his desk."

That usually meant I'd get a call back in a week. I wondered if it was time to do some name dropping. Huntington had given me the name of Horace Manning to verify his CIA story.

"Really. This is very important. It involves a matter of national security."

"National security?"

"Yes, my client is Robert Huntington. His company is called Continental Exporters. You can verify the urgency of the situation with Congressman Horace Manning."

There was a moment of silence and then Perez said, "All right, Mr. Turner. Agent Barton will get right back to you."

It appeared that Agent Perez indeed knew the congressman. I wondered how he fit into this bizarre case. Twenty minutes later Jodie buzzed me and to let me know that David Barton was on the line.

"I got a message you called," Barton said.

"Yes, I represent Robert Huntington. He advises me that you have garnished his company's bank account."

"Let me see. Yes, that would be Continental Exporters. . . . Let me see, according to the bank we've captured enough to pay the entire liability."

"So, I've heard. But the fact is, I need to see if there is any chance you might release the account. The money you captured doesn't really belong to Mr. Huntington. He has to wire it to a third party by Friday."

"What are you talking about? The money was in a Continental Exporters' bank account and its tax identification number was on the account, so it clearly did belong to them," Barton replied.

"True, but the money was just in the account pending disbursement to the rightful owner."

He laughed. "That doesn't make any difference. Your client had legal custody over the money, so there is an absolute presumption that it was their money."

"You don't understand. We are not dealing with ordinary businessmen here. If these people don't get their money, they will get violent."

"What people?"

He had me there. I didn't really know the answer to that question. "Ah. . . . The rightful owners of the money are Chinese and they don't take kindly to being stiffed. They won't just sue my client, they'll want blood."

"Oh, come on. Don't you think you're over reacting a bit?" Barton said.

"I wish I were. But my client expects that his local agent will be kidnaped and possibly murdered if the money doesn't show up in the account on Thursday."

"I'm sorry, that's not my concern."

"What about Manning? Did you talk to Congressman Manning?"

"No, I didn't. What does he have to do with this?"

"I'm not sure, but my client seemed to think you ought to talk to him."

"I've got a call into him, but I can't imagine he would have anything to say to me that would alter my stance on this issue."

I obviously wasn't getting anywhere, so I decided to go back to a more direct approach to break the logjam. The fact was I had no idea why the Continental Exporters' account had been garnished. A garnishment meant that taxes hadn't been paid. Perhaps if I explored the source of the tax liability I might find a solution to the problem.

"So, what kind of tax liability do we have here anyway?"

"Income tax—over a quarter of a million dollars. Continental Exporters hasn't filed a tax return since it started doing business."

"So, you've just estimated the tax liability?"

"Right."

"Based on what information?"

"Bank records. Your client runs a lot of money through its accounts."

"So, if the tax returns were actually filed and showed no tax liability, would you release the garnishment?"

"Maybe. If you could convince me that the tax returns were correct."

"So, you need 1985 and 1986?"

"Right."

"Okay. Let me try that angle. In the meantime, try to get a hold of Manning."

"Hey. I've got a call into him. If he calls me back, I'll talk to him."

It didn't appear that Mr. Barton liked Manning very much. After I hung up with Barton I called Huntington to see why he hadn't filed the Continental tax returns and to see if maybe we could get them filed quickly. Unfortunately, he didn't answer and I had to leave a message on his voice mail. I prayed he'd check his messages soon because time was running out for his partner.

4

Money to Burn

On Wednesday, after getting my nails done and having a quick massage, I went to see Jimmy Bennett. Stan couldn't make it as he was at Lottie West's funeral. I hadn't had an opportunity to talk to Jimmy since he had gotten out of jail and we needed to get started on his defense immediately. While civil cases tended to drag on and on, criminal cases usually were put on a fast track as society demanded swift justice and defendants were entitled to a speedy trial. He agreed to meet me at the corporate headquarters of Baker Construction Company located in Las Colinas.

The Baker Construction Company offices took up two of the nineteen floors of the plush Williams Square complex. I parked my BMW in the garage next to the building and took an elevator to the seventh floor. The offices were ornately decorated with original oil paintings and sculpture depicting the American West. I marveled at the collection. The receptionist said Jimmy would be right with me. I took a seat and waited. Five minutes later Jimmy showed up and took me back to his office. I sat on a big leather sofa and Jimmy took a seat in a side chair across from me.

Jimmy's spacious office was neat and tidy and his big natural wood desk was as clean as any I'd ever seen. As hard as I looked, I couldn't find a lick of dust anywhere. It was clear that Jimmy was not your usual cowboy.

"Quite a place you have here," I said. "You've got some pretty impressive pieces of art."

"Yes. They're part of my father-in-law's private collection—works by Paul Kane, Herbert Dunton, Charles Russell, and Thomas Moran plus some Indian art as well. He accumulated them over the past thirty years. Every piece is an original."

"Really," I said, thinking how valuable the collection would be today—more motive for murder.

Jimmy, sensing my mental calculations, looked at me, smiled proudly, and said, "The collection has been appraised at $1.1 million."

I raised my eyebrows, smiled, and replied, "It's a shame Don won't be around to enjoy it."

Jimmy shrugged and then our eyes met. He smiled but didn't say a word. He wasn't a bad looking man but I wasn't the least bit attracted to him. His stare was beginning to bother me, so I looked away and said, "Well, we've got a lot of ground to cover so we better get busy. I guess the first thing I'd like to know is what you and your father-in-law were fighting about."

Jimmy shrugged, took a deep breath, and replied. "Well, the truth is I just got fed up with his shit."

"Fed up?" I asked.

"Taking orders from him. Doing all his dirty work. You wouldn't believe the shit he was in to. You know, there's just so much a man can take."

"What do you mean? What dirty work," I asked. "You're going to have to be very explicit. Remember. I don't know anything about you or your father-in-law."

"Right. Well. . . . Shortly after marrying Betty, Don insisted I go to work for him. Since I worked construction, it was only natural that I went to work for BC."

"BC?" I asked.

"Baker Construction."

"Right."

"He hired my brother too. He said he liked family in the business because you could always trust family, right?"

I nodded and pulled a notepad from my purse.

He continued. "Don and I hit it off pretty well and before I knew it I was a crew supervisor. After work, he'd often come get me and my brother and we'd hit a few bars together. Even though I would have preferred to go home to Betty, he'd insist we go out to clubs—strip clubs mainly."

"Really?" I said. "He wasn't protective of his daughter?"

"No," he laughed. "He bought me prostitutes."

"Really," I said, shaking my head in disbelief. "And you went along with it?"

He shrugged. "Reluctantly. I felt lousy about it, but what could I do? He was my father-in-law and my boss."

"Okay, go on," I said.

"Anyway, he paid Betty and I a lot of money—"

"Betty worked for him too?"

"Not really, but she still got a paycheck—$500 a week."

"How much did you get?"

"$1,500 a week plus expenses. Don was making a lot of money and he was used to throwing it around. When we went to a strip club, he would always bring a wad of fifty-dollar bills. The girls knew him and when they saw him coming they'd flock to him. We'd often take a couple girls home with us to the condo."

"The condo where the murder took place?" I asked.

"Yeah, the company owned it. We used it for private parties or for guests to stay at."

"What kind of guests?"

"Friends, customers, potential investors, politicians—you know—anybody Don needed in his pocket.

"I see. So, you'd take your guests and the girls there and—"

"Party, smoke a little marijuana, you know, whatever we felt like."

"How often did you do that?" I asked.

"A couple times a week," Jimmy replied. "Amanda lived there during the day. Don stayed with her at night."

"So, Amanda was a steady girlfriend?"

"Yes, an expensive steady girlfriend. He paid for her apartment, provided her a new Mercedes, lots of jewelry, and an allowance."

I'd heard stories of corporate executives living this way, but I had never actually met someone involved in that kind of game. It sounded like fun, but obviously was a very dangerous way to live.

"Wasn't Don married?" I asked. "How did he get away with doing all this?"

"Margie, his wife, is a zombie. He could have brought Amanda home and done-her on the living room sofa while Margie was watching TV and I doubt Margie would have noticed."

I laughed. "How long has Amanda been his girlfriend?"

"A year or so."

"And Margie didn't know about her?"

"Seriously. She is blind and deaf—or at least pretends to be. I guess, when you have so much money to spend, it's easy to get distracted. Most of the time she was at Buffalo Ridge anyway."

"Buffalo Ridge?"

"Yeah, the company has a thousand-acre ranch near Abilene—The Buffalo Ridge Ranch. She spends a lot of time there with her horses and their trainer."

"Their trainer?"

"Earl. Earl Modest. It's never been a big secret that she and Earl were lovers. She tries to act like she's the faithful wife, but everyone knows the truth."

"What did Don think about Earl?"

"He was glad she had Earl. Earl kept her out of his hair."

"I see."

I didn't see. It all sounded pretty screwed up to me, but I figured I'd sort that part of the story out later. Right now, I wanted to find out what happened on the day of the murder and Jimmy seemed to be avoiding the question.

Okay, so you were fed up with the mandatory weekend carousing with your father-in-law. Is that what you were arguing about?"

"More or less. Don had some people coming in from Washington and he wanted me to wine and dine them, take them to a club, get them drunk, and then take them to our condo."

"What people?"

"Potential investors who supposedly could bail out

Metroplex."

"So, you didn't want to take them out?"

"No, the feds were snooping around and Betty was getting sick and tired of me supposedly working every night. She wasn't as oblivious to the world as her mother. She suspected there were other women and she was beginning to get a resentful attitude. I figured if I didn't take a stand, my marriage would be over."

"Okay—"

"Besides I'm thirty-five years old with three kids that I love. I was becoming an alcoholic and half the time I couldn't remember what I had done the night before."

Jimmy stood up and went to the window. He looked toward DFW Airport. A big American Airlines Jet was gliding in for a landing. I could understand how he might be fed up with his life, but there was obviously more to his sudden attitude change—there had to be.

"So, when you told him that, I take it he didn't like it?"

"No, we argued and he said I was an ungrateful son of a bitch. He threatened to fire me. I wanted to beat the shit out of him, but out of respect for Betty I didn't touch him. I just left and took a drive to cool off."

It sounded like a plausible story but I wasn't sure it was the truth. If Jimmy was about to get fired, it was convenient that Don was killed before that happened. With Don gone Margie would likely turn the business over to Jimmy to run. Then Jimmy would have all that money to throw around. It sounded like a pretty good motive for murder.

5

The Funeral

Rebekah and her mother volunteered to do all the arrangements for Lottie West's funeral. I was greatly relieved as I didn't like funerals. I guess that was because I'd only been to two funerals in my entire life—my father's and my aunt Helen's. Both of their deaths haunted me. For years all my father talked about was retiring and traveling around the country with my mother. But shortly after his 65th birthday he developed cancer of the oesophagus and travel was out of the question. For the next six months, we watched him slowly starve to death.

My aunt Helen had lived near us when I was a child. I spent a lot of time with her, playing tennis, going to movies, and just hanging out. When I was about ten years old she developed dementia and had to come live with us since she couldn't be alone anymore. I loved her and it was difficult for me to watch her slowing losing her mind.

It was a perfect day for a funeral. The sky was clear, the wind was still, and temperature was a pleasant sixty-three degrees. The service drew a respectable crowd of twenty-five souls paying tribute to a mysterious woman whom they knew nothing about. As three vocalists led us in *Rock of Ages,* I wondered about Lottie West. Who was she? What had happened to her friends and family? And why had she died alone?

After the funeral, Rebekah, Derek, and I went to Lottie's home to do an inventory of her property. The house reeked of natural gas, dog odor and was in such disarray that we considered abandoning the venture and hiring someone to do it. But after a few minutes we got used to the smell and started rummaging through Lottie's property.

"I'm going to see if I can find any records," I said. "Rebekah, why don't you take a legal pad and start making a list of what personal property she has."

"Okay," Rebekah said, grabbing a legal pad from my briefcase.

"I'll check out the house—see what's working, what's not," Derek said.

"Good," I replied and headed for the bedroom.

Lottie's bedroom was in much better shape than the rest of the house. She apparently had kept the dogs out of her room. I was glad to discover this, as the thought of her sleeping with a dozen dogs was unsettling. I noticed several family photos on a desk. The first was a man in a full-dress Army uniform who looked to be in his early 30s. He was tall, fair skinned, and handsome.

The second photo was a family shot of Lottie, the tall stranger, another woman and two children—a boy and a girl. I sat down and started going through each drawer one by one. In the bottom drawer, I found a stack of envelopes held together by two rubber bands. When I picked up the stack, the rubber bands broke and the envelopes scattered.

"Shit," I said and then heard a dog barking and growling in another room.

"Ahhhh! Stan!" Rebekah screamed from the kitchen.

I jumped up and ran into the kitchen. A skinny black dog had Rebekah penned in the corner. It was pacing back and forth and growling at her.

"He's going to bite me!"

Cautiously I approached the dog and said, "Just be still, honey. He won't hurt you. Will you, nice doggy?"

I eased myself between Rebekah and the dog. The dog continued to growl and bare his teeth. Then the back door opened and Derek walked in. Seeing the opened door, the dog bolted for it and was gone. Rebekah breathed a sigh of relief.

"Where did *he* come from?" I said.

"Somebody shut him in the closet, I guess," Rebekah replied. "When I opened it, he ran out. Scared the livin' crap out of me."

I couldn't help but laugh.

 "It isn't funny," Rebekah said, still shaking.

"You're lucky he didn't take a bite out of you. By my calculations he hasn't eaten for at least three days," Derek noted.

"How did he survive the gas?" Rebekah asked.

"And how about the crime scene crew? I can't imagine how they could have overlooked him," I said.

Derek walked over to the closet where the dog had emerged. He turned on the light and looked inside. "There's a hole," he said.

I walked over and looked over Derek's shoulder. There was a passageway big enough for a dog or a child to go through. "It must lead to the crawl space under the house," I said.

"Maybe we should check it out," Derek suggested.

"Why?" Rebekah said. "There's probably nothing under there but rats and spiders."

I smiled. "Probably, but there may be other dogs trapped in there. I suppose we should take a look."

"Let animal control do it," Rebekah said shuddering. "I don't like the idea of either of you going under this house. This place gives me the creeps."

"Don't worry, I'll get a flashlight and take a look from the outside before we go in," I said ignoring Rebekah's protests.

"I've got one," Derek said. "I'll go get it."

Derek left to go get a flashlight and I went outside to look for a way into the crawl space. In the backyard, I found a wooden door that led under the house. When Derek came back with the flashlight, I kicked the door open with my foot and shone the light inside. There didn't appear to be anything under the house but some old paint cans and a lot of cobwebs. Then I noticed a red cooler over in a corner.

"Somebody left their Igloo under here," I said.

"Probably the plumber—had a few beers while he was working," Derek surmised.

"I doubt it. He'd have taken it with him. I think I'll crawl under there and see what's in it."

"No!" Rebekah moaned. "Don't go under there. Come on. It's just a stupid cooler."

"Oh, don't worry. Derek will keep the flashlight on me."

I crawled through the hole and carefully made my way to the cooler. The cobwebs were thick. I prayed that none of them had been spun by the infamous brown recluse spider which was common in North Texas. Their bite was deadly. When I got to the cooler I tried to pull it around so I could open it, but it wouldn't move.

"I don't know if this is just heavy or it's caught on something," I said.

"You want me to come help," Derek asked.

"No," I said as I finally got the cooler to move. "That's weird," I said, noticing the cooler was padlocked.

"What?" Rebekah asked.

"It's got a padlock on it. I guess somebody took their beer drinking seriously."

After I had towed the cooler out from beneath the house with much difficulty, we all stood over it wondering what was inside. Since we didn't have a key, Derek went back to his car for a tire iron. When he returned, he stuck the narrow end of the tire iron under the lid and pried it open. The old plastic gave way without much of a battle. As the contents of the cooler came into view, Rebekah exclaimed, "Oh, my God!"

We all stared into the cooler in disbelief. It was filled to the brim with gold and silver coins. Derek said, "Well, look at that little stash. And I was worried about having enough money to pay for her funeral."

"I wonder what all that is worth," I said.

Derek knelt down and picked up a handful of the coins. They were a mixture of old silver dollars, gold pieces, and other coins that I didn't recognize.

"Thousands—maybe hundreds of thousands. Some of these coins may be pretty rare."

"What are you going to do with them?" Rebekah asked.

"Inventory them and then get an appraisal," I replied. "I guess I'll have to get a safety deposit box too."

"We better check this place out very carefully. No telling what else Lottie may have stashed around here," Derek said.

We continued our search of the house all afternoon but found nothing but a lot of books on art history. Apparently, Lottie West had been an art lover. The final shock of the day came when I got back to my office. Detective Besch of the Dallas Police Department had called. He wanted me to know that Lottie West's death hadn't been accidental. The gas had been intentionally injected into the house from the gas furnace through the heating and air condition ventilation system.

I wondered why someone would murder an old lady who lived alone. Then it dawned on me why she had so many dogs. She was scared, needed protection, and a good alarm system in case whoever was looking for her got too close. Unfortunately, dogs were as susceptible to natural gas as humans. I wondered how much the killers had stolen after they killed her. There was obviously a lot I didn't know about Lottie West and needed to find out to protect the estate from further looting.

6

Surprises

After meeting with Jimmy Bennett, I was anxious to talk to his wife, Betty Baker-Bennett. She would obviously have a different perspective on the conflict between her father and her husband. I wondered how she would be taking her father's death and whether she thought her husband could have killed him. She agreed to meet me at her spacious home high upon a hilltop looking over Lake Lewisville. As drove up I-35 from Dallas, I noticed a storm was brewing to the West. In fact, it was getting so dark I had to turn on my headlights. Several press vehicles were parked at the front entrance to the estate. The reporters milling around watched me as I showed my credentials to the gate attendant and he waved me in. It was another half mile to the main house where I parked my car and waited until precisely 9:00 a.m.

I looked in the mirror to make sure my lipstick hadn't smudged, grabbed my umbrella just in case the brewing storm let loose, and walked to the front door. I knocked and a minute later Betty opened the door and invited me in. She was a friendly, darkly tanned brunette about 5'1" in height. She wasn't the type of person I would have expected to be married to Jimmy since he was more than six feet tall. I pondered a second on how that would work in bed. . . . Anyway, she wore sky-blue pedal pushers and a short yellow top which seemed rather cheery considering she'd lost her daddy just days before. She showed me around her house and then led me to a sun room where she had coffee and pastries for us to munch on while we talked.

"I'm sorry about your father. I appreciate you taking the time to talk to me during what must be a difficult time for you."

She shrugged. "You have to do your job. I understand. I want to help in any way I can."

"I appreciate that. It must be difficult to be around your husband knowing he might be responsible for your father's death."

"I don't believe it for a minute. Jimmy didn't kill my father. I'm absolutely sure of that."

"Why are you so sure?"

"Jimmy's a lot of things, but he's not a murderer. Anyway, he loved daddy just like I did."

"Really?"

"Yes. I don't have any brothers, just a younger sister, Margo. Daddy always wanted a son. When I started dating Jimmy in high school, Daddy kind of adopted Jimmy as his own son. They went fishing, hunting, and played golf together. It was pretty sad actually, since I had to compete with my father for Jimmy's attention."

I wondered if she had intentionally left bar-hopping and picking up loose women off her list, but I didn't ask. "Wow. That would be difficult," I said.

"Daddy just assumed I would marry Jimmy—not that I

didn't want to marry him. I love Jimmy and we have three great children. We've been together for nearly ten years now. When you've been with a person that long, you get to know them."

"Sure, so you don't think he had anything to do with your father's death?"

"No. It must have been a business associate or one of his customers at Metroplex. God knows he had plenty of enemies."

"Really? What kind of enemies?"

"Metroplex was in trouble. Examiners from the OTS were out there every day."

"OTS? Let's see. That's the—"

"Office of Thrift Supervision."

"Oh, right."

"They're like the FDIC."

"Uh huh."

"They demanded the board of directors put another two million dollars of capital into the business. Many of the board members blamed daddy for Metroplex's problems."

"I can understand why the board would blame him, but why would his customers be angry with him?"

"The examiners reviewed every loan and if they didn't think there was adequate security or if the paperwork wasn't perfect they'd require it be fixed within ten days. If the problems couldn't be fixed in that time frame, they'd make daddy call the note."

"Oh, boy. That would make a customer angry."

"Yes. I can't tell you how many poor souls daddy had to put out of business. He read me some of the letters he received. It was pretty scary."

"Can you think of anyone in particular who was angry with your father? Did anyone threaten him?"

"There's a file at the office where he kept all the hate letters. He liked to show them to his friends when they came in to visit him."

"Really? Why?"

She shrugged. "I don't know. He would jokingly say that if he ever got knocked off, we'd only have to check out the alibis of the customers who'd sent him hate mail."

We looked at each other intently for a moment. We must have both been thinking the same thing. Was the murderer's identity in the hate mail file? "I doubt the person who killed your father would be dumb enough to send a letter threatening him," I said.

She nodded. "My thoughts exactly. It would be too easy."

"Nevertheless, I'd like to see that file," I said.

She nodded again, "No problem. I suppose you'll be going over to the office to interview the staff."

"Right. I'll need to do that."

"Just have Ruth, Don's secretary, find it for you."

"Ruth?"

"Ruth Rutherford. She's actually my aunt—my mother's sister. She's been dad's secretary for years."

Despite Betty's insistence that her husband was innocent, I had to discuss the possibility that he might have killed her father. I wasn't sure how to lead into that question, but eventually figured there wasn't any easy way to do it.

"You know. The police will be probing deeply into Jimmy's life to try to prove him guilty. In order to defend him I've got to know everything—personal as well as business."

She sighed. "So, where do we start?"

"Tell me about your relationship with your husband. I've heard that you were unhappy with Jimmy's long hours and . . . and—"

"Infidelity? Is that what you're trying to say?"

"Right. I'd heard—"

"That he had a mistress stashed up at the condo?"

"No. I hadn't heard that. Did he?"

"No. Daddy did, but not Jimmy. I'm sure he screwed around a time or two, but it didn't mean anything. He's an attractive guy and the women flock to him."

Betty didn't sound so sure that it was just a time or two, but I didn't question her assessment of the situation. She was being remarkably candid and I didn't want that to stop.

"I understand your father encouraged it?"

She took a slow deep breath and twisted her neck slowly around in circles apparently trying to relieve the stress she must have been feeling. Finally, she said, "Yes, he did." She confirmed what Jimmy had told us earlier that her father insisted Jimmy be his drinking companion. She denied knowing any of the details of their escapades, but only that Jimmy was gone most of the time and she was sick of it.

"So, when did Jimmy get home that night?"

"Late. I went to bed at midnight. I was asleep when the police came at about 12:30 a.m. I told them he wasn't home so they left, but they apparently left one patrol car down the street to wait for Jimmy to come home. I had no way to warn him. They arrested him a little after 6:00 a.m. in the driveway right after he got out of his car. I didn't even get to talk to him before he was taken away."

"What did he tell you the next day when he was released on bond?"

"He told me about the fight and said he'd taken a drive to cool off. I told him he should have come got me. I would have kept him company." She confirmed the story Jimmy had told us pretty much verbatim. I wondered if it had been rehearsed. The thought occurred to me that Betty might have a lot to gain by her father's death too. I wondered if he had a will. Surely the chairman of a major thrift would have a detailed estate plan. I needed to know who stood to gain by Don's death.

"Did you father have a will?"

She nodded, "Yes, and a trust—a living trust, I think."

"Really. Who's the trustee now that your father is dead?"

She didn't answer right away. Her eyes glazed over like she was in deep thought.

"Is your mother the trustee?"

My question jerked her back to the present. She shook her head. "No, I'm the trustee. Mom can't balance her checkbook."

I didn't say anything. At least Jimmy wasn't the trustee. That would have really put a nail in his coffin. I couldn't help wondering though, if both of them were working together to hide the truth. They had plenty of motive and apparently no love for dear old dad.

After a couple of hours, I had exhausted my welcome and knew it was time to leave. There was a lot more to learn about Betty and Jimmy Bennett, but it would have to wait for another day. "Well, I've got to be in court at one, so I better get going," I said and stood up and began packing my briefcase to leave. I looked up, smiled at her, and continued, "I appreciate you taking the time to fill in all the blanks. It's very important that I know everything if I'm going to effectively defend your husband. If you think of anything else that I should know, give me a call, would you?"

Our eyes met as I started to leave. She forced a smile. I sensed she had something more to say. I braced myself for I knew it couldn't be good by the look on her face. She took a deep breath and said, "There is one other thing apparently Jimmy didn't tell you. You're gonna find out anyway, so I better tell you now."

"What's that?" I said and then held my breath.

"I filed for divorce last week."

My heart sank. "Oh, my God!"

We talked a few more minutes about the pending divorce. I could feel Betty's agony as she talked to me. She said she told Jimmy about it the same day her father had been murdered. Obviously, the filing of the divorce was what prompted the argument between Jimmy and Don. What they argued about exactly, I didn't know, but I assumed Jimmy had blamed the destruction of his marriage on his father-in-law. I asked Betty if there was any hope of reconciliation. She said all the lonely nights had taken their toll. She didn't think the love she had once felt toward Jimmy could ever be rekindled.

I thanked her and showed myself out. As I stepped out the front door, I was awed by the light show in progress. Frequent burst of lightning illuminated the turbulent waters of Lake Lewisville. Miraculously it hadn't started to rain yet. There was a big jet drifting through the clouds on its final descent into DFW Airport. I watched it for a moment thinking about Jimmy and Betty and how turbulent their lives had suddenly become. They had been given everything a person could ever want in this life, yet they never found happiness, and now they were both alone. I got in my car and drove off feeling sad, not because I felt sorry for Betty, but because I knew all about loneliness.

7

Late Return

It was Thursday before I got another call from Tex. The week had been hectic so far with two funerals, Huntington's predicament, and the beginning of another major murder case. Jodie indicated he was on line three. I picked up the phone and Tex immediately began complaining about Metroplex.

"So, did you work something out with them?"

"Shit no. I just got a letter. They've called my note, the bastards."

"Oh, God. I'm sorry, Tex. Damn it!"

"Now what am I going to do?"

"What happened to the money from Ecuador?"

I was referring to $900,000 dollars Tex had pocketed from a scam he had pulled off in Quito, Ecuador the previous year that had nearly got us both killed. While I was on vacation in Colorado, Tex had wired $1.8 million dollars into my trust account without any explanation. At the time Paula and I were defending a man accused of killing an IRS agent and, accordingly, were under close scrutiny by the feds. When they discovered I had received $1.8 million dollars from Equador via the Cayman Islands, they jumped to the conclusion that I was connected somehow to a guerilla organization in Equador. Even though Tex hadn't received the money honestly, the FBI had no proof of that and didn't want it to end up in the hands of the guerillas, so they let him keep the money.

"A lot of it went down the tubes on Monday. The rest I invested in the business. I'm broke, Stan. There is no way in hell I can pay off that note."

"What about some of your business partners, can't they help you out?"

"They all took a good hit on Monday too. I've talked to most of them and nobody is in a position to help me out."

"I wonder if maybe you could move the note?"

Tex shook his head. "That would take some time. I doubt I could pull it off even if I found a bank that was actually lending money right now."

Tex was right. It was unlikely he could move the loan with banks and savings and loans falling like rocks in a landslide. The idea of chapter 11 was sounding better and better. We discussed it again and for the first time Tex seemed interested in the idea. Chapter 11 was difficult and expensive but it would force the bank to continue to carry the note for a while. Down the road, after the stock market rebounded and the banking system had been stabilized, Tex could find new financing for his venture and take Metroplex Savings and Loan out of the equation. Tex said he would seriously consider this option knowing, at the very least, that he could buy some time and save himself from complete financial ruin.

After Tex had hung up, Jodie advised me that Robert Huntington had arrived to work on his tax returns. I had finally gotten hold of him and suggested we get his company's tax returns done to see if it really did owe the IRS all the money that they claimed it did. Jodie showed him in and he took a seat. He didn't look happy.

"So, did you find all your records?"

"Such as they are. A lot of what we need is at our other office."

"Well, can't you call your partner and have him give us the numbers over the telephone?"

"I guess. But do we have time?"

I shrugged. "I don't know, but I don't see any other way. The IRS isn't going to release the garnishment and we don't have time to go to court to try to get the money freed up. This is really our only hope."

"I can't believe they are doing this after all I've done for this damn country. Did they call the congressman?"

"Yes, but Barton didn't seem impressed when I dropped his name."

"Did he talk to him?" Huntington asked.

"He hadn't yet. He said he would."

"Well, we've got to get him to talk to Manning."

"Why don't you call Manning and have him call Barton?"

"I can't do that. There can't be any contact between me and Manning."

I sighed. "Well, let's get to work on those tax returns. It could take us all day to get them done. Then we have to file them with Barton and convince him that they are accurate and that Continental Exporters doesn't owe the IRS any money."

Huntington opened his briefcase and started stacking papers on my desk. After we had worked on the tax returns for several hours, it appeared there wasn't going to be any taxes owed as the company had actually lost money both years. I thought it was time I called Barton and arranged for a meeting. I told Jodie to get Barton on the line. She did.

"Listen, we've just about got the Continental Exporter's tax returns done and wanted to make arrangements to file it with you. I think when you see them, you'll agree nothing is owed and will want to release the funds."

"Yeah, well. I can't just drop everything for your client, Mr. Turner. I'm booked up until next Thursday. You'll have to wait until then."

"You know we can't. A man's life is at stake here."

"You keep saying that, but I'm not buying it."

"Did you talk to Manning?"

Barton didn't answer right away. Finally, he said, "No, we've been playing telephone tag."

"Try him right now, would you? This is important and he could clear things up for you."

He laughed. "I don't see how."

"Just call him. I'll hold."

I took a deep breath and whispered to Huntington, "He's calling Manning right now."

Huntington nodded and replied, "Good."

There was what seemed like five minutes of silence and then Barton came back on the line.

"All right. I think I understand your predicament a little better now," Barton said. "Why don't you come in tomorrow morning at 8:00 a.m.? I'll squeeze you in before my nine o'clock meeting."

I gave Huntington thumbs up and then thanked Barton. He cautioned that he wasn't making any promises, but that he would take a look at the returns and make a decision at that time. Huntington was relieved but still was quite anxious. I knew there was a lot he wasn't telling me and I had no idea what Manning had told Barton, but whatever it was it did the trick. We worked another couple hours on the returns. Huntington had to make a few calls to his partner to get some of the missing information we needed. Finally, a little after five o'clock they were finished.

"Well, we did good," I said. "Continental Exporters did lose money both years as you suspected. That should satisfy Barton.

"I hope so. I've got to get that money freed up tomorrow."

"Keep your fingers crossed," I said smiling. "It won't be long now."

Huntington left with the understanding that we would meet the next day at Barton's office in the Earle Cabell Federal Building in downtown Dallas. I was feeling very good about what we had accomplished, however, we still had one problem. A lot of the backup and supporting documentation for the return was at the other office. Whether IRS would accept all our numbers without seeing the backup was a question mark. Normally when a return was filed the IRS would accept it at face value. Later on, if it were selected for an audit, the numbers could be challenged or backup could be requested. In this case, however, with the money already garnished, they might want to audit the returns immediately. This could take time and delay the release of the money. I didn't want to alarm Huntington, but realistically if he got his money the next day it would be a miracle—or by the grace of Congressman Manning.

As I was contemplating the situation, I heard voices. Jodie had already left so I assumed Paula was still there. I got up and walked into her office. She and Bart were in the middle of a passionate kiss. "Oh, sorry," I said, making a quick U-turn.

Paula broke away from Bart and said, "No. It's okay, Stan. Bart was just leaving."

Bart smiled and gave me a wave. I nodded.

"I'll see you later, stud," Paula said.

"Right. Later," Bart replied and made a hasty exit.

"I'm sorry," I said, embarrassed I had interrupted them.

"Don't worry about it. I was just feeling kind of sad and lonely after interviewing Betty Bennett today."

Paula filled me in on her interview.

"I wonder why Jimmy didn't tell us about the divorce?" I said.

"I don't know, but it kind of makes you think he's hiding something," Paula replied.

"I suppose we better assume we can't believe anything he tells us."

Paula nodded. "I'll start digging around and see if I can corroborate what he's told us so far."

"Good. You headed home?"

"Yeah, dinner, a little wine, and a warm body are just what a girl needs when she's sad and depressed."

I frowned. "So, why are you so sad and depressed? You got the big murder case you wanted."

Paula took in a deep breath and then rolled her eyes. "Right. I've got everything a girl could ask for. Have a great night, Stan. I'll see you tomorrow."

She grabbed her purse and left. If she was trying to

lay a guilt trip on me, she had succeeded. I felt badly that I couldn't be more to her than a partner, but she knew my situation when she signed on. I just prayed she'd fall in love with Bart or find someone else and give up on me. Until she did that it was awkward and a bit dangerous being around her.

8

Settling Down

On Friday morning, I didn't want to get up. I saw that it was nearly 7:00 a.m. and time to get ready for work, but I felt so warm and content next to Bart, I didn't want that feeling to come to an end. Finally, guilt overcame me and I vowed to get out of bed. Bart had one arm around me so I couldn't move without waking him. Finally, I gently lifted his arm and squeezed out from underneath it. He stirred but didn't wake up. The cold morning chill on my naked body made me shutter. I walked quickly to the closet, grabbed a robe, and then headed to the kitchen to make a pot of coffee.

When I got back to the bedroom, Bart was up and taking a shower. My efforts not to wake him apparently had been unsuccessful. Taking advantage of the opportunity, I dropped my robe and joined him in the shower. He was glad to see me. We made love under a stream of steaming hot water. It was definitely a very refreshing way to start the day.

Neither one of us had time for breakfast, so we grabbed a couple breakfast bars and left about eight. As I drove south on Preston Road, I couldn't help but think how nice it was waking up next to Bart. I wondered whether he had enjoyed it as much as I had. I had never considered settling down with anyone ... except Stan, of course. Was it time to face reality and move on? As painful as that thought was for me to contemplate, I had to face reality. Stan wasn't destined to be my lover, as much as I wanted it to be. Bart was a good man and we were quite compatible. Maybe it was time to give our relationship a chance to move to the next level. It might be just what we both needed to bring some joy in our lives. God only knew we could both use some of that.

By the time I got to the office I had convinced myself that I needed to chart a course in that direction. I'd very subtly suggest that we might want to live together awhile just to see how it worked out—no commitments—just an experiment. Men usually hated commitments, so my plan seemed perfect. I couldn't wait until evening to see how he reacted to it.

When I ran into Jodie, she informed me that Stan wouldn't be in until noon as he had an appointment at the IRS office with his new client Robert Huntington. I was a little disappointed because I wanted to tell Stan about my new plan. I wondered how he'd take it. After organizing my desk and planning my day, I left to go to Baker Construction to meet with Ruth Rutherford, Don Baker's sister-in-law. There was a lot of traffic on LBJ Freeway so it took nearly an hour to get to Las Colinas. As I approached Williams Square I marveled at the herd of bronze horses galloping across the courtyard. They were so well crafted by the artist who had sculptured them that they appeared almost alive. I regretted that I personally had no artistic talent whatsoever.

Once inside, I announced myself to the receptionist. Jimmy Bennett came out to say hello. He was in a good mood laughing and flirting with one of the receptionist. I took the opportunity to ask him why he hadn't mentioned the divorce to me. That sobered him. He didn't have a good explanation. We talked a minute longer and then he led me to Ruth's office. She was an attractive middle-aged woman with dark hair and big brown eyes. The years had been good to her or she had found a good plastic surgeon, I wasn't sure which. We all chatted a moment and then Jimmy left us alone.

"So, how has everyone around here been taking Don's death?"

Ruth shrugged and replied, "Well, actually Don hadn't been spending a lot of time here since he acquired Metroplex Savings. He's pretty much left everything to Jimmy. Consequently, his death hasn't affected business that much. There's a lot of turnover in this industry anyway, so there was only a handful of the employees who knew Don very well."

"I see. Were you here last Saturday?"

"Yes."

"Did you witness the altercation between Don and Jimmy?"

"Part of it. I heard them arguing and, of course, stopped what I was doing so I could listen."

"Did you know that Betty had filed for divorce?"

"No. Not until Jimmy told Don that during the argument. I was shocked to hear it."

"Tell me what you heard them say?" I asked.

Ruth took a deep breath then replied, "Don was telling Jimmy about some potential investors who were coming into town to inspect the bank. Don had to come up with two million dollars in cash in a hurry or the OTS was going to shut them down and declare it insolvent. When Don asked Jimmy to pick up the investors from the airport and take them out on the town, Jimmy refused."

"Really. How did Don react to that?"

"He was very angry. He wanted to know why Jimmy wouldn't do it. Jimmy told him that he was through getting whores for him. That's when the news of the divorce came out. I don't think Jimmy had intended to tell him, but it just came out in the heat of the moment."

"So, then what happened?"

"At first the news shocked Don and he didn't say much. But then he started berating Jimmy. He told him he didn't blame his daughter for wanting a divorce. He told Jimmy he was an ungrateful leech who'd be living on the street had he not married the bosses' daughter.

"Jimmy responded with a few obscenities and then pushed Don. At this point Jimmy's brother John and a couple other employees interceded preventing the confrontation from escalating into a fist fight."

"I understand Jimmy left immediately after the altercation?"

"Yes."

"Did he say anything to you or anyone else before he left?"

"He talked a couple minutes with his brother and then stormed out. I heard the tires on his Dodge Ram squeal as he left the parking lot."

"Did Don leave at the same time?"

"No, he worked a little while longer in his office before he left. I put a couple calls through to him."

"Who did he talk to?"

"He called Congressman Manning who was his contact man for the new investors. I don't know what he told him. Then his girlfriend called."

"So, he didn't make any attempt to conceal his relationship with his girlfriend?"

"No, my sister knew about it. She put up with it because Don felt so guilty about what he was doing that he gave her whatever she wanted. She could travel anywhere, buy anything, and see anybody she felt like. It was a pretty sweet deal for her—at least she thought so."

"She never expressed any jealousy or resentment?"

"Not that I ever heard."

"I understand Don had some enemies both at work and amongst the customers of Metroplex Savings and Loan."

"I wouldn't know. The only person I know for sure didn't like Don was Jimmy's brother, John."

"Really? Why do you say that?"

"Don asked John to go out on the town with him and Jimmy on several occasions but John declined. He's a very religious person and hated that Don was encouraging Jimmy to cheat on his wife—not to mention drinking and smoking pot. He tried to get Jimmy to stand up to Don, but Jimmy thought he had to please his father-in-law or risk losing his job and his wife."

"Why? I'm sure that someone with as much talent and experience as Jimmy could easily find another job."

"Yeah, except for one minor problem."

"What's that?"

She frowned and shook her head. "He didn't tell you?"

"No. What?"

"He's got a little drug problem."

I sighed. "Oh. Jesus. That's just wonderful."

"It's not a big secret. I'm surprised he didn't mention it. He got fired from his last two jobs on account of it."

"What kind of drugs?"

"Cocaine. I'm afraid there's not another construction company in Texas who'd hire him."

I shook my head in disbelief. What else could I find out about Jimmy Bennett that would make his case any more difficult? Jesus! I had been searching for evidence to prove his innocence, yet aside from a few letters from angry customers, all I'd found was more and more evidence pointing to him as the killer.

I thanked Ruth and asked if she'd tell John Bennett I was ready to talk to him. I figured John would know a lot about his brother Jimmy and could elaborate on some of the revelations of the past twenty-four hours. John was supposedly a religious man, so I hoped that meant he would be honest and forthright. But I wasn't taking anything for granted. I'd known plenty of men of the cloth who used the Lord simply to lure their victims into a false sense of security.

Ruth showed me to John's office. He stood up and we shook hands. There were two side chairs directly in front of John's elegant desk. I set my purse down on one side chair and sat in the other one. John Bennett was shorter than his brother and more muscular. He asked if I wanted a coke or a cup of coffee which I politely declined.

"Thanks for taking the time to talk to me," I said with a smile. "In the initial stages of an investigation I try to get to know my client and those around him as well as possible before I widen my inquiry."

John nodded. "That makes sense."

"Jimmy has told me a lot but there is still much more to learn. Clients forget or are reluctant to be perfectly candid for one reason or another. Even though what they tell me is privileged, they still often hold back. That's why I need you to tell me everything. Better I find out anything damaging now than later."

"Okay."

"Just in the last twenty-four hours I've learned two critical facts that Jimmy didn't tell me."

"Like what?" John asked.

"His drug problem and pending divorce."

He nodded. "You'll find Jimmy is a little paranoid from his drug addiction. He doesn't trust many people."

"You wouldn't know talking to him that he had an addiction."

"No, we got him to go to a clinic a few years back and he worked out the problem, but he has a lapse now and then."

"Is he under treatment now?"

"Nothing formal. He has a shrink that he visits when he needs help."

"What's his name?"

"Dr. Winston Rutledge III."

I wrote down the name and then asked, "Do you think when he found out that Betty had filed for divorce that he went looking for some cocaine?"

"It's possible, but I didn't see any evidence of it."

"When was the first time you saw him after the

murder?"

"The next day after he posted bond."

"Your aunt told me that Jimmy talked to you just after his altercation with his father-in-law. I'm curious as to what he told you."

John's face dropped. He looked away and took a deep breath. I raised my eyebrows in anticipation. He turned and looked at me. "He said. 'I'm gonna kill that son of a bitch!'"

"Oh, great. That'll play well in court."

"You've got to understand, Jimmy has a short temper but he's not really the violent type. I've never known him to hurt anyone. He may threaten to kick your ass, but it's just talk."

"Well, unfortunately the jury isn't going to understand that. They're going to assume his threats are serious."

John nodded, "I've warned him many times to keep his big mouth shut, but he doesn't listen. It's just his nature to talk tough."

"Help me out, John. I'm trying to build up a defense here, but so far I've come up with nothing. I've either got to find an alibi for Jimmy or find someone else to pin the murder on. You have any ideas?"

John took a deep breath and exhaled slowly. "I'm not sure he was just driving around all by himself letting off steam."

"What do you mean?" I asked. "You think he was with someone."

"Jimmy's not a loner. He usually seeks companionship when he's upset. He may have picked up someone to keep him company."

"You have any idea who it was, or why he would lie

about it?"

"No, it's just a feeling."

"Hmm. If you think of anyone, please let me know."

"I will."

"Before I leave, I'm afraid I've got to ask you some delicate questions. Please don't take offense, but I've got to be thorough."

"What do you mean?"

"It's been suggested that you didn't like Don much."

He laughed. "That's a given."

"And you probably didn't like Amanda Black much if it's true she was a hooker."

"Don was a sinful man if I ever knew one. He lacked any sense of morality or conscience. He was a greedy, power-hungry tyrant who would do anything to get what he wanted. Even though Jesus teaches us to love all God's children, I found it hard to even tolerate Don Baker. As for Amanda, well she wasn't a bad person, just weak as we all are."

"So, where were you the night Don and Amanda were killed?"

"At home with my wife and family."

"Do you have a big family?"

"We have two children. They were out with their friends that night, but they were all home by midnight."

"You don't mind if I talk to your wife, do you?"

"No, be my guest."

So far John was the closest thing I had to another suspect. He definitely had a motive to kill Don, and Amanda was a sinner in his book, so it may not have bothered him too much to kill her as well. His alibi was weak in that his wife would surely lie for him if she thought it would protect him. But he didn't seem like a killer. His religious beliefs seemed sincere. As much as I wanted to have another suspect, I was afraid John Bennett just didn't fill the bill.

9

No Show

On Friday morning, I got up at 6:00 a.m. since I knew it would take better than an hour to get down to the Federal Building by 8:00 a.m. Over the years I had become a night person, so getting up that early was a real chore. Rebekah fixed me breakfast and I drank an extra cup of coffee to help wake me up. The drive down Central Expressway was a nightmare this time of morning. At 7:57 a.m. I pulled into the parking lot just west of the Earle Cabell Federal Building. It was five after eight when I stepped into the IRS field office on the 9th floor.

The room was deserted. I looked around at the decor— matching salmon sofa and love seat, glass coffee and end tables, and two coral lamps—not bad for the IRS. Then I noticed a single table with a book and a sign that read: "Please sign in and take a seat."

I signed the book and then sat on the love seat. I looked at my watch and saw it was 8:10 a.m. Where was Robert? After another ten minutes, a door opened and a short bald man appeared. He scanned the room and then looked at me. "You're alone?"

I stood up and said, "Yes, Mr. Huntington should be here any moment."

The man looked at his watch, shrugged, and said, "I'll check back in few minutes. I hope he gets here soon. I don't have much time."

I nodded and replied, "I'm sorry he's late. I can't imagine what has happened to him."

He shrugged again and closed the door. I went out in the hall and found a pay phone. Our staff didn't get into the office until 8:30 so there was no use calling there. I got Huntington's telephone number off the file and dialed it. There was no answer. With no place else to call I went back into the IRS office and waited. Five minutes later the baldheaded man appeared again and frowned when he saw I was alone. "Still no client? he asked.

"No, something must have happened. Listen, I know you've got to go into a meeting so let's get started without him. I've got a power of attorney and the returns, so I can go through them with you."

He nodded and replied, "Okay. Come on in."

I followed him into a room full of private cubicles. He picked the first one and took a seat at a round table. I joined him and opened my briefcase. We introduced ourselves and then I gave him the completed tax returns and we went through them together. He acknowledged that the company did indeed appear to have lost money but indicated he didn't know if the collection division could turn loose of the money without at least a review of the return. I reminded him of the importance at getting the funds released immediately.

He said, "Give me a minute. I've got to run this by my supervisor. While I'm gone, you can see if your client has arrived."

"Okay," I said and then got up and went back out into

the waiting room. Huntington was nowhere to be seen. It was now nearly 9:00 a.m. so I went to the pay phone and called the office. Jodie answered.

"Jodie. Have you heard from Huntington?"

"No, isn't he supposed to be with you?"

"Yes, but he's not here and it's a little difficult convincing the IRS agent of the urgency of releasing the garnishment when my client can't even make it to the meeting on time."

"I'm sorry. He hasn't called. I checked with the answering service and the only one who called is Luther Palmer."

"Luther Palmer? That's Huntington's partner."

"Really? Hmm. Well, the connection didn't sound too good. I thought maybe he was calling from a cell phone."

"Did he say what he wanted?"

"Yes, he needs to talk to Mr. Huntington immediately. The message said he's been trying his home number but there is no answer."

"I know. I've been calling that number too."

"I wonder why he doesn't answer?" Jodie said.

"That is strange. Maybe I'll drop by his place on the way back to the office. He might be sick or something."

"Good idea. Should I call Luther back?"

"Yes. Tell him we're looking for Huntington and will let him know when we find him."

When I got back to the conference room, Barton was filling out a form. I sat down and said, "Sorry, I took so long but I was trying to locate Huntington. He seems to have disappeared."

Barton shrugged and replied, "Well he'll probably

surface pretty quickly when he discovers his account has been released."

Barton signed the document he was working on and handed it to me. "Here's your release. It seems we have to presume a tax return is correct until it is tagged for auditing. That takes some time."

"Well, thank you, Mr. Barton. I certainly appreciate your help straightening this matter out."

"Oh, don't thank me. Had it been my decision you would have had to wait your turn to get a release considered. Lucky for your client he's a friend of Congressman Manning."

After Huntington had dropped Manning's name, I did some research on him. He was a conservative Republican and a key member of the House Banking Committee. No wonder the IRS jumped when he asked them to consider Huntington's request immediately. The question now, however, was the whereabouts of Huntington. If we couldn't find him soon, we couldn't wire the money to Luther. Once the deadline had passed, there was no telling what might happen to him.

Huntington lived in a townhouse just off of Northwest Highway near Preston Center. I opened a wrought iron fence gate, walked up to the front door, and knocked. There was no answer so I knocked a second time. The drapes were drawn so I couldn't see inside. I went around the back and into the backyard. It was a mess with garbage cans, old boxes, and lots of weeds. There was a doorbell on the back door so I pushed it. Chimes could be heard from inside, but there still was no answer.

After a couple of minutes of pondering the situation, I

went to a neighbor's house and knocked. An elderly lady with thick glasses appeared at the door.

She squinted at me and said, "Yes, what do you want?"

"Sorry to bother you, but I'm looking for Mr. Huntington."

"Who?"

"Your neighbor, Mr. Huntington."

"Is that his name? I've never talked to him. He's not a very friendly man."

"Really? Well, have you seen him today?"

"No, haven't seen him since yesterday afternoon. He left about 5:30 with another man."

"Can you describe the man?"

"I don't know. I wasn't paying too close attention."

"Was he tall or short—black, white?"

"He was Spanish lookin'."

"Someone from Latin America?"

"Right. Kinda short, dark hair, dark skin."

"Whose car did they leave in?"

"They left in a taxi."

"A taxi? What kind?"

"One of those Golden Cabs, you know, like you see at the airport."

"Right. Did you hear them say anything when they left?"

"Yes, but they weren't speaking English."

"Spanish?"

"No, it didn't sound like Spanish. Something similar to Spanish."

"What was their tone? Was it friendly?"

"It sounded like they were arguing. They were yelling at each other."

"Hmm. Well, thank you very much for the information. I really appreciate your help."

It didn't make much sense that Huntington would run off voluntarily when we were on the verge of freeing up his money. I had bad feelings about his disappearance. The thought occurred to me that some answers might be inside the townhouse. The thought of going to jail for breaking and entering didn't appeal to me, so I decided to call a detective I knew, Bingo Besch, at the Dallas Police Department. It took a few minutes, but I finally got through to him.

"Sorry to bother you, but one of my clients is missing. He missed an important meeting this morning and he's not answering his telephone."

"So, maybe he got lucky last night and spent the night with a broad, got drunk, you know."

"No, this was way too important a meeting. Lots of money was at stake. He's either too sick to call or someone has kidnapped him."

"So, you want to come down and fill out a missing person's report?"

"No, I want to go in his townhouse and look around."

"I don't know. It's probably premature to do that."

"What if he's sick or someone shot him?"

"Did you see any evidence of that?"

"No, but—"

"Call me when he's been missing twenty-four hours. Then I'll send someone over to take a look around."

"Did I tell you he's a friend of Congressman Manning?"

"No, you didn't mention that."

"Yeah, the Congressman had something to do with this transaction that I was working on. Like I said, this was an important meeting that Huntington wouldn't have voluntarily missed."

"Okay, I'll meet you over there in thirty minutes."

"Thanks. I really appreciate your help."

After I hung up, I wondered if bringing in the police was a wise move. What if Huntington was doing something illegal? If he was, he should have told me about it. Since he didn't, I had to assume everything he was doing was on the up and up. Detective Besch showed up right on time with another officer and, after knocking hard on the door, told the officer to pick the lock. It only took him about two minutes to get us inside.

The room was dark and sparsely decorated. There were a few old newspapers and magazines but no books, knickknacks, or photographs to be seen. I went into the kitchen and Besch headed for the bedroom. The refrigerator had a half gallon of milk, a carton with three eggs in it, and jar of strawberry jelly. In the cupboards were a few dishes, cups, and glasses but not enough to host a dinner party. The pantry had only a half a loaf of bread and a box of Frosted Flakes. I joined Besch in the bedroom where he was examining the closet.

"It doesn't look like your guy planned to stay here long," Besch said.

"No, apparently not."

"What kind of business is he in?'

"Exporting. I think he travels a lot."

Besch closed the closet and looked at me. He said, "Looks like he left in a hurry."

I nodded. "It appears so."

"Detective! Come here. You need to see this," the officer said.

We walked quickly through the kitchen toward the back door where the officer was standing. I looked around the room. There was a broken pot that had been knocked off a window sill. Drawers were half opened. A box of Tide was on its side with it contents spilled out onto the floor. The officer was examining the back door. The inside latch was broken and there was splintered wood from where it had been torn from the door frame.

"Looks like there might have been a little scuffle here. Perhaps Mr. Huntington didn't leave with his Latin friend voluntarily after all."

"I don't think he did," I said. "It looks like he was persuaded to leave."

Detective Besch nodded and said to the other officer, "Let's get us a crime scene unit up here."

There was nothing I could do at Huntington's place while the crime scene unit was working, so I went back to my office to call Luther and talk to him. Jodie tried to get him on the line but there was no answer at the number he had left. Had we been too late? Then I realized it was nighttime in China. We'd missed the deadline. I thought about the money sitting in the account I'd managed to get the IRS to release. How long would it be before it disappeared? I put in a call to Metroplex's attorney. His name was Arthur Lott. I'd met him while serving on a committee for the Dallas Bar Association. He answered and we chatted a minute about Chamber activities then Art asked, "So, your partner is defending Jimmy Bennett?"

"Yes. We got lucky. It turned out Jimmy was a friend of one of my old clients."

"Well, I met Jimmy once or twice. He seems like a decent guy. I can't see him killing Don, but you never know about people these days."

"No, anything's possible I guess. How is everyone at Metroplex taking Don's death?"

"Not well. It came at a bad time with the regulators breathing down our throats. I guess you've read in the newspapers that if we don't come up with two million by the end of the month, they may shut us down."

"Yes, I read about that. You think you'll find the money?"

"Maybe. There are several groups of investors looking at it seriously."

"Good. . . . Listen. I'm calling you about the IRS garnishment of the Continental Exporters's bank account."

"Okay."

"I've got a release to send you.".

"Good. How did you pull that off?" he asked.

"My client called in a few favors from some friends he had in Congress."

"Your client must be an important man."

"Yeah, apparently so. Unfortunately, he's disappeared. There may have been foul play."

"Really?"

"So, I think I'll sit on this release a while so that the money in the account doesn't disappear. . . . That is, if you don't mind."

"No, but I've got to warn you it's only guaranteed up to $100,000 and, like I said, Metroplex is hanging on by a thread."

"Oh, Christ. I don't know what else to do. I don't have the authority to move the money."

"Well, nothing is likely to happen in the next 10 days."

"Good. Hopefully we'll find Mr. Huntington by then. Let me know if anyone inquires about it, okay? If my client has been kidnaped or killed, the persons responsible may try to access the money."

"Sure, no problem. You'll be the first to know."

"Thanks, Art. I really appreciate it."

After working a few hours, I put a call into Detective Besch back at his office. I wondered if the crime scene investigators had found anything. I doubted they had, but you never know. He wasn't back yet, so I left a message. Before I left to go home, he called.

"Stan? You called?"

"Right. Did your crew find anything?"

"No, everything had been removed and the place was wiped clean."

"Anybody, other than the lady next door, see anything?"

"No, no other witnesses."

"So, what are you going to do now?"

"I'm going to need you to come down and tell me everything you know about this guy and help our sketch artist draw a picture that we can send out to other law enforcement agencies. Tomorrow we'll contact the FBI."

"Really? Well, I'll be happy to come down there anytime. Just let me know when."

"Drop by first thing Monday morning, okay?"

"Nine o'clock okay?"

"Yes, I'll see you then."

All I needed was to waste a day with the Dallas Police department when I had so many other things to do. I wasn't relishing the idea of talking to Besch anyway, since I had the attorney-client privilege to worry about. If I came clean with Besch, I could be violating my professional responsibility. If I withheld anything though, it might hinder the police in their investigation and delay them in their search to find Huntington. If he was in trouble, any delay could endanger his life.

Paula was going to be pissed off too since Huntington hadn't paid me a red cent and probably never would. I cursed myself for taking the case without a retainer. Then I remembered I did have a check for $5,000 and an IRS release. All I had to do was give the release to the bank and I could cash the check. But then the account would be vulnerable to the thugs who had Huntington. I thought about Mo and wished I could call him, but he made it clear he couldn't talk to me about anyone that the Company sent my way. Now I was getting a little glimpse of what it was like to be a CIA agent and I wondered why anyone would ever make that career choice.

10

Hate Mail

After interviewing everyone at Baker Construction Company my next stop was Metroplex Savings & Loan. So far, I had made no progress at all in building a defense for Jimmy Bennett. I prayed my fortunes would change. Stan had briefed me on Metroplex Savings. It was in serious trouble and almost every day there was an article in the newspaper about some sort of investigation involving the thrift. I didn't know much about what had gone on there, but I had a hunch this would be the place I'd find Don's killer.

My appointment was with the executive vice-president, Gerald Hatfield, who had taken over for Don Baker after his death. Hatfield was a tall deliberate man about thirty-five years old. He had been Don's right-hand man and would be very knowledgeable about what the bank was going through and who might have had it in for Don. I was escorted to Hatfield's office and seated in a burgundy leather side chair across from his big oak desk. We talked a few minutes about Don's funeral where we had briefly met and then got down to business.

"If I'm going to successfully defend Jimmy Bennett, I've got to find out who might have had reason to kill him. He must have had a lot of enemies considering the situation the bank was in."

"He did," John said, but I just can't see any of them committing murder."

"I understand that, but somebody out there is the murderer and we've got to figure out who it is."

"I'm not so sure Jimmy didn't do it."

"How well do you know Jimmy?" I asked.

"We don't socialize or anything like that, but I see a lot of him. He would come by the office pretty much every night to pick up Don."

"So, what makes you think Jimmy might be the killer?"

"He's a very intense guy and he's got a bad temper. I've never liked him. Frankly, he scares me."

"Did you tell anyone you didn't like Jimmy?"

"No, of course not. I'm just giving you my candid opinion of him."

"Can you think of something specific about him that you didn't like other than the hot temper?"

"He's cocky, arrogant, and ungrateful. Don gave him everything but he was never happy."

"Do I detect a hint of jealousy?" I said.

Hatfield shrugged. "I guess. I've always had to work hard to get the things I wanted. Jimmy's had everything handed to him on a silver platter."

"Perhaps he had more handed to him than he asked for," I suggested.

"What do you mean?"

"Maybe he just wanted to do his job and be left alone."

Hatfield laughed. "Bullshit. He enjoyed the money, the women, and especially the drugs."

"I thought he was off the drugs."

Hatfield frowned. "That's a joke. He couldn't go a day

without a fix."

"You know this for a fact?"

"I've caught him snorting in the head a few times."

"Recently?"

"Yeah, within the last 10 days."

I shook my head. My case was continuing to nosedive. I wondered if I would ever find another suspect. If I were going to do that I'd have to steer the conversation away from Jimmy and find out about the other people in Don's life. Hatfield didn't seem to want to talk about Don's other enemies but I had to press the issue or I'd never find out the truth.

So, what's this I've heard about some hate mail?"

Hatfield nodded. "Right. Don got a few letters from unhappy customers."

"Ruth said Detective Perkins took Don's files, but she thought there may be copies in the files here.

"Right."

"Can I see them? "

Hatfield picked up his phone and instructed his secretary to bring in the files with the hate mail. A few moments later his secretary walked in with a half dozen files and set them on Hatfield's desk. He picked up the top one and opened it. After a moment of silence, he took out a letter and handed it to me.

"This one is from a builder up in Collin County. Chuck Walters. You've heard of Walter's Homes.

"Sure," I replied.

"We had been financing a new housing development for him. He's been a client with us for more than ten years and never gave us a lick of trouble. Then the federal regulators came in and complained that the property appraisals on some of his units were out of whack. They made us get new appraisals and they came out substantially lower than the original ones. They insisted we get another $150,000 of collateral or the loans be reduced. Unfortunately, Walters couldn't do either one since the real estate market had collapsed."

"So, you called the note?"

"Right. Walters lost everything and got pretty belligerent about it as you can see from the letter."

Hatfield handed me the letter. It was hand written and difficult to read as Walters' handwriting was rather shaky.

Don,

After all these years how could you pull such an underhanded trick. Boy, did I misjudge you and Metroplex Savings. I believed all that talk about having a banking partner you could trust. What a joke, huh? You must have got a good laugh when your PR people came up with that one.

Well, you've messed with the wrong man. I won't sit idly by and watch you steal my business. Be advised. You haven't heard the last of me. Justice will be done.

Chuck Walters

I looked up at Hatfield. "This isn't so bad. He may just mean he's going to sue the bank. He didn't threaten physical violence or anything illegal."

"I agree. He's just pissed off and I don't blame him."

"So, let's see what else you have."

Hatfield handed me the files and I read them one by one. They were all quite similar—marginal businesses that toppled when the bank closed their lines of credit or called in their notes. One of the letters was from a man who had immigrated from India and had sunk his families' life savings into purchasing a building for a new restaurant. He planned to get the restaurant going and then bring his family to America one by one. After he had acquired the property, the bank refused to fund the finish-out as they had promised. The customer was irate and promised Don would be punished for his transgressions. This seemed more promising but I still doubted any of these people were responsible for Don's brutal murder. Then Hatfield handed me the last file. I looked at the name printed in bold letters. It read *Tex Weller*. My heart skipped a beat.

11

The Key

When I got to the office the next morning, I called Luther Palmer again, hoping that I'd just missed him the last time I had called. This time I asked the overseas operator to tell me Luther's location. She said it was Tehran. That shook me up as Huntington had told me he was in Beijing. I wondered why he had lied to me? He obviously didn't want me to think he was exporting to Iran. Beijing or Tehran, it didn't matter, I still had to assume Luther was in trouble.

There still was no answer. I racked by brain trying to think of a way to find out what had happened to him, but I didn't have much to go on. We didn't have a U.S. Embassy in Iran anymore, since the last embassy delegation had been kidnaped and held hostage for 444 days. I decided to look for an embassy of another country, one friendly to the U.S. Great Britain was the obvious pick since they spoke English and were ally. The Embassy was located in Teheran. The operator put me through to a low level public relations officer. I explained the situation.

"We don't keep track of U.S. companies operating in Iran. Frankly, there aren't many of them these days."

"Can you look into it, Mr. Palmer's life may be in jeopardy?"

"I will, but I suggest you contact the International Red

Cross. They are much better at this sort of thing than we are."

That seemed like a good idea so I called them next. They took my inquiry and said they'd look into it. I looked at the clock and noted it was 8:30 and time to go see Detective Besch. After a tedious bumper-to-bumper trek to the police station, I spent the rest of the morning telling Besch everything I knew about Robert Huntington, which wasn't much. I know he thought I was withholding information, but I really wasn't. Huntington hadn't told me much about himself or his business. Besch told me to contact him immediately if I heard from Huntington or anyone associated with him. Then he switched gears.

I understand you're the executor for Lottie West's estate."

I nodded. "Yes, I am."

"Well, I guess you and I are going to be spending a lot of time together. I've been assigned that case as well."

"Oh, really?"

"Yes. I need to find out what you know about the victim."

"Not much. I met her a couple times when she retained me to do her will. I guess somebody was after her money, huh?"

"It looks that way," Besch said, "From what I've been told it was a miracle they didn't find it."

"Yeah, it was right in plain sight under the house. Had the killer known it was there, he could have just crawled under there and taken it. Pretty good hiding place, actually."

"Filling the house with gas was a pretty tricky way to kill everyone. One spark and the place could have blown up."

"Yeah, but it was a good way to get rid of the dogs and Lottie all at one time. I imagine the killer opened all the doors and let the gas clear out before he started his search."

"Maybe," Besch said. "I wonder if he knew what he was looking for and, if so, whether he found it?"

"I don't know. What do you think?" I asked.

He shrugged. "I was hoping you'd find that out."

I laughed. "Me? I thought this was your investigation."

Besch smiled. "As Mrs. West's executor, don't you have an obligation to find out who killed her too? What if the killer found something of great value and stole it?"

He had me there. Locating and gathering the estate's assets were my responsibility. Since there it was likely that the killer had taken property of the estate it was my job to investigate that possibility. Fortunately, the estate now had assets to fund such an investigation. I took a deep breath and closed my eyes. All I needed were two murder investigations going on at the same time. Rebekah was going to be beside herself when I told her. I didn't want to go home and give her the bad news.

Since I had prepared the will, I knew the probate would be a pretty simple procedure. All I'd have to do was file the will with the Court, get sworn-in as Independent Executor, and file an accounting. There would be no court supervision under Texas' simplified probate procedure. The accounting would be the most difficult chore since we didn't know the extent of Lottie's assets. Another difficult task would be finding her heirs—particularly since she had denied that she had any. As it stood the SPCA stood to get everything unless an heir contested the will. That would likely happen with so much money at stake. If there were heirs, they could contest her mental capacity at the time she executed the will, particularly since she had forgotten she had heirs.

The first step would be to go through all her personal records and property that we'd found in her house. The police had taken it all, but Detective Besch had made arrangements for me to have access to it. Later that afternoon Derek and I went over to a police storage facility to go through it. Derek had volunteered to help, so I took him up on the offer. He knew Lottie better than anyone, so it made sense to have him around.

We each opened one of the dozen or so boxes the police had packed everything into. Derek's box contained photos which he began going through. I told him to check for anything written on them or other clues as to the identity of the persons in the photos. I pulled out a stack of letters from my box and began reading. They were love letters exchanged between a new bride and her husband who had been called off to war. They were dated between February and April 1945 when Lt. William Tidwell West was stationed in Berlin.

There were the expected proclamations of love between the two and Lottie's expressions of worry and concern for her husband's safety. The letters also described Lt. West's participation in the occupation of Berlin after Germany's defeat, but there was nothing to shed light on Lottie's death. As I continued to dig through the property I found a small wooden file box. Inside there were index cards with names and addresses on them and at the bottom of the box there was a key. "Look at this," I said and held up the long thin key.

Derek looked at me. "A safety deposit box key."

I nodded. "Yes. It has a number on it—A327."

"Huh. I wonder where it's from."

I turned the key around and around examining it carefully. "I don't know. There's no name on it."

"Well, if we find any banking records they may shed some light on that question."

We kept digging through the boxes of records and found an account at Republic National Bank. The branch Lottie patronized was in Oak Cliff. I added a visit there to my list of things to do. From the index cards and photographs we came up with twenty-one names of people who somehow had been a part of Lottie's life. Unfortunately, tracking these people down wouldn't be easy. The addresses looked to be very old and the likelihood that any of these people still resided at the addresses listed was remote.

"I think I'll let Besch check these names out," I said. "He's got better resources than I do for this kind of thing."

"What about the safety deposit key?" Derek asked.

"I think I'll run that lead down myself since whatever is in that box belongs to the estate."

It was late when we finished up at police headquarters. I took Central Expressway north toward Richardson. Along the way I noticed a car behind me. It seemed to be following me. At first I thought I was just being paranoid so I made some random lane changes. The car made the same changes. I began to feel uneasy so I made an unexpected exit off the expressway and down a side street. The car followed me. My pulse quickened as I now had no doubt I was being followed.

The car was a white Chevrolet Impala with a big CB antenna mounted on the roof. A lone white, dark-haired man was driving. He didn't try to pass me but just kept right on my tail. I saw a busy gas station ahead so I decided to pull in and get gas. I didn't figure the man would try anything around a lot of people. In fact, I was pretty sure he'd just go on by pretending not to be interested in me. To my surprise when I turned in and pulled up to the pump he followed and pulled up behind me.

I just sat there stunned looking in my rearview mirror. Neither one of us moved. Now what? Should I get gas and ignore him? Confront him? Get the hell out of there? I could feel my heart pounding as I pondered my next move. Suddenly, I found myself getting out of the car and walking straight toward the stranger. As I approached, he frantically started his car, backed up, and tore out of the gas station like a scared rabbit. His tires let out such a squeal that all heads turned to watch him go. Who was this guy? I'd never seen him before. The only thing I did know was that he'd be back.

Fortunately, I had got a clear look at his license plate—ZPG 973. It was a Texas plate with a frame advertising Friendly Chevrolet. I called Detective Besch when I got back to the office and told him what happened. He told me he'd check out the license number and let me know who it belonged to.

After I hung up the phone, I studied the safety deposit key. It had nothing written on it but the number A327. No hint as to what bank housed the safety deposit box. I pondered how I could figure that out. Lottie West didn't have a car, so I figured the box must be in a bank within walking distance of Lottie's house. I got in my car and drove over to Lottie's neighborhood.

There were three banks within walking distance of her house—Cullen Frost, First National, and Guaranty. Unfortunately, they had all closed at noon since it was Saturday. On Monday morning, I stopped at each bank, went inside and showed them the key but Lottie's key hadn't come from any of those branches. I wondered if the key would actually open a box somewhere or if it was just an old key that opened nothing. Then I remembered Lottie had an account at Republic National Bank in Oak Cliff. I stuck the key in my pocket and headed for Oak Cliff.

The bank was situated in a tough neighborhood. Guards with shotguns were stationed at each entrance. I went inside and asked a secretary where to find the safety deposit box manager. She pointed to a thin, black lady sitting at her desk. I walked over to her and introduced myself. Then I showed her the key.

"This isn't one of our keys. Did Mrs. West have an account here?"

"Yes, she did. That's why I thought she might have rented a safety deposit box here."

She stood up and said, "I'll go check our records."

Ten minutes later she returned and advised me that William West at one time did have a box in the bank, but that it had been closed when his will was probated in 1980. I left the bank a little disappointed. Finding Lottie's safety deposit box had turned out to be more difficult than I'd anticipated.

12

Conflict Of Interest

When I got back to the office I rushed into Stan's office. He looked up and smiled. I didn't reciprocate.

"You won't believe what I found out when I met with Gerald Hatfield at Metroplex," I said.

"What?"

I suddenly felt sick. I walked over to a side chair and sat down. This couldn't be happening.

"Are you okay?" Stan asked.

"Not really," I said.

"What's wrong?"

"Did you know Tex Weller had a loan with Metroplex?"

"Sure. He's been banking with them for years."

"Well, did you know there was a letter from Tex in Don's hate mail file?"

"What?" Stan exclaimed. "I knew Tex was upset when they made him sign that consulting agreement, but he never mentioned sending Don a letter."

"Well he did, and it isn't a letter I'd like read to a jury."

"Oh, my God. Come on. You can't believe Tex could have killed Baker," I said.

"Well, I wouldn't put it past him considering what a greedy bastard he is."

I was referring to his propensity to get involved in shady, get-rich quick schemes, the last of which nearly got he and Stan killed.

"I don't know."

"It's pretty clear that money is all he cares about. You said he was livid when he got the news his loan had been called."

"Still, I can't see him doing that. I've known him for years. He's not a violent person. Besides, the note was called after the murder."

"He knew it was coming when the stock market crashed. Didn't you two talk about the likelihood that Metroplex would call the note?"

"Yeah, but—"

"I can't believe you'd defend him after what he did to you."

"I'm not defending him. I'm just trying to analyze the situation. I'll admit he may have had a motive, but I'd be shocked if he were the killer."

"It doesn't matter if he is or he isn't. Either way, now I have a conflict of interest. I'm going to have to withdraw from Jimmy's case. Damn it! I can't believe the bastard has screwed up my murder case."

"Wait a minute. Don't jump to conclusions. You don't necessarily have a conflict of interest."

"Yes, I do. Tex is a suspect now and the firm represents him. We can't represent both he and Jimmy."

"Maybe Tex has an alibi. If he does, then he wouldn't be a suspect."

"He'd better have an alibi," I said. "If I have to withdraw on account of him, he might end up dead. Then you'll really have a conflict of interest."

He laughed. "Okay, calm down. I'll go talk to him."

"Right now, I hope. I can't even think. I'm so upset."

Stan left and I started to return phone calls but I was so sick inside I didn't feel like talking to anyone. There was a lot of other work I could have done, but no matter how hard I tried, I just couldn't concentrate. Finally, I grabbed my purse and headed home. All I wanted was a hot bath and a bottle of Chardonnay—or, better yet, vodka.

The place was dead quiet—too quiet. I turned on the stereo and put on the new Randy Travis album, *Always and Forever.* Now there was a man who knew about love. I kicked off my heels, grabbed the vodka, and headed for the bathroom leaving a trail of discarded clothing in my wake. Steam billowed up and filled the room quickly as the scalding hot water poured into the tub. When it was full, I slipped in and sunk into the hot bath.

The hot water and few shots of vodka put me in a trance. I had everything I ever wanted except, of course, the love of my life. But I was prepared to sacrifice that love for fame and fortune, if that was the price. I was there, right on top, the envy of every judge and lawyer in the state of Texas. The press loved me. I could get an interview with any reporter or talk show host in the blink of an eyelash. At least today I could. Tomorrow I might be washed up on account of Tex Weller—the greedy little bastard. I wondered if he *had* killed Don Baker. I prayed he hadn't. I couldn't defend Tex Weller. My heart just wouldn't be in it.

When the bath water cooled, I got out, dried myself with a big fluffy towel, and rubbed lotion all over my body. It felt good and the smell of lilac was exhilarating. I was feeling better and my thoughts turned away from Tex to Bart. Where was he? Maybe he'd like to go out for dinner. I found the phone and tracked him down at the medical examiner's office. He thought dinner sounded good and said he'd pick me up at six. I looked at the clock on the dining room wall and noted it was quarter to five—plenty of time to get ready.

It took a while to find the perfect outfit. I had decided tonight was the night to heat things up a bit with Bart. Deep down I was sure he wanted a permanent relationship but whether or not he would acknowledge it, I didn't know. A tinge of fear shot through me. What if he said no? What if my ploy backfired and turned him off? I may be screwing up a perfectly good relationship by putting unnecessary pressure on it. I moaned.

What was I doing? What happened to the confident seductress who was always in control? What would people think if they knew of the turmoil boiling inside me? I cringed at the thought. I looked at the clock radio and saw it was 5:55 p.m. I heard the front door open. I smiled. Bart had arrived.

Bart took me to a cozy little restaurant nestled in one of the few hills in Dallas near downtown. It was called Baby Doe's. We started with a bowl of their famous cheese soup made with Premium Coors Beer. Bart had a bottle of Coors too and I was drinking a Chardonnay. The crowd was thick and the music loud. We were both having a good time. The moment had come.

I looked at Bart with loving eyes, "Honey. I've been thinking."

Bart looked at me and smiled. He seemed to sense I was about to say something important. I liked that about

Bart. He listened to me and gave me his full, undivided attention. Not many men did that.

"About what?"

"About us."

"Us?" Bart said, gazing into my eyes.

"Yeah, us. Is that a big surprise?"

"Kind of," he said.

His comment stung. I looked at him wondering what was going through his mind. He forced a smile.

"I'm sorry," he said. "Go on. What about *us*?"

I took a deep breath. "Well, I like being with you and I think you enjoy my company, right?"

"True."

"So, I was thinking . . . maybe . . . you know . . . we should spend more time together."

He smiled. "That would suit me fine, but what about your practice. How much more time could you afford to spend?"

"Well, that's what I'm getting to. Maybe . . . maybe you should . . . you know . . . consider moving in with me."

Bart gave me a look I'd never seen before. I couldn't tell if it was shock or dismay. He looked away and fumbled with his napkin. I closed my eyes fearing the worst. Finally, he looked at me and said, "What about Stan?"

"What about him?" I said, even though I knew exactly what he meant.

"You over him?" he asked.

I swallowed hard. "Yeah. I'm over him."

He turned his head and smiled. "That's not what your eyes say."

I shrugged. "I'm over him. Okay? I'm over him."

Bart sighed. "I don't know if I believe you. I want to. There is nothing I 'd like more than to wake up next to you every morning for the rest of my life. But I won't be a stand-in for Stan Turner."

Tears welled in my eyes. I said, "You won't be. I promise."

He took my hand and said, "Then marry me. Be my bride."

The words took my breath away. Tears flowed from my eyes. I lost control. I was so embarrassed. I hadn't cried since I was a child. Bart came over to me and put his arms around me.

"I hope those are tears of joy?" he said.

I embraced him and replied, "They are."

13

The Alibi

After Paula's shocking news about Tex, I told Jodie to reschedule my afternoon appointments and then I called Tex at his home. He wasn't there but his wife Toni told me he was due back in about a half hour. That was about how long it would take me to get to Grand Prairie where he lived, so I told her I was on my way to see him. He answered the door on the first knock and let me in.

"Stan. Toni said you were coming. What in the hell's going on?"

"We need to talk."

"It must be serious for you to make a house call."

"It is."

"Okay, let's go in the den. I'll get us a couple of beers."

"Fine," I said and followed him through the living room to the den. He pointed to an overstuffed chair, so I took a seat. He disappeared into the kitchen. A moment later Toni walked out with two beers.

"How are you, Stan?"

I shrugged. "I've been better. You know how stressful these murder trials can get."

"I can imagine. How's Rebekah?"

"She's well. Busy with the kids."

"I bet. Say hi to her for me."

"I will."

Toni left and Tex returned with a can of peanuts. He sat on a love seat across from me.

"So, what's up," Tex asked.

"You don't know why I'm here?"

Tex squinted. "Well, not exactly. I suspect it has something to do with Metroplex Savings. Did you talk to their lawyers?"

"One of them. But that's not why I'm here. Paula questioned Jerry Hatfield today about Don Baker's death."

"Yeah, I bet he didn't shed any tears over Baker's murder."

"Why do you say that?"

"Baker didn't know the first thing about running a savings and loan. Jerry ran the place and Don got all the credit. If that wasn't bad enough, Don treated Jerry like dirt."

"How do you know this?"

"I did business with them. I watched how they operated. Don was strictly a PR man, and it was common knowledge."

"Is that why you hated him? Because he was a fraud?"

Tex smiled and replied, "That and a no good, underhanded, son of a bitch."

"Is that a quote from your letter?" I asked.

"What letter?" Tex asked.

"Jerry showed her a file of hate letters addressed to Don and guess what she found."

"Oh, shit," Tex moaned shaking his head. "It wasn't a hate letter exactly. It was just a letter complaining about the way they did business. I was a little pissed off, if you recall."

"Yeah, well your language was a little too colorful and

your threat much too explicit to ignore."

Tex took a deep breath. "So, now what do we do?"

"You've got Paula and me in a mess. Now you're a suspect and we've got a conflict of interest."

"A suspect? Are you out of your mind?"

"No. You had as good a motive as anybody to kill Baker and the threatening letter shows you were actually thinking about doing it."

"I didn't mean it."

"It doesn't matter. You think anyone would believe that it was all a big mistake?"

"I guess not. So, what are we going to do?"

"I don't know. First, I need some answers. Where were you on Sunday night?"

"Here with Toni watching the Cowboy game."

"That would be a great alibi except a wife would be expected to lie for her husband. Do you have anyone else who can vouch for your whereabouts?"

Tex thought a minute, then replied, "No. I can't think of anyone."

"Listen, if you had anything to do with Don Baker's murder I need to know. Paula and I can't defend Jimmy Bennett if you're a suspect too."

"I didn't have anything to do with his murder."

I looked at Tex straight in the eye. He didn't flinch or look away and there was enough intensity in his voice that I felt he was telling the truth. I took a deep breath and smiled.

"Good."

We both took a swig of our beers and ate a few peanuts. There was an awkward moment of silence, then I said, "So, what's happening with your Metroplex loan."

"Well, they accelerated the note on Tuesday so I've got 28 days to come up with the full balance."

"You think you can move the note in that length of time?"

"I'm working on it, but frankly I doubt it's going to happen."

"You give any more thought to my Chapter 11 suggestion?"

"Yeah, I suppose if nothing else works we'll have to do it. I hope it doesn't come to that though. I hate the idea of filing bankruptcy."

"Chapter 11 is a big undertaking, so I'm going to have to start working on it now. It's not something you can do in 24 hours. I'll need to get with your accounting people to start working on the schedules and statement of financial affairs."

"Okay, whatever you need. Just let me know."

"In the meantime, don't disparage Don Baker and, if anyone wants to talk to you about him let me know. If Detective Perkins decides you're a suspect in Don Baker's murder, then we'll have to withdraw from the case and you'll have to hire another law firm."

"But why? You were *my* lawyer first."

"It doesn't matter. We have confidential information about both you and Jimmy Bennett. It wouldn't be fair for us to represent either one of you."

"Well, that stinks! I'm in trouble and I can't even use my own attorney."

"I'm sorry. But that's the way it is. So, see if you can come up with someone to corroborate your alibi. That would eliminate the problem and I'd sleep a hell of a lot better."

"Okay. I'll give it some thought, but I doubt I'll be able

to do it."

After the meeting with Tex, I went straight home. It was after seven when I walked in the door. Rebekah had put my dinner in the refrigerator and while she was warming it up, I tried to call Paula to tell her not to worry about the potential conflict of interest but there was no answer. Rebekah was setting my dinner on the table when I walked back in.

"Paula isn't home," I said. "I wonder where she went."

"Why do you need to talk to her?" Rebekah asked.

"She was worried about a conflict of interest when she found out Tex had sent a nasty letter to Dusty Baker just before he died."

"So, what are you going to do?" Rebekah asked.

"Tex insists he's innocent and I believe him."

"Yeah, but even so, you could still use the letter to create reasonable doubt, couldn't you?"

"Yes, I know. We'll have to disclose the potential conflict of interest to Jimmy Bennett and see what he wants to do. It's his call. I don't think Tex was involved in the murder, but, you're right, the letter could be useful."

"So, just withdraw. You don't need this case."

"It wouldn't matter to me, but Paula would be devastated."

"Too bad. There will be other cases. Tex is your friend and if he's a suspect you should be defending him."

"If Tex is a viable suspect, I couldn't defend either one of them."

"Good. I don't like you doing these murder trials. They're too dangerous. I nearly lost you the last time you got involved in one."

I got up and embraced Rebekah. "I know, but I don't think I'm in any danger in this case, honey. You don't need to worry about me. I'll be fine.

She wiped the tears from her eyes with both hands. "Right. You didn't think you'd get kidnapped in Ecuador either and you didn't expect to get ambushed on your way to Dusty Thomas' ranch, did you?"

"Okay. Maybe this is a way to bow out gracefully. I'll try, but I can't promise anything. It's a complicated situation."

"Do it for me, Stan—and the kids. Okay?"

I sighed and said, "I'll see what I can do."

14

Engagement

After Bart's proposal, everything went crazy. We talked for over an hour about our wedding and our future together. Then we went to a club to celebrate our engagement. We drank way too much and had to take a cab home. I know it was after midnight when we were finally dropped off. We made love a couple times and then finally fell asleep.

When I woke up, it was after 9:30 a.m. I couldn't believe I'd slept so late. Bart was already up and rummaging around in the kitchen. As I was trying to muster enough energy to get up, Bart walked in.

"Got to go, love. I'm late for court."

"Why did you let me sleep so late?"

"I just woke up a few minutes ago myself. Quite an exciting evening, huh?"

"Yeah. Did we really get engaged or was I dreaming?"

He smiled. "Engaged? What are you talking about?"

I frowned. He laughed, came over to the side of the bed, and leaned down. We kissed. As our lips parted he said, "Yes, we did and tonight we need to go shopping for an engagement ring."

I raised my eyebrows as thoughts of diamonds danced

in my head. "Hmm. I can handle that."

We kissed again, longer this time. Bart broke away, "Okay, I gotta go. I'll meet you here at six."

I pulled him back for one more kiss—a long passionate one. Then he was gone. I rolled out of bed and headed for the bathroom. Thirty minutes later I was going out the front door when I remembered I didn't have my car. It was back at the nightclub where we'd ended the evening. I let out a groan of frustration, turned around, and went back inside to call Jodie. She said she'd be right over to pick me up. It actually turned out well because I had some time to tell Jodie about our engagement. She was shocked, but seemed pleased. I asked her if she'd be in my wedding party as my pool of friends and family was kind of light. Being the career girl that I was, I'd lost track of most of my college and law school friends. The law is a merciless slave driver.

By 10:30 I was sitting at my desk in a daze. I still couldn't think of anything but my wedding. Had I been hasty in opening the door to Bart's proposal? I liked my freedom. What would it be like being tied to one man? As I was stressing out, Stan walked in and gave me a hard look.

"What's up with you?" he said. "You look . . . happy."

I looked at him and smiled broadly. "I am happy. Very happy. I'm . . . I'm getting married."

The look of shock on Stan's face jolted me. What had I done? A shroud of fear swept over me. I'd never have him now. He just stared at me for a long moment with his mouth half opened. He seemed to be struggling to keep his composure. Finally, he said, "Wow. I didn't know you were serious with anyone. Is it Bart? It must be Bart."

I forced a smile. "Yes, he asked me last night."

"Gee. . . .Wow! . . . Congratulations. I'm happy for you."

"You don't sound too happy," I said bluntly.

"No. I am. It was just so unexpected."

"Don't worry. I'm not leaving the firm or anything. We're going to wait until after the Bennett murder trial to get married. Did you talk to Tex?"

"Yes, he assures me he had nothing to do with Baker's murder and that there is no conflict of interest."

"Yeah, but do you believe him?"

"I don't know. Rebekah wants us to withdraw from the case."

"What?"

"She's never liked me handling murder cases, plus if it turns out Tex is involved, she'd want us to defend *him*."

"Oh, God," I sighed. "What are we going to do?"

"Well, we have a contract with Jimmy and as long as he doesn't have a problem with the potential conflict of interest, then we have to go forward."

"What about Rebekah?"

"She's a little scared after the Dusty Thomas case and the attempts on our lives. But she'll get over it."

Stan had been kidnapped several months earlier while in Ecuador looking for Tex and we had been shot at during our defense of Dusty Thomas in our last murder trial. Rebekah had gone through a lot and she was understandably concerned about Stan's safety. I didn't blame her for wanting us to bow out of the case, but I was glad Stan hadn't given in to her.

"They'll both have to sign waivers," I said. "We have to cover our ass on this one."

"Right. It won't be a problem with Tex. I don't know about Jimmy."

"I'll talk to him," I said. "I'll convince him."

Stan left and I managed to focus again on Jimmy's case. Feeling much better after hashing out the conflict of interest issue, I started going through my notes. Stan hadn't seemed concerned about it, so I certainly wasn't going to let it keep me from moving forward. I had learned quite a bit about Jimmy and Don Baker but I hadn't investigated Amanda Black as yet. I wondered how she fit into the scheme of things. Was she an innocent victim or was she intentionally murdered along with Don? I had learned that she worked out of a strip club on Greenville Avenue called the Blue Diamond Saloon. It was lunch time when I walked in and a dozen men were enjoying a free buffet while they gawked at two strippers dancing on stage. I asked one of the waitresses if I could talk to the manager. She said she'd get him. I sat on a stool at the bar and waited.

The manager looked like a relic from the 60's with his long greasy black hair combed way back. He sat down on a stool next to me and asked if I was looking for a job. I laughed and then told him who I was and why I was there.

"I loved Amanda. She was one of my best girls. I can't believe she's dead."

"I'm sorry for your loss. I promise you I'll do everything in my power to find her killer and bring him to justice."

"Thank you. I'm glad to hear that. A lot of people wouldn't care whether her killer was punished or not."

"I care. Can you tell me something about her? I'm trying to figure out the reason she was killed."

"She's from a wealthy family in Houston. She dropped

out of SMU and started dancing here a couple years ago. I guess she just wasn't the academic type."

"Where did she live?"

"Before she moved into Don's place, she lived in an apartment not too far from here. She had a roommate—Melody Hayes. She's a dancer here too."

"How did she meet Don Baker?"

"Don spends a lot of time here. He likes pretty women and spreads a lot of money around amongst the girls. They all smoother him with attention whenever he shows up. Amanda was not only beautiful but had some brains too, so Don took a particular interest in her."

"He dated her?"

"Sure. But it was more than that. He used her to entertain investors and get them to open up their pocketbooks. She was more like a partner in crime."

"What was in it for her?"

"Money, jewels, cars—whatever she wanted Don gave it to her."

"What about Jimmy? Did he have a relationship with Amanda?"

"Yes, Jimmy had a fling with Amanda before Don met her. When it cooled down Don stepped in and took up the slack."

"How did Jimmy handle that?"

"He claimed not to care, but I could tell he was jealous as hell. I never understood how Jimmy could put up with the crap Don dished out. I'd have killed him long ago."

"So, you think Jimmy killed him?"

"I'd bet money on it."

The manager found Melody Hayes and graciously

sent her to talk to me. She was a short brunette with a slim physique and big brown eyes. She told me about the frequent trips her and Amanda had made to the company condo. I asked her if Don and Amanda had any problems.

"Amanda wanted her own place. She wanted Don to deed the company condo over to her or get her one of her own. Don said he'd do it if she'd help him raise the money he needed to keep Metroplex in business."

"So, exactly how did Amanda help raise money for Don?"

"Don would introduce her to potential investors and she would spend a lot of time with them learning their secrets and identifying their weaknesses. Don would use the information to close the deal. They'd do whatever it took to induce the investors to fork over the desired cash, including blackmail and extortion."

This was blowing my mind. I'd never run into such a sinister operation. I couldn't quite figure out why Don would have to resort to such tactics to keep his savings and loan afloat. I had always thought a savings and loan would be a very lucrative business without such aggressive marketing. Why was it necessary to get all this capital investment? It didn't make sense to me. I had learned a lot from Melody, but I needed some fresh leads.

"So, in the last couple of weeks before her death, who was Amanda working on?"

"You mean for Don?"

"Right. Who were these investors that Don was courting from back east?"

"The last one I saw her with was a professional baseball player from the Red Sox."

"What was his name?"

"Oh, God. I'm bad with names. Wait, it was Oscar, I think."

"When did you see them together last?"

"Oscar was in town last weekend. Amanda picked him up at the airport on Friday the 16th, I think."

"What did they do all weekend?"

"I don't know. I had to work at the club. The last time I saw Amanda was Friday night when she left to go pick up Oscar."

"Did she say what she planned to do with him?"

"They were trying to get a $250,000 investment out of him. Don had a big presentation set up for Saturday and Amanda was supposed to butter him up and have him in a good mood for the presentation. That's all I know."

"Well, you've been a big help, Melody. I appreciate your candor. I may need to ask you some more questions later."

"No problem. I want to help find the bastard that killed Amanda. She wasn't a saint, but she didn't deserve to die."

"We'll get to the truth. Don't worry. I won't let up until I figure out what happened to Don and Amanda."

It was late afternoon when I got back to the office. When I pulled into the parking garage, I noticed a car parked on the curb. Two men were in the car talking. I thought it strange that they would be just sitting there. Were they cops or private investigators? If so, who were they staking out? I wondered.

15

Heirs

When I got to the office on Monday morning there was a message from Detective Besch. Curious as to what he wanted I called him immediately. He said he had the name and address of the owner of the car that had followed me and was going out to question him. I asked if I could tag along. He agreed. Thirty minutes later he picked me up. We drove to a quiet upper-class neighborhood near the intersection of Hillcrest Boulevard and Walnut Hill Lane where we parked across the street from the home of Otto Barringer.

"So, do you know anything about Mr. Barringer?" I asked.

"Not much. He's married with a couple of teenagers. No record. Apparently, he's self-employed."

"I bet he'll be surprised to see us."

Besch smiled. "That's a good bet."

We walked up the door and Detective Besch rang the doorbell. A minute later a middle-aged woman appeared. She introduced herself as Mrs. Barringer. Besch asked if Mr. Barringer was in and she indicated he was. She invited us inside and escorted us to the den. She said he was upstairs and she'd go get him. When she returned, she advised us he'd be right down and asked if we wanted some tea. We both declined.

It was a long five minutes before Otto Barringer made his appearance. He was a slender, pale man of about 45 years of age. He did a double-take when he saw me. Besch got right down to the nitty gritty.

"Mr. Turner here tells me you've been following him."

Otto turned a little red and replied, "No, he must be mistaken."

"I don't think so. He got a good look at you and wrote down your license plate number. I brought him along so he could identify you." Besch turned to me and asked, "Is this the guy?"

I nodded. "Yes, this is the man."

Otto twisted in his chair and ran his fingers through his hair. "Okay. Okay, I'll admit it. I was following you. I'm sorry. I meant you no harm."

Besch frowned. "Why don't you enlighten us as to why you were following Mr. Turner?"

Otto took a deep breath and looked over at his wife who also seemed anxious to hear what he had to say. He exhaled and said, "It's a long story."

Besch replied, "Then get on with it."

"Mr. Turner is the executor of my aunt's estate."

"You're Lottie West's nephew?" I asked.

He nodded. "I haven't spoken to her for many years. She and my parents were estranged. When I read her obituary, I got to thinking about her and felt badly that I hadn't seen her for so long. When I was a child, I saw a lot of her and we did many things together. When she and my parents got at odds, she moved away and I lost track of her.

"

"So, why follow Stan?" Besch asked.

"I was trying to get up the nerve to talk to him. I wanted to find out what Lottie had been doing for the last fifteen years. I thought maybe I could get a memento or something."

"Or claim an inheritance?" Besch suggested.

"Well. It did occur to me that I might be an heir. She always liked me."

It all made sense now. Otto Barringer was embarrassed that he hadn't visited his dear aunt in fifteen years, but not too embarrassed to claim his inheritance. I shook my head in disgust. I told him to make an appointment and bring any records he had to prove his relationship to Lottie West. He assured me he would do so. Besch had a few more questions.

"Did you know where your aunt was living?"

"No, she disappeared years ago. I just happened to see her name in the obituaries."

"Are your parents alive?"

"Yes, they live in Dennison."

"What are their names?"

"Loretta and James Barringer."

"Did you tell them Lottie had died?"

"Yes."

"Why didn't any of you go to the funeral?"

"Well, actually I didn't see the obituary until after the funeral."

"Why was that?"

"I was in Atlanta the week she died but my wife was home. She saw the obituary and called me. Unfortunately, I couldn't get back in time for the funeral."

"Why didn't your parents go?" Besch pressed.

"We didn't tell them that she had died until after I got back home. I know that sounds strange, but you've got to understand there was a lot of bad blood between them. We almost didn't tell them at all."

"Why was there bad blood?"

"I'm not sure. I was young when it all happened. My father and my uncle didn't get along—you know—personality conflicts."

"Did your grandmother stay in contact with anybody in the family?"

"No. Other than my parents and me, there is just my sister Alice who lives in Philadelphia. I don't think she had any contact with Aunt Lottie either."

Besch took a deep breath and looked over at me. "I think we're done here, Stan."

I nodded and we all stood up. As we were leaving Besch stopped, turned and said, "Oh, I guess you heard Lottie's death wasn't an accident."

Otto frowned, "It wasn't?"

"No, the gas line was cut and fed into the air ducts. It was murder. You wouldn't know who might have wanted Lottie dead, would you?"

"God, no. Like I said, I hadn't seen her for a long time."

Besch nodded, turned, and we left. On the way back to the office, Besch said he didn't believe much of Mr. Berringer's story. I concurred. Why follow me? He could have just called me on the telephone. It was obvious that he hadn't told us the truth. Besch suggested I go talk to Lorretta and James Barringer. He said he'd get someone to interview

Otto's sister in Philadelphia. We agreed for the moment that Mr. Otto Barringer was now a suspect in Lottie West's murder despite his alibi. Besch said he'd check that out and also see if Otto's spending habits had changed recently.

When I got back to the office there was a message from Arthur Lott. For a moment, the name didn't ring a bell, then I remembered he was the attorney for Metroplex Savings and Loan. I dialed his number and his receptionist put me through.

"Someone tried to do a wire transfer on the Continental Exporter's account today," Lott said.

"It didn't go through, did it?"

"No, there's still a hold on the account, but they had all the right numbers and passwords."

"What was the destination of the wire?"

"The request stipulated the money was to be wired to a bank account in Panama City."

"Panama City? What's in Panama City?"

"I don't know. You asked me to call if there was any activity on the account. Have you had any luck finding Mr. Huntington?"

"No. He's totally disappeared. How did you get the request for the wire transfer?"

"By telephone."

"Any idea where the call came from?"

"No, sorry.

"Well, I appreciate the information. Let me know if there is any additional activity."

I was about to call Detective Besch to tell him about the attempted wire transfer on the Continental Exporter account when Paula walked in. She had a worried look on her fact.

"Stan, did you know someone is watching us?"

"No. Who?"

"I don't know who they are—FBI, police, private detectives, maybe just a couple of thugs—but they're in the parking garage right now."

"Did you get their license numbers?" I asked.

"Yes."

"I was about to call Detective Besch. I'll give him the numbers and maybe he can find out who it is. I can't imagine why the FBI would be watching us."

"Me either. It's just unsettling to have someone following you and watching every move you make."

"I know. Don't worry. We'll get to the bottom of this."

Paula left and I called Detective Besch. He was surprised to learn someone was watching us. He said he'd check with the FBI agents he was working with on the Huntington case and see if they knew anything about it. I told him about the activity in the Continental Exporters' bank account.

"The kidnappers are behind it I'm sure," Besch said. "They want the money in the account. How secure is it?"

"Well, like I said, there is an IRS garnishment on it now so until the bank gets a release in hand they won't let loose of the money."

"And you've got the release?"

"Yes."

"Where is it?"

"In the Continental Exporter's file, right here in my office."

"I'm not comfortable with that. Someone could break in

and steal it. I think I'll see if I can get a judge to put a freeze on that account."

"Good idea. Hanging onto the release was just a temporary fix at best. I was hoping you'd find Huntington quickly, but that doesn't seem likely now."

"No, and if the kidnappers have the account number and passwords, they don't need Huntington anymore. They may have already killed him."

"Who do you think is behind this?"

"Probably someone close to Huntington—a partner or someone he does business with. This isn't a random kidnaping."

After hanging up with Besch, I got the Continental Exporters' file and looked inside. Much to my relief the release was still there. I wondered where I could put it to be sure it was safe. I remembered several years ago losing a file. We searched the office high and low for it but couldn't find it. Somehow it has slid behind and underneath one of my desk drawers. Only by taking the drawer entirely out could you find the file. It was only by accident that I found it several years later. I put the release in an envelope and slipped it in my secret hiding place. Since I was the only one who knew it existed, I was confident it would never be found.

A few hours later as I was straightening up to go home, the telephone rang. I picked it up and recognized Besch's voice.

"The money's gone. We served the papers to freeze the account on an officer at Metroplex Savings and he advised us the money had already been wired to Panama."

"What? That can't be. I just talked to Arthur Lott this

morning.   He said they wouldn't release it without the release and I've got the release right here with me."

Besch sighed. "Well, call him and find out what happened, would you? There was 3.2 million dollars in that account."

"Three point two million dollars? I didn't realize there was that much in there. Now that I think about it though, Huntington never said exactly how much there was in the account. He said he needed $150,000 right away but never mentioned the balance in the account."

"Really? The officer we talked to said $3.2 million was wired to Panama. I guess Huntington didn't want you to know any more than you had to."

Still in shock from Besch's bombshell, I put a call into Arthur Lott, but he was gone for the day. I told his secretary that it was urgent and that I needed to talk to him immediately. She said she'd track him down and give him the message. I left her my home telephone number in case she was able to find him that evening. I couldn't believe the account had been drained. How could that have happened? Then I remembered the retainer check I hadn't been able to cash. Now it would be worthless. The bastards had stolen my retainer too!

16

The Congressman

Arthur Lott called me back the following morning and was shocked when I told him the Continental Exporters account had been cleaned out. He claimed to know nothing about it but said he'd look into it and get back to me. He seemed sincere and I had no reason to believe he knew what was going on. Less than an hour later he called back.

"I talked to my contact at Metroplex and they said a copy of the IRS release was delivered to them so they released the account. They assumed it had come from you," Art explained.

"No. I've got the original in my possession and I didn't send a copy over to them."

"Well, Stan. I'm sorry, but with the release in the file we had no choice but to release the hold on the account."

"Damn. I can't believe this."

After thinking about it I decided the copy of the release must have come directly from the IRS, so I called Anthony Perez to see if he knew anything about it. He didn't seem surprised to hear from me.

"Yes, I sent the release over to Metroplex. Your client's friend, Congressman Manning called. He said he had been told the lien had been released but the bank claimed not to have received the paperwork. I told him you had the release but apparently hadn't delivered it to the bank yet. He asked me to send a copy over to them."

"Oh, my God. I can't believe this."

"Is something wrong?" Perez asked.

"No, nothing that concerns you. Thanks for your help."

After hanging up with Perez, I called Congressman Manning's office to see if I could talk to him, but the receptionist claimed he was out. What was going on? I had just helped somebody steal 3.2 million dollars and it pissed me off. I called Detective Besch and told him what I had found out.

"Congressman Manning? Are you sure the call came from him? It might have been an impostor."

"Well, maybe, but I doubt the IRS would be fooled by someone claiming to be Manning. They seem to know him pretty well over at the Dallas field office. I think Perez has met him and knows his voice."

"Well, I'll pass this information onto the FBI. With a U.S. Congressman involved that will knock the priority of the case up a notch or two. What are you going to do?"

"I was thinking of calling Congressman Manning. Would you have a problem with that?"

"No. It's a free country. Promise me, though, that you'll tell me what he has to say."

"You bet. If he won't talk to me, I may have to go to Washington and confront him in person."

"Actually, he probably won't talk to you by phone or in person."

"Oh, he *will* talk to me whether he wants to or not."

Besch laughed. "Well, if you need a friend in law enforcement up there in Washington, you can contact

Willard Marshall of the Metropolitan Police. Just drop my name and he'll be your best friend. We were in the army together in Vietnam. He's a good detective."

"Thank you. It will be a comfort to know I have someone to turn to if need be."

"Be careful, Stan. You're into some pretty sticky shit here."

He was right about that and I wondered if I should just leave it alone. But the more I thought about it, the angrier I got. One of my clients had been kidnapped and now he'd been robbed of 3.2 million dollars. I just couldn't blow it off. I had to get to the bottom of it. Huntington's life might depend on it.

I asked Jodie to see if she could get Congressman Manning on the line. She tried, but was told he would be in committee hearings all day and his appointment calendar was full all week. They said it was unlikely I'd be able to talk to him until next week. After thinking about it briefly, I knew it was unlikely that Manning would ever talk to me. It was clear I'd have to pay him a visit.

17

The Ring

Bart made it home early for our shopping trip. He brought me a dozen red roses to get the evening off to a good start, he said. I felt like a school girl getting ready to go out on a prom date. Bart seemed more excited and happier than I'd even seen him. He really did love me. I could see it in his eyes. As we got in Bart's car and headed for North Park, where our search for a ring was to begin, I felt very strange like I was in a dream that could be interrupted at any moment. I kept looking around, wondering when I'd be awakened.

North Park was crowded as usual but nothing could dampen my enthusiasm on this particular night. We browsed in the first two jewelry stores we encountered, but didn't find anything that struck our fancy. In the third store, however, I found a three-stone designer engagement ring that we both loved. It was expensive, but Bart said if I liked it, it was mine. Fortunately, they had one in my size, so Bart slipped it on my finger and I promised never to take it off again.

The rest of the evening was a blur. We had dinner at the Mansion, found a club afterwards where we were able to dance, and listen to great music. Then we went home and finished off the evening in each other's arms. The next morning was so blissful I didn't want to get up. We lingered in bed until almost nine o'clock when the telephone rang. It was Stan and he was upset.

"I've got to catch a plane to Washington," Stan said. "I wanted to let you know that I was going. I should be back tomorrow."

"Why are you going to Washington?" I asked.

"I've got to see Congressman Manning and get some answers."

"Answers to what?"

"Why he called a friend at the IRS and got them to release the Continental Exporters' bank account. The money is gone because of him."

"Why would he do that? What does he have to do with Continental Exporters?"

"I don't know, but I intend to find out."

"Be careful, Stan. Someone has already kidnapped Huntington. I don't want you disappearing too."

"Don't worry. I'm just going to visit a U.S. Congressman. How dangerous could that be?"

Stan's telephone call scared me. I had a very bad feeling about his sudden trip. Obviously, he was in the middle of some serious business that neither of us understood. Even Detective Besch and the FBI seemed to be clueless as to what was happening. I wished I could have done something, but I didn't have the slightest idea what it would be. All I could do while I waited, was to focus on Jimmy Bennett's case. Hard work would keep my mind off Stan and the danger I knew was awaiting him in Washington.

When I got to the office, I reviewed the witness list and decided it was time to visit Don Bennett's wife, Margie. Fortunately, she was still dealing with Don's affairs and hadn't returned to the ranch. She agreed to see me that afternoon in their plush abode that made Jimmy's place look like servants' quarters. As I drove up to the place, I wondered why any human being needed so much space. I imagined Don and Margie arguing and hearing echos billowing through the huge house.

Margie wasn't what I expected. She was homely if not downright ugly. She also wasn't the friendliest human being on the planet either. I counted three servants waiting on her but she never once offered me even a cup of coffee. I now understood why Don Baker didn't mind that she was off with her boyfriend at Buffalo Ridge most of the time.

"I just needed to ask you a few questions as part of my investigation," I said.

"I don't know what in God's green earth I could tell you that would help."

"Well, I thought maybe you might know who your husband's enemies were. Perhaps Don told you something or you observed things that concerned you."

"The police have the right man. Jimmy's been looking for a way to get control of Don's money. I told Don he shouldn't trust that SOB. He's a two timin' snake."

"What did he do that made you hate him so much?"

"He married my daughter for starters. I forbid her to marry him, but she didn't listen. He's a snake charmer, that boy is. Don took to him like he was a long-lost son, too. But, I could see right through him. Jimmy's a leach. Never did an honest day's labor in his life."

"I heard he did a pretty good job running Baker Construction."

"No. His brother's a good boy. A real Christian. He's the one that kept Baker Construction doing so well. Jimmy just likes to act like a big shot."

"Still, I sense there is something you're not telling me about Jimmy. What happened between you two to make you so angry?"

"Nothing. He's just a two-bit drug addict. Even Betty finally figured that out. It's about time she had the sense to divorce the asshole. I hope he rots in prison for the rest of his life."

Margie's hostility toward Jimmy shocked me. I figured she wouldn't like him, but her emotional tirade made me think he'd hurt her deeply somehow. It was clear I wasn't going to find out what was going on between them from Margie. Jimmy himself would have to enlighten me.

18

Nightmares

I called Rebekah and Paula and told them I was catching the next flight to Washington DC. Needless to say, neither one of them was thrilled to hear that news. Rebekah did reluctantly agree to pack me an overnight suitcase. I told her I'd stop home and pick it up on the way to the airport.

The American Airlines flight took off right on time. It was about a two and a half-hour flight to DC so I figured I'd have plenty of time to think and plan my strategy upon arrival in Washington. I had been acting on anger and outrage and as the flight drew on I had second thoughts about my trip. What if I couldn't talk to Manning? What would I say to him if I did get the chance? After a while, I felt sleepy and dozed off.

I was in a bar with a woman and two other couples. My companion was a short brunette. I felt awkward being with her. I could tell she felt equally uncomfortable being with me. We left the bar and went to a hotel—the sign read Howard Johnson. We were both a little drunk and stumbled into our room. We took off our shirts. She began to give me a massage. Her fingers felt good—oh, so wonderful.

The scene shifted. I was in a courtroom waiting to be called as a witness. Suddenly a horrible feeling came over me. I stood up and ran into the next room. A woman was in a bathtub. She was pale white and her eyes fixed. I lifted her out of the tub and tried to revive her. She didn't respond. I held her tightly as tears flowed from my eyes. A paramedic put his hand on my shoulder. Let her go, he said.

"No! No! She can't be dead!"

The plane lurched as it hit the tarmac at Washington Dulles International Airport. I awoke amazed that I was in an airplane. The people around me were all looking at me oddly. I couldn't believe I'd slept so soundly. It seemed like just seconds earlier I had settled back for the long flight.

After deplaning into the mobile lounge, we started our short ride to the terminal. Memories of meeting Rebekah and my friend Steve here at Dulles seventeen years earlier played in my mind's eye. They had come to be with me when I was on trial. A jolt, as the mobile lounge made contact with the terminal, woke me from my daydream. The doors opened and we all entered the terminal.

Once inside I recovered my luggage and headed for the car rental plaza. Jodie had reserved me a car and it was ready for me when I got to the rental desk. A wave of anxiety washed over me at the thought of confronting Manning. *This is crazy.* I found my car and read the directions the attendant had given me for the trip to my hotel. I was staying at the Howard Johnson. The same one I'd stayed in while I was in the Marine Corps in the spring of 1970. When I saw the old hotel, memories flooded through my mind of Nicole Schultz, the sexy brunette massage therapist who'd spent the night with me in one of those rooms when I was on trial for allegedly murdering my drill sergeant. I wondered what she was doing and if she still lived in Washington.

It was after 7:00 p.m. when I closed the door and gazed around the small room—nothing fancy but adequate for a good night's sleep. I was hungry, so I decided to see if the old Omaha Corral Bar & Grille was still in business. I called the desk clerk and asked and she said it was. After changing into something casual, I left the hotel and started walking in the direction I remembered it being. A few blocks down the street I got an eerie feeling that I was being watched. I turned around quickly and surveyed the crowded street. Nobody seemed to pay me any mind, so I turned back around and continued on my way. Finally, I saw the big Omaha Corral sign flashing ahead. I quickened my pace and when I got to the front door I went inside.

A pretty girl in a jean skirt, yellow and white plaid blouse, and alligator boots greeted me. She asked if I was expecting anyone and I said, "I don't think so." She gave me a funny look and then found me a table near the bar. As I was being seated, I noticed two men walk in. They looked at me and then quickly looked away. Both men were overdressed for a Midwest style steakhouse. She seated them across the room.

After downing a couple beers, the waitress brought me the big T-bone steak I'd ordered along with beans, fries, and Texas toast. I had just started eating when I noticed one of the two men get up and use the telephone on the wall. I took a deep breath and told myself they had nothing to do with me. After all, Manning had no way of knowing I was in town—at least not yet. But then I remembered Paula had seen someone outside our office in Dallas. Suddenly I wasn't so hungry and wished I'd ordered room service.

I lingered in the restaurant hoping the two men would leave but they weren't going anywhere. Finally, I got up my nerve and left. Just outside the door I stopped and waited. A second later the two men came out quickly and nearly ran me down. I got a good look at them. They excused themselves and kept walking. Spotting a cab coming down the street, I hailed it and quickly got inside. The driver took me back to the Holiday Inn and I went straight to my room.

The next morning, I headed toward the Capitol and Rayburn House Office Building where I had been told Manning had his office. It was difficult finding a place to park and I ended up having to walk six blocks away. Finally, at 10:15 a.m., I walked into Manning's congressional office. The receptionist asked who I was, so I told her and gave her a business card. She looked at her book and said I wasn't on the Congressman's appointment calendar.

I nodded and said, "Yes, this just came up. It's an emergency. Just tell the Congressman I'm Continental Exporters' attorney and I'm here to discuss the Robert Huntington kidnaping."

She gave me a skeptical look and went into an adjacent office. I looked around and noticed a lady dressed in black sitting behind me next to the door. I had walked right by her coming in and hadn't noticed her sitting there. She looked at me curiously. It was several minutes before the receptionist came back. "I'm sorry, Mr. Turner, but the Congressman can't squeeze you in today. He said to call him next week and he might have time to see you then.

"Tell him that's okay," I said. "I'm sure I can get an appointment today with the FBI or maybe a newspaper reporter who's not busy."

I started to walk out when a man stepped into the reception area. He was a tall, distinguished looking gentleman who looked familiar. I'd seen Congressman Manning on the evening news, but hadn't paid much attention to him. He motioned for me to follow him. I did and he led me into his office.

"Mr. Turner, I'm a Congressman for godsakes. You can't just barge in and expect to get an appointment immediately. And what exactly would you tell the FBI or the press?"

"Thank you for seeing me, Congressman. I apologize for coming without notice, but the matter is urgent."

"Well, nearly everything I deal with is urgent to someone."

"Anyway, I'll get to the point. I wanted to thank you for helping us free up the Continental Exporters' bank account."

"It was nothing. Just a telephone call to my old friend Tony Perez."

"You must have heard that Robert Huntington was kidnapped."

"Yes, a dreadful thing. Has the FBI made any progress in finding him?"

"No. He seems to have just vanished off the face of the earth."

"Well, of course, I'll do what I can to help find him, but you didn't come here to discuss his kidnaping, did you?"

"No, I wondered why you called Mr. Perez last night inquiring about whether the lien on the Continental Exporter's bank account had been released?"

"Well, . . . it was just routine follow-up. I was just curious."

"Nobody called you and asked you to check on it, did they?"

"Why, no. Nobody. I just followed through and made sure the job got done."

"So, you thought it was necessary to have Mr. Perez hand deliver a copy of the release to Metroplex Savings?"

"Yes, I'm an expert at cutting through red tape and I could see what had happened. The paperwork had just got stalled."

"But you knew Huntington had been kidnapped? Why was it so important the release be delivered to Metroplex?"

The Congressman shifted in his seat uncomfortably.

I said, "Did you know the money was going to be wired to Panama the moment the lien was released?"

The Congressman stood up. "Good God, no! Is that what happened?"

The Congressman may have been a great politician, but he wasn't a great actor. I could see he was up to his thick neck in whatever sinister business was going on with Continental Exporters. It appeared I had gotten my questions answered and I wasn't going to accomplish anything more with further inquiry of the Congressman. I got up to leave.

I said, "Thank you, Congressman for seeing me and answering my questions. I think I understand what's going on now."

The Congressman leaned forward, narrowed his eyes and replied, "Mr. Turner, you don't understand a damn thing and you best stay out of business that doesn't concern you."

A cold chill darted through me. I'd just been threatened by a U.S. Congressman. Puzzled by the threat, I replied, "Or what?"

The Congressman stood up abruptly ignoring my question. It was clear it was time to leave, so I turned and left his office without another word. The receptionist gave me a hard stare as I walked past her. The girl in the black dress suddenly stood up and stepped in front of me. We collided and I felt her hand slip something in my inside coat pocket. She winked at me and began to apologize profusely. Curiosity as to what had been placed in my pocket welled inside me, but I knew I was being watched so I resisted the desire to pull it out and look at it. Just outside the office building I saw the two men who had been following me. They took up their posts again and followed me to my car. Fortunately, the lot was busy so I got to my car without incident.

Very carefully, I slipped my hand in my pocket and pulled out the folded piece of paper that had been deposited there by the mysterious lady in black. I opened it and found an address written hastily in blue ink. It read "22 East Commercial Way, Washington, D.C."

Not wanting the men following me to suspect I had received a message, I tucked the note back in my pocket and started the car. As I drove out of the parking lot I noticed the two men get into a blue Mercury Marquis and take off after me. I thought about the note and wondered what it meant. I had no idea where the address was, so, if I did decide to go there, I would need to get directions. It occurred to me that it could be a trap. The Congressman could have had the lady in black slip me the note to lure me to a quiet place where he could have me beaten or murdered. They'd make it look like I got lost and was the victim of a street gang. Then I remembered Detective Besch's friend Willard Marshall. I stopped at the next telephone booth I saw and called him.

"Hi. This is Stan Turner. I'm an attorney from Dallas. Detective Bingo Besch told me to look you up if I needed any help while I was in town."

"He did, did he?"

"Yeah, I'm sorry to bother you but I've run into a bit of a problem." I told him briefly about Huntington's kidnaping and Congressman Manning's involvement. He listened without comment. "When I was leaving Congressman Manning's place one of his staff members slipped me an address. I don't have any idea whose address it is but I need to check it out just in case it means something."

"Give me the address and I'll have someone find out where it is and who owns the place."

I read him the address and continued, "I have another problem too." I told him about the men following me.

"Do you have any idea who they are?"

"No, not really, but they're driving a blue Mercury Marquis Virginia license number TXU 232," I said.

"Okay, We'll check that out too. Hang on."

There were a few minutes of silence and then Willard came back on, "The address is a warehouse in a commercial district northwest of the capital. It's owned by CTW Investments, Inc. of Philadelphia and currently leased to a company called Continental Exporters."

"Continental Exporters?"

"Right. That's what it says."

"That's my client's company. We definitely need to go check it out."

"Okay, where are you? I'll come pick you up. I'll make sure your friends are detained why we go take a look at the warehouse."

"Thank you. I really appreciate all your help."

"No problem. Any friend of Bingo's is a friend of mine. How's the old rascal, anyway?"

"Doing well. Working hard."

"I bet. Hang loose. I'll be there in about five or six minutes."

"No problem. I'll see you soon."

I looked over my shoulder and saw the blue Mercury parked a block down the street. I wondered who they were and what they wanted from me. Suddenly two police cars came barreling around the corner. The first one stopped in front of the Mercury and the second one came to a screeching stop next to my rental car. I got out and jumped in next to Williard Marshall. He tore off leaving the other police car and the two men behind.

"So, did you find out anything about those two men?" I asked.

From what we could find out about their vehicle they are definitely not FBI. They're either private investigators or CIA."

"Really?"

We got to 22 Commercial Way in about twenty minutes. It was a large warehouse in an industrial area. When we approached the building, we realized it was closed and boarded up.

"There still may be some important evidence inside," I said. "Can we go inside and search?"

"Not without a warrant."

"Maybe if you called Detective Besch, he could give you what you need for a warrant?"

"You got his number?" Willard asked.

I had called Detective Besch enough times that I had memorized the number. I gave it to him and he dialed him on his car telephone. They talked for a few minutes and then he turned to me and said, "He's gonna call his contact at the FBI to get the warrant. We should have it in a few hours.

I nodded and replied, "Good. I hope we find something in there to make all this hassle worth the effort."

"Well, we'll just have to wait and see. In the meantime, I know a place we can get a cup of coffee while we wait."

I nodded and replied, "That sounds good to me."

Detective Marshall drove me to a diner. It didn't look like much but he said the coffee was good. We got a booth and a waitress poured us each a cup. As I drank, I wondered about his relationship to Besch.

"I appreciate you jumping right in to help me out," I said. "I didn't expect you to drop everything on account of me."

"Well, if Bingo told you to call me, I knew it must be important, and, after talking to him, I can see you may be onto something big."

"I don't know what to make of it. It's the most bizarre situation that I've ever been in."

"I wouldn't say that," Besch said. "If you're the Stan Turner I've heard about, your life *is* the definition of *bizarre*."

"You've heard about me? Wow."

"Well, you had us spellbound with the Dusty Thomas' trial."

"It was my partner who really should get the credit for breaking that one. She was on it like a hound dog from day one. She's a great criminal attorney."

"What's her name?"

"Paula Waters. She's back home right now trying to figure out who killed Don Baker."

"Right. I've read about that one in the papers too. Do you really think your client is innocent?"

"I don't know. He says he is, so I guess that's all I need to hear, right?"

Marshall nodded, "I guess for a criminal defense attorney that's enough."

"My hunch is that he is innocent. Don Baker had a list of enemies as long as a lizard's tongue."

Marshall laughed. "Yeah, well I bet a lot of bankers are unpopular these days with banks and thrifts failing left and right."

"I don't feel at all sorry for those greedy bastards. It's just too bad they're taking good folks down with them."

"So, who is this mysterious lady in black? Do you know her name?"

"No, she had a desk in the Congressman's office so she must be staff or an intern?"

"How old was she?"

"I bet she was an intern. She looked like she was in her early twenties."

"I'll make some inquiries and find out who she is. She might have some additional information that would be useful."

We talked for another half hour and then Marshall looked at his watch and said, "I suppose we should be getting back to the warehouse. That warrant ought to be coming through here pretty soon."

I nodded and we both got up. We left the diner and drove back to the warehouse. The place was surrounded with police cars and a detail of FBI agents were unloading equipment out of one of their vans. I followed Detective Marshall up to the agent in charge.

"Jordan," Marshall said. The man turned and smiled at the detective.

"Hey, Detective Marshall," Agent Jordan said. They shook hands. "Thanks for the tip, We've been dead in the water on this Huntington kidnaping."

"Don't thank me," Marshall said looking toward me. "Thank Mr. Turner here."

Agent Jordan extended his hand and I shook it. "I just hope you find something in there that leads us to the kidnappers."

A blue Buick sedan drove up and a man got out holding a document. He brought it to Agent Jordan. Jordan looked at it and said, "Here's what we've been waiting for." He motioned to his men and they all gathered around. "Okay, it looks vacant but we don't know for sure if that's really the case, so be careful. Let's proceed as we discussed earlier."

Everyone nodded and they broke away into their teams. One unit went around the back of the building while another one readied a frontal entry of the building. An agent planted some kind of small explosive device on the front door and then backed off. It exploded blowing off the lock and quickly two agents kicked open the door and entered the building. Marshall told me to wait outside and then he entered the building with several of his men.

There was silence for several minutes and then one of Marshall's men came out and motioned for me to come in. I quickly followed him through the front door, down a long hallway, and into a huge open warehouse. The agents were scurrying around searching every inch of the place.

Jordan saw me approach and said, "Well, no evidence of grapefruit or any other commodity."

"Really?"

"Yeah, everything's been wiped clean, scrubbed down, and vacuumed. There's not a print, a scrap of paper, or even a fiber in the whole damn place. Whoever cleaned up this joint didn't want anyone to know what they'd been up to.

19

Searching For An Alibi

Jodie seemed as excited about my wedding as I was. One afternoon we took a long lunch and went to Nieman Marcus to shop for wedding dresses. I must have tried on twenty dresses before I narrowed it down to three possibilities: a sleeveless satin sheath with a chapel train, a satin embroidery with a scooped neckline and a sweep train; or a chiffon over crepe with a scooped neckline and cathedral train. They were all so beautiful I couldn't decide which one to buy. I was glad Jodie was helping out because my mother had died of breast cancer a year after I graduated from law school. One of her greatest regrets about dying so young was that she'd never see me get married. I prayed that she'd be watching from heaven.

When I got back to the office, I called Jimmy Bennett and told him we needed to talk. I wanted to go over with him what I had learned in my investigation so far and get his reaction. I had discovered a lot since I had talked to him last and now I had a long list of questions. He came to my office late that afternoon. We met in the conference room.

"Why does Margie hate you so much?" I asked.

Jimmy shrugged, "Because I was from a poor family,

never went to college, and I'm from Arkansas. Bottom line—I'm not good enough for her daughter."

"Yes, but it must go deeper than that. She really went on a tirade when I asked her what she thought of you."

"Well, I was the one who informed her that Don was sleeping with her sister."

"What?"

"I caught them going at it one night at the office. I couldn't believe it. I wasn't going to say anything to her about it, but she got me pissed off one night and it just came out."

The door opened and Jodie advised me I had a phone call from Stan. I excused myself and took the call. Stan told me about the FBI raid on the Continental Exporters' warehouse. He wanted me to know he'd be delayed in returning for a couple of days. I told him to be careful and to keep me posted on what was happening. After hanging up, I went back to the conference room.

"Okay, I know Metroplex was in trouble, but tell me more about the specific problems it was having? Why was it in trouble?"

"The biggest problem was loan defaults. Don had a lot of friends he lent money to and he didn't always get enough collateral. They had an appraisal company they contracted with that would evaluate the collateral and put a value on it. The amount that could be lent depended on the value of the collateral. What usually happened was that Don would call the appraiser handling the job and suggest to him what value the appraisal should show. The appraiser would then make sure it coincided with the needs of the bank. The collateral on Metroplex loans were usually 25-50%

overvalued."

"Who were some of his friends?"

"Congressman Horace Manning and Speaker John Potts were the worst offenders."

"Really? What did they finance with the money they borrowed?"

"That's a good question. I'm not sure if they used it to finance their campaigns or invested in some private business ventures, but they borrowed nearly five million dollars between them. When they defaulted, Don nearly had a stroke. The OTS came in a hurry when they saw the nonperforming loan report that next week."

"So, what did the bank do about the delinquent loans?"

"The feds insisted they turn them over to an attorney. I believe there is a lawsuit pending against the Congressman and the Speaker."

"I haven't heard about any lawsuit in the newspaper. You'd think if a prominent person like a Congressman or a state representative defaulted on a loan, it would be big news."

"Those two men are very powerful and they know how to keep a lid on things."

"Apparently so," I said.

"Does it benefit the Speaker or the Congressman in any way that Don Baker is dead?"

Jimmy thought for a moment and replied, "Well, Don was up to his elbows in their shady dealings. If he ever turned on them, they'd be in serious trouble."

"What kind of shady dealings?"

"I don't know exactly. It was all hush-hush. But it had

to be illegal otherwise there would have been no reason to keep it secret."

"Didn't you question him about it?"

"Sure, but it didn't do any good. I think Don enjoyed keeping me in the dark. He liked to play games like that. I guess it made him feel important."

"Were there any other problems between Baker and his partners?"

"Baker Construction didn't pay payroll taxes. They considered everyone contract labor if they worked full time. The Texas Employment Commission did an audit and determined they should be withholding. That forced the IRS to follow suit. Don was assessed hundreds of thousands of dollars in civil tax penalties."

"How did that play out?"

"They pulled some strings to make it go away."

"I see. The Congressman made a phone call to IRS and the Speaker made a phone call to the TEC."

"Exactly."

"Unbelievable. I didn't think that sort of thing went on any more."

Jimmy laughed. "You don't even know. Don's given me grocery sacks full of money to deliver to people."

"And you delivered it."

"Yeah."

I shook my head in disbelief. "Okay, another question. You told me the last time me met, that on the day of the altercation with Don, you went for a drive up I-30 toward Oklahoma."

"That's right."

"You said you were alone, but some of the people in

your office think you had company with you. They claim you had a girlfriend. If that's true, I need to know about it. Withholding critical information could seriously jeopardize your defense."

"They're full of shit. I don't have time for a girlfriend. Sure, I've been with a lot of girls while I was out with Don, but none of them meant anything to me. I certainly wouldn't confide in them."

"If you were with a woman, she could provide you with an alibi. Are you trying to protect someone?"

"No! I told you. I was alone."

"You've got to account for every minute from the time you left the office until they arrested you. I need you to sit down and make note of everything that you remember. I don't care how insignificant it is, write it down anyway, as it may help us find an alibi."

I didn't know whether to believe Jimmy or not. He seemed sincere, but I wasn't a hundred percent sure. His drug problem was next on my list, but I was a little bit scared to bring it up. It was sure to be a sensitive issue. I took a deep breath and asked, "When's the last time you used drugs?"

Jimmy studied me, took a deep breath and said, "I told you, I'm off drugs."

"That wasn't the question. When was the last time you smoked a joint, took a snort, injected yourself, or whatever you do?"

He frowned and looked to the side like he was thinking. Was he trying to remember or deciding whether to lie? He took a couple short breaths and replied, "Shit, I don't know."

"Have you taken any drugs since Don was killed? I've got to know. It will come up at your trial. If you have been on drugs, we'll have to develop a strategy for dealing with that issue."

He gave me a hard stare. "Okay, I still take a snort now and then, but I can handle it. It doesn't affect me on the job."

"How often?"

"Not more than once or twice a day."

I shook my head. "When did you start up again?"

He shrugged. "A few months ago. I've been under a lot of stress at home and at work as you know. I needed something to help me get through each day."

"So, on the day Don and Amanda were murdered you had at least one hit of cocaine?"

He nodded.

"If this gets out, it's going to hurt your defense. Have you ever blacked out or had a lapse of memory?"

"Yeah, sometimes."

"So, you've woken up somewhere and can't remember how you got there or what you did for the previous twenty-four hours."

"It's only happened a few times. I'm pretty good at pacing myself. I don't do more than I can handle."

"Do you drink a lot too?"

He shrugged. "A six pack of beer after work usually."

"Is it possible that you had more than one hit of cocaine—a few extra beers perhaps—and while you were out driving you got angry and turned around and went to the condo? You might not remember it. But it is possible you killed Don and Amanda, isn't it?"

"No! I remember exactly where I was and what I did, and I didn't go to the condo. I thought you were on my side?"

"I am, but we've got to be prepared for this type of questioning. If you do testify, the DA will come down on you pretty hard. I need to know if you can handle it."

"I can handle it from the DA, but not from my own lawyers."

"I'm sorry. But this isn't a game. Your life is at stake and I don't care whether you like me or not. My job is to give you the best possible defense at trial and that's what I intend to do."

We continued our discussions for another hour and then Jimmy left. If there was anything I *was* clear about in this case, it was that Jimmy couldn't testify at trial. The DA would destroy him. We'd have to find the actual killer or prove reasonable doubt, neither of which would be an easy task.

20

Stolen Treasures

It was several days before I was able to get back to Dallas. The FBI wanted me to fill them in on everything I knew about Continental Exporters. I didn't know much, but I did tell them about Luther and the $150,000 that was supposed to be wired to Huntington's Beijing office. They contacted the person I had talked to at the Red Cross to see if Luther had been located and he told them he had not. It occurred to me that perhaps Luther was never in any jeopardy and that Huntington had simply used him as a pawn in his game of deception.

My suspicions increased when Paula informed me of the Metroplex loans to Congressman Manning and Speaker Potts. Could all this be a coincidence or was there a connection between Continental Exporters and Metroplex Savings & Loan? It certainly was a possibility that couldn't be ignored.

Detective Besch called and said he wanted to stop by the next morning to see me so I could brief him on what happened in Washington. He also wanted to fill me in on the latest in the Lottie West investigation. I remembered I was supposed to go visit Lottie's daughter and son-in-law, James and Loretta Barringer in Dennison, so I had Jodie get their address for me. It was nearly 6:00 p.m. when I knocked on the front door. A woman in her 70s appeared. She opened the door a crack.

"Yes, may I help you?"

"Mrs. Barringer?"

"Yes, I'm Loretta Barringer."

"Hi, sorry to disturb you, but I'm Stan Turner. I'm an attorney in Dallas and I am the designated Independent Executor of the estate of Lottie West."

"Oh, my. You're handling Lottie's estate?"

"Yes, I wonder if I could speak with you for few minutes?"

She opened the door and let me come inside. Her home had a warm and friendly feeling with its early American decor, a large brick fireplace, and many beautiful antiques. She showed me to a sofa and invited me to sit down. A few moments later a tall, skinny man with a scowl on his face walked in the back door. His wife introduced him as her husband James Barringer. She explained to him who I was and he took a seat on a piano bench across from me.

"I ran into your son, Otto, and he informed me that Lottie indeed had living relatives. I had thought that she did not."

"Well, we disowned her years back," James said.

"That's what I heard. Have you talked to Otto lately?"

"No, not for a couple of weeks. He did tell us Lottie had died, but it was after the funeral."

"Then I have some disturbing news to tell you," I said.

"What's that?" Lorretta asked.

"It seems Lottie was murdered."

"Murdered, oh my," Lorretta replied.

I told them about the circumstances of Lottie's demise. They didn't seem overly upset or surprised by the revelation. I wondered if that meant they knew something about it or, simply, that they didn't care. Either way their cold, aloof attitude bothered me.

"Do the police have any suspects yet," Loretta asked.

"No, not really. They've just started their investigation. Do you know anyone who would have reason to kill Lottie?"

They both shook their heads no.

"Well, needless to say, Lottie didn't leave either of you any property. I am curious, though, as to why you were estranged."

James' expression didn't change. He looked away and took a deep breath. Lorretta said, "It was her husband's doin'."

"Really, is that the military man I saw her with in several photos."

Lorretta nodded. "Most likely. They were married just before the war started. He seemed like a decent man. He served several tours in Italy, France, and then Germany when the war was finally over. He was a first lieutenant in the army. When he came back from Germany after his last tour, he was a different man. War changes men, I guess. He pretty much became a loner and didn't want to socialize much at all. He wouldn't even let us visit Lottie and they never came to see us. It was real strange behavior. We finally gave up on keeping up any kind of a relationship with them."

"I see. That's too bad. But, I'm curious. Why didn't you get back together after, after—what was Lottie's husband's name?"

"William West," Lorretta replied.

"After William died—why didn't you get back in touch with your sister?"

"We tried, but she had grown bitter over the years and become a little paranoid—you know—locking herself up with all those dogs. My word. She wouldn't speak to us at all. She said we were just after her money."

"Did she have a lot of money?" I asked. "After they killed her, they ransacked the place. I have no way of knowing what they took because I don't know what property she had. All we found were some gold and silver coins that were hidden in a place a thief wouldn't have found them."

"We don't know for sure, but we heard—there was talk that they had millions," James replied.

"Really? What line of work was William in?" I asked.

"He was an antique dealer—mostly European stuff. He had a retail store on McKinney Avenue in Dallas for many years."

"That wouldn't be an easy trade to learn. Did he work for a dealer to learn the business?"

"Apparently he got interested in art and history while in Germany. I guess he had a lot of free time after the war was over, so he took it up as a hobby. He brought a lot of stuff back with him when he came home and just opened up his own place."

"Interesting. So, I guess it turned out to be a lucrative business?"

James shrugged. "I believe it was but I'm just guessing. William and Lottie never talked about money or their business the few times we did get together."

"There are some personal effects that are of no value to anyone but family. You're welcome to come look through them and take what you like," I said.

Lorretta's eyes lit up. "Oh, yes. We'd like that. She was my sister and it was terrible the way William stole her from us. I curse the day she met that man."

"Just call my office and Jodie, my secretary, will be happy to arrange a time for you to stop by and look through it."

"Thank you, Mr. Turner," Lorretta said. "May I ask you one more question?"

"Sure," I replied.

"Who will be getting Lottie's money?"

I smiled sympathetically and said, "The SPCA."

Their faces dropped. I added, "She was very fond of her dogs."

James shook his head and stormed off. Loretta escorted me to the door. As I left, she said, "We'll be by to go through Lottie's things."

I smiled and left. It amazed me how a strong loving family could be so quickly and easily torn apart for no apparent reason. Unfortunately, it was a pretty common phenomenon and this wasn't the first time I had been caught in the middle of a nasty feud. It was even worse if there was money involved which was apparently the case with Lottie West. I was pretty certain now that whoever killed Lottie West walked off with a lot of valuables—possibly cash, works of art, jewelry, and antiques. I wondered if I'd ever know the extent of what was stolen.

The next morning Detective Besch came by and I filled him in on what had transpired in Washington and what I'd learned about Robert Huntington and Continental Exporters. When I was done, he told me Otto Barringer hadn't been making any unusual expenditures in the past few weeks. That didn't eliminate him as a suspect. He could have still killed Lottie but knew better than to start spending the loot. Besch had also made contact with Otto's sister, Alice St. James, in Philadelphia.

"What did she tell you?" I asked.

"Her story was very similar to her parents," Besch replied. "Except she indicated the estrangement took place in the mid-sixties when rumors surfaced about the possibility that William West might have stolen art treasures from Germany."

"Really?"

"Yes, apparently he tried to sell some of the pieces to a Dallas art dealer. He met with him and showed him some slides of an ancient manuscript. He claimed to have inherited them from his father but the pieces were so well known and obviously stolen, the dealer wanted no part of it."

"Jesus. That would explain a lot."

"Later on, the dealer checked with some art authorities and realized that he had been shown the Ludinburg manuscripts—probably the most valuable art objects to even enter the state of Texas."

"Oh, my God."

"These manuscripts were part of a collection that included a 9th century version of the Four Gospels, the Reliquary, and other gifts from kings and emperors who ruled numerous German states in the 9th and 10th century."

"So, Lottie's killer was after these treasures?" I said.

"That's my guess."

"So, what now?"

"I've notified Army intelligence and they are going to send me all the information they have on these missing art treasures. In the meantime, I've got men checking all the local art dealers and pawn shops to see if anybody has tried to sell anything like that over the last few weeks."

"Sounds good. Is there anything else I can do to help the investigation?" I asked.

"Yes, I've been told the Ludinburg Church has a committee or commission of some sort trying to locate these art treasures. You might want to contact them and find out how to contact these people."

"Sure, I'll get right on it."

Besch left and I sat for a while trying to digest all I'd learned about William West and his underground art business. It was a complicated scenario but it was starting to come into focus. William West had to be secretive as he was sitting on millions of dollars of stolen art treasurers. He couldn't afford to have Lottie's family snooping around his home or his business. His reclusiveness was for a good reason. I wondered if Lottie knew what her husband was involved in. Was she the innocent spouse or willing accomplice? I understood now why she was so paranoid. Who else knew about William West's business? It occurred to me if I was able to answer that question, I'd be a lot closer to knowing who killed Lottie West.

21

Frantic Call

After my second interview with Jimmy Bennett it was clear we were going to have to delve deeper into the relationship between Metroplex Savings and Loan, Congressman Manning, and Speaker Potts. I asked Stan what he thought about it.

"The secret alliance among the three men certainly could have led to Don's murder. I wonder if Don was upset at the Congressman for not making his problems with the federal regulators go away?"

"I bet he was," I replied. "Perhaps out of frustration he threatened the Congressman."

"Right. And the Congressman decided it wasn't healthy to have Don alive anymore."

"So," I asked. "How do we prove that?"

"Well, maybe somebody, a neighbor or jogger, saw something at the condo the night of the murder."

"I'm sure Detective Perkins talked to everybody?" I replied.

"True. But they may not have asked the right questions or they may have only listened to what they wanted to hear," Stan suggested.

"Well, I'll be happy to go canvass the neighborhood. If there is a connection between the Congressman and Don's death that should go a long way to creating reasonable doubt."

"Sounds good," Stan said and then excused himself to let me get back to work. As I was opening my mail Jodie buzzed to tell me that Jimmy was on the line. I picked up the telephone.

"I'm at the Condo," Jimmy said. "They followed me here."

"What?"

"They're up in the trees. They have guns."

"Who's in the trees?"

"The feds, the IRS, hell I don't know who they are?"

"Have they talked to you?"

"You need to do something. They're going to kill me?"

"Why would they want to kill you?"

"Aren't you going to do something? Shit! *Click*"

The phone went dead. I rushed over to Stan's office and told him what had happened.

"He said the Feds were after him?" Stan asked.

"Yes, he was frantic. He sounded like he'd gone mad."

"Let's call his wife and maybe she can go over to the Condo and find out what's wrong with him."

I nodded, buzzed Jodie, and asked her to get Betty Bennett on the phone. A minute later she buzzed back and said Betty was on the line.

"Mrs. Bennett. We just got a very strange telephone call from Jimmy. He said there were people up in a tree with guns who were trying to kill him."

Betty sighed. "Oh, shit. He's on a cocaine binge."

"What?"

"When he gets high on cocaine, he becomes very

paranoid and often imagines people are after him. I've gotten calls before like the one you just got. Sometimes he'll get in the car and drive hundreds of miles thinking he's running from someone. He called me one time from Florida."

"Jesus, I didn't realize his addiction was that bad."

"That's another reason I'm divorcing him."

"Well, should we do something?"

"I'll go over to the condo and make sure he's okay."

"Thanks," I said.

Stan and I discussed Jimmy's condition and decided we couldn't really do anything about it, so we'd just have to come up with a strategy to mitigate its impact on the jury. That usually meant bringing it up early and being honest about it. It would take some fancy footwork but it wasn't an insurmountable problem. Jodie buzzed in again and said Betty was back on the line. I picked up the phone.

"Jimmy's not here. He may have taken a road trip," Betty said.

"What do you mean?"

"He took some clothes and a suitcase?"

"Oh, my God. They'll revoke his bond if he leaves the state."

"My guess he's half way to Louisiana by now."

"Why Louisiana?" I asked.

"He likes to get out of Texas, and north and east are the quickest ways to do that."

"Maybe we can catch him before the cops do?" I said. "Hold on."

I put Betty on the speaker phone.

"There's no way we could catch him unless he stops," Stan said.

Betty replied, "That a strong possibility. When Jimmy travels, he stops frequently for coffee or food. I'll go east on I20 and check all the roadside restaurants and convenience stores. You go north on I35 and do the same. I think there is a fair chance we can catch him. We've got to catch him. He'll go crazy if they lock him up in a jail cell.

"Okay. Call me on my car phone every thirty minutes," I said. "The number is on my business card."

"I will. Thanks," Betty replied.

For the first time since I had met Betty, she seemed concerned for Jimmy's well-being. I guess there still was some love left for him after all. I knew Jimmy loved her. He had made that abundantly clear each time I'd interviewed him. In fact, if Jimmy was guilty of killing Don Baker it would be because Don was responsible for Jimmy losing Betty, the woman he loved.

We didn't figure Don would stop right away so we didn't start hitting convenience stores and restaurants until we got to Denton. We got off on the access road at the Triangle Mall exit and went by each restaurant, gas station, and convenience store very slowly looking for Jimmy's pickup. After the eighth or ninth establishment we pulled into a roadside bar next to a Cracker Barrel Restaurant. We were looking for a big black Ford F150. Betty had given us the license plate number. We drove all the way around the lot and didn't see anything until we had gone almost a full circle. Then we saw it. We parked next to it and rushed inside.

Jimmy was at the bar smoking a cigarette and talking to the young lady bartender. Stan and I slipped up and sat on each side of him. He looked at us and did a double take.

"Counselors? What are you two doing here?"

"You called me, remember?" I said. "The FBI was after you."

"Oh, right. . . . I lost them," he said taking a drag on his cigarette. "Thanks for coming, though. I'm okay."

Stan said, "Where are you headed?"

"Just out for a drive?"

"Not out of state, I hope," Stan asked.

Jimmy shook his head and smiled at the barmaid, "No, just out and about hoping to get lucky."

The barmaid blushed and walked to the other end of the bar. Jimmy took another drag on his cigarette. Stan looked at me and shook his head.

"Why don't you come back with us?" Stan said. "In your condition, you're likely to get stopped and if they see your suitcase they may think you're skipping out on your bond."

"Nah., I'm all right," Jimmy said. He stood up and then nearly collapsed. Stan grabbed him under one arm to keep him on his feet. We helped him out to Stan's car.

"You take him home in your car," I said. "I'll follow you in the pickup."

Stan nodded and closed the passenger side door. It was about a forty-five-minute drive back to the condo where Jimmy had been living since Betty kicked him out. Betty must have called right after we left because she was there to meet us. We took him inside and put him to bed. When Betty returned, she asked us if we wanted a cup of coffee. We accepted.

"I so sorry you two had to waste the afternoon chasing Jimmy. Now you can see why I'm getting a divorce."

"Yes, I don't blame you," I said. "It must be very difficult."

"Yes, it is. . . . So, how is your investigation going? Do you think there is any chance Jimmy can be acquitted?"

Stan looked at me expectantly. I smiled at him. "Actually, to be honest with you it's not looking very good. The state's got a pretty good case against Jimmy, even if it is circumstantial."

"But Daddy had so many enemies, so many people who were angry with him. Don't you have any other suspects?"

"Sure, what do you know about Congressman Manning and Speaker Potts?" I asked.

"They were very good friends. Daddy took them fishing at Lake Fork a lot. They came over to the house quite often before I got married and they did some business ventures together."

"Yes, and we believe some of those ventures were not entirely legitimate. It's a possibility that when Metroplex Savings and Loan got into trouble that your Dad got at odds with Congressman Manning and the Speaker. If that is true, they may have felt it necessary to kill your father."

"What? No way. I know both of them very well. They are both honorable men. They wouldn't be involved in murder."

"I don't know. If they had a lot at stake, they might."

"Do you think you can prove that?" Betty asked.

"Luckily, we don't have to," Stan said. "Our goal is to get enough evidence of that relationship to create reasonable doubt."

Despite her spirited defense of Congressman Manning

and Speaker Potts, Betty didn't seem all that shocked by the notion that Congressman Manning and the Speaker might have killed her father, or had him killed. It was clear she knew or was, at least, aware that they were involved in some illicit ventures. All we had to do now was to gather some credible evidence of those illicit deals so we could convince the jury that Jimmy was innocent. The problem with that strategy, however, was that the Speaker and the Congressman wouldn't take kindly to us snooping into their affairs.

22

Break In

One morning several weeks after returning from Washington, I arrived early to my office. I had a chapter 13 bankruptcy docket at 8:30 a.m. and needed to get prepared for it. When I went to open the front door of the office, I noticed the lock had been broken. I pushed the door opened and proceeded cautiously into the reception area.

The first thing I noticed was all the drawers in Jodie's desk were open. From Jodie's work area, I went to the file room. It was a mess—file drawers half-opened, files laying on the floor, and papers everywhere. I went into my office next and it looked like a tornado had struck. My locked middle drawer had been pried open with a screwdriver. Drawers were emptied out on the ground, pictures had been knocked off the walls, and books were all over the place.

For a moment, I just stood there in shock. Then I heard the door open and Jodie walked in. "What the hell?" she said. I joined her in the reception area.

"I guess somebody was looking for something," I said.

"Shall I call the cops?" Jodie asked.

"Yes, call Detective Besch. Whoever did this probably

has a connection to one of the two cases he's handling. You better call the trustee's office too and get me a pass this morning. I won't be able to make the 8:30 a.m. docket. "

Jodie picked up the telephone and called Besch's number. She talked to him a minute and then hung up. "He's on his way over with a crime scene team. He said not to touch anything."

"Okay, I guess we'll have a cup of coffee while we wait."

She nodded and replied, "Sure, I'll put a pot on. Detective Besch and his men will probably want some too."

We walked into the kitchen and Jodie turned on the coffee maker. I sat down and thought about who might be responsible for trashing the office. I couldn't come up with an answer.

"You must have something that somebody wants pretty badly," Jodie surmised.

"Yeah, I wonder what it is?"

"Well, what do you have that belongs to Huntington or Lottie West?"

"The IRS release," I said. "But the funds have already been stolen."

"Anything else?"

"No, the police have all of Lottie's stuff."

"Maybe, it had nothing to do with either of them. It could have been a thief looking for money or equipment to steal."

"I don't know," I said. "I guess we'll have to let Besch figure it out. He's the detective."

Ten minutes later Besch showed up with his crime scene investigators. They began carefully processing the room looking for prints or other evidence of the intruder. Besch joined us in the coffee room while they worked.

"This might actually be a break," Besch said. "If they left a fingerprint or someone saw them enter or exit the building, we might be able to get an identification."

"I've racked my brain trying to figure out what I would have that someone might want, but I can't think of a thing," I said.

"Maybe they were looking for something to do with the Jimmy Bennett case," Jodie suggested.

"Let's just wait and see," Besch said. "In the meantime, we need to focus on William West. I believe he's the key to figuring out who killed Lottie. We need to know more about him.

"His family doesn't have much to say," I said.

"Well, there must be neighbors and friends who knew him. They would probably be less reluctant to talk," Besch replied.

"What about the people who did business with him?"Jodie asked.

"Well, we've determined he died of cancer in 1980. I've already had someone check all the art dealers in town. Nobody claims to have known him," Besch said.

"Perhaps that's because he wasn't selling to the general public. He might have been dealing with private collectors."

"So, how do you make contact with private art dealers," Jodie asked.

"You ask legitimate dealers. They often know who the crooks are," I said.

"Or you send someone in looking for stolen art or a

piece of art that isn't for sale," Besch said.

"I'll do that," Jodie said.

Besch looked at Jodie, then at me. I shrugged. "She's a pretty good actress, actually."

"No. I'll let one of our people do it."

"I'd really like to do it," Jodie replied. "I need a little excitement in my life. It gets boring around here typing and answering the phone all day."

"Actually, I do have something for you to do," I said.

"You need to contact the Ludinburg Church in Germany and contact that organization that is looking for art stolen by the Nazis during World War II. You like art, don't you? You can be our in-house art expert. I have a feeling we're going to desperately need one before this case is over."

"Okay, that sounds like fun," Jodie said tentatively. "But I don't know much about art."

"Don't worry, neither do we," I said.

Detective Besch got up. "We'll I've got to get going. I think my people are about done. I'll let you two get started cleaning this place up. Sorry, I can't stay to help."

Detective Besch and his team left and Jodie and I started cleaning up the mess. Two hours later everything was in its place and we went back to work. I thought about our discussion about William West and finding black market art dealers. It was time to start the hunt. I picked up the big Dallas Yellow Pages. There were 103 listing but luckily many could be eliminated just by examining their names—American Museum of Miniature Arts, Dallas Museum of Art, etc. After culling through the list there were only eighteen that looked like serious art dealers who might deal in the type of art works that William West had for sale. After calling each of them and asking general questions, I further narrowed the list to four that seemed very sophisticated and particularly knowledgeable. It was nearly noon so I decided to get a bite to eat and then go visit the four galleries.

The first gallery was manned by a college student who barely knew how to run the cash register. He said the owner was out of town for a few days. The owner of the second one was suspicious of my intentions, rude, and completely uncooperative. I was starting to get a little frustrated when I entered Euro Art of Dallas beneath One Main Place in downtown Dallas. It was a modest looking gallery with a large inventory of prints and quite a few original looking works of art on the walls. A partner in the business, who identified himself as Hans, greeted me. I introduced myself and told him the purpose of my visit.

"We don't touch stolen art," Hans advised.

"I didn't think you did, but I thought maybe being in the business you could point me in the right direction."

"I'm sorry. I can't help you. I don't know anyone like that."

"I'm not out to get anyone. I'm just looking for information to help me find out who murdered a client, Lottie West. Her husband William West acquired some art while he was in Europe and may have tried to sell it. He died seven or eight years ago.

"He never actually brought the pieces with him—just pictures of them."

The voice came from behind me. I turned and saw a tall, heavy set man speaking. He introduced himself as

Leonard Linus—the other partner in Euro Art, I surmised.

"You knew him?"

"Like I said, he came by with photos of pieces of his stolen art and wanted me to buy them, or find a buyer. I, of course, wouldn't touch them."

"How did you know they were stolen?"

Mr. Turner, "These pieces were very well known—rare manuscripts in jewel bindings from Germany. They are historical pieces of great value. There have been people looking for these treasures for more than forty years. In fact, a person can earn a substantial reward simply by providing information that eventually leads to their recovery."

"Really? Who pays for the reward?"

"Either the church, the government, or the German Cultural Organization."

"Did you ever report Mr. West to the authorities?"

"No, but I contacted the German Cultural Organization and told them about it."

"When did all this happen?"

"Oh, it's been ten or fifteen years at least—I'm not sure."

"What did they do?"

"They told me they would pay a one million dollars reward for the return of the treasures—no questions asked."

"Really?"

"Yes, the primary purpose of the organization was to recover the goods, not prosecute the thieves. They didn't want anyone who had these pieces to be afraid to return them for fear of going to jail."

"So, what did you do?"

"I called Mr. West and told them I would buy the

pieces from him for a million dollars, but he said he'd already sold them."

"To whom?"

"A private collector—Zimmerman—I think his name was."

"I see."

"So, I contacted him and offered him the money, but he wasn't interested in selling so cheaply."

"Do you know his first name?"

"Yes, I can look it up," he said as he started going through a stack of index cards. "He bought some other pieces from us, so I have his name and address. But don't tell him where you got it. He's a powerful and ruthless man."

"I won't," I said, puzzled that he would give me this information so freely. "I really appreciate you telling me all this. I am curious though. If he's so dangerous, why are you being so helpful. If you hadn't of stepped forward, I would have left and known nothing."

Linus shrugged and replied, "Mr. Zimmerman doesn't care so much about art as he does making lots of money. He has no scruples whatsoever. He's a rude, arrogant man who will do whatever it takes to get what he wants. It's about time someone put him in his place."

"Luther," he said reading from a card he had selected. "His first name was Luther."

It was clear Leonard Linus had no love for Luther Zimmerman. He wouldn't go into more specifics as to why he hated him so much, but I was sure it would be juicy. Linus went into the back room for a moment and then returned and handed me a piece of paper. It had Luther Zimmerman's address and telephone number on it. I thanked him, gave him a card, and asked him to call me if he thought of anything else that might be helpful. He said he would.

On the way back to the office, I was excited. Luther Zimmerman sounded like a great suspect. He knew the value of Lottie's treasures, didn't mind dealing in stolen goods, and apparently lacked any sense of morality. Now all I had to do was find out if he had an alibi.

23

Quicksand

It was late December when Judge Wingate sent us a scheduling order in Jimmy Bennett's case. According to the order the trial was to begin on April 5, 1988. That left us only three months to get ready for trial. Now that we were engaged, Bart and I were anxious to get married. Once we got the scheduling order, we set our wedding date for the last Saturday in June.

I cringed at the idea of planning the wedding in the middle of a murder trial, but Bart and I decided we had no choice. When the Jimmy Bennett case was over, it was likely there'd just be another case, so there was no way to avoid a conflict. We'd just have to get a good wedding planner. I asked some of my friends and was told they'd heard Monique Lebon was good.

Monique stood barely five feet tall, but it was five feet of pure energy. She was constantly in motion and ordered people around like she was a female Napoleon. A French Canadian by birth, she had been forced to relocate to Texas to be with her husband who had been awarded a professorship at the University of Texas at Dallas. We met and hit it off immediately, so we hired her.

Once we made a decision on the date the first order of business was to reserve the church. I called Father Bob at

All Saints Catholic Church and asked him if he'd marry us. He said he would be honored to do it. I was glad because I'd known him since I was a child and he had been particularly helpful to me when my mother was sick.

The service was set for 4:00 p.m. and my father insisted we have the reception at Prestonwood Country Club where he was a member. There was so much to do and so many decisions to be made, I was having trouble concentrating on Jimmy Bennett's case. Finally, I flipped open the file and looked at my notes. The last time Stan and I had talked about the case I had made a note to go talk to some of the neighbors around Don Baker's condo. It was possible that somebody might have seen someone come or go on the day of the murder. We needed to get a connection between one of our suspects and the crime scene. I told Jodie where I was headed and took off.

The condo was not too far from Jimmy Bennett's offices in Las Colinas. It overlooked a lush pond on the fringe of the Las Colinas Country Club. There were twenty-four units in the condominium so I had lots of work to do. Since it was a gated community, I went to the manager's office to inform them of what I planned to do. An attractive blonde manned the reception desk.

"Hello, I'm Paula Waters with Turner & Waters, Attorneys."

The lady looked up, "Oh. Pleased to meet you. What can I do for you?"

"Well, I'm one of Jimmy Bennett's defense attorneys and I'm looking for witnesses who might have seen something the night he was murdered."

"Sweet Jesus. Not another investigator."

"What do you mean?"

"First Detective Perkins, the FBI, and now—what was your name?"

"Paula Waters."

It surprised me that the FBI had been out to the Condo, but as I got to thinking about it, it made sense. The murder of the President of a thrift on the brink of failure had to turn some heads in Washington. I figured they must have sent the FBI down to check into it. I wondered if they were in communication with Detective Perkins and, if so, if they'd share any evidence they found with us. I suspected they wouldn't.

"So, what do you want to know?"

"Were you here the night of the murder?"

"No, I close up at 5:00 p.m."

"Before you left did you notice anyone around who wasn't a resident?"

"Just the pool man. He worked all afternoon fixing a crack in the deck."

"Was he your usual pool repairman?"

"I guess. The company sends out different men. I don't know them all."

"Had you ever seen this guy before?"

"No, can't say that I had, but he stayed pretty busy fixing the deck."

"What did he look like?"

"Tall, slim and good lookin'. I'd guess he was a cowboy but I couldn't say for sure. But he'd definitely look good on a horse."

I laughed. "Were there any strange cars around the day of the murder?"

"Not that I recall."

"Do you know Congressman Manning or Representative John Potts?"

"I saw Manning give a speech one time at a real estate convention."

"Have you ever seen him around here?"

"No. Can't say that I have."

"What about Potts?"

"Wouldn't know him if I saw him."

"Is there anything you know or saw that might shed some light on who murdered Don Baker and Amanda Black?"

"Well, Amanda had a lot of visitors. She was a popular girl. I . . . I wondered sometimes if she wasn't doing business out of the condo."

"Doing business?"

"You know—hooking. She was a stripper wasn't she? She had a lot of good lookin' boys visit her during the day. At night it was all Don Baker, but during the day that girl liked to party."

This was the best news I'd heard since I started working the case. Did Amanda have a jealous boyfriend or a John visit her that night? Could their death be as simple as a jealous rage of a would-be lover? The possibilities were staggering.

"Well, thanks for your help. If you don't mind, I'll just start knocking on doors and talking to people."

"Okay, but don't expect a warm reception. People around here are getting tired of hearing about Don Baker and Jimmy Bennett."

"I will, thanks."

There weren't a lot of people home during the middle of the day but I did manage to talk to a half dozen or so of the residents. One of them, a young black woman named Sylvia Stock, lived just down the hall from the Baker condo. She claimed to be a friend of Amanda Black."

"We did our laundry together," she said.

"Really? Did you see Amanda on the day of the murder?"

"Yes, I saw them come in that evening about 7:30. They were loud as usual. It sounded like they'd just come from Happy Hour."

"After they came home did you see them come out of the condo?"

"No. All I could hear was the TV. It was on pretty loud."

"Did Amanda have a lot of friends come by her place during the day?"

"Sure. She was a popular girl. A lot of girls from the club came by to hang out."

"What about men? Did she do any business in the condo?"

"I don't know about that. I've seen guys there, but she's a beautiful woman and men are attracted to her. When she goes to the pool to take a swim during the day, you wouldn't believe how many men drop whatever they're doing to get their swim trunks on."

I laughed. "Was there anybody that might have been overly obsessed with Amanda?"

"Gee. I don't know. There was this guy who showed up in the laundry room one time when we were doing our clothes. He talked to Amanda like they were friends—more than friends. She told me after he left that she had dated him a few times, but that it was over between them."

"Did the other guy act like it was over?"

"No. He was still hittin' on her—trying to get another date, but Amanda wasn't interested."

"Hmm. Did you get a name for this guy?"

"Phil, I think. She didn't say what his last name was?"

Did you see anyone else outside the condo the night they were murdered?"

"Yes, a man walked by my window and headed toward Amanda's place about 10:35 p.m. I had been watching the news and remembered thinking it was strange for someone to be visiting at that hour. I didn't hear him knock either, which surprised me, so I peeked out the front door to see what he was doing."

"What *was* he doing?"

"I don't know. He had disappeared."

"Can you describe him?"

"Tall, dark skin, lean," she replied. "I didn't see his face."

"Could it have been the same person you met in the laundry room?"

"Possibly? Like I said, I didn't see his face."

A sick feeling came over me. Jimmy was tall, deeply tanned, and lean. Could he have come to the condo? Had he been lying to me? If he was on one of his cocaine trips, he might not even remember going there and killing Don and Amanda. I needed to find out who it was Sylvia had seen that night. If it was the spurned lover that would be wonderful, but if it was Jimmy, he was in quicksand and sinking fast.

24

The Bribe

In mid-January my son Mark, who was a sophomore in high school, asked me to be a judge in his debate tournament. I didn't really have time to do it, but I didn't have the heart to tell him no. Fortunately it was just a one day event. The topic of the debate was: "Should the United States trade arms with Iran in exchange for the release of hostages?" The debate got me thinking about the lady in black from Congressman Manning's office. I hadn't heard anything from Detective Marshall about her nor had the FBI informed me about what was happening in the search for Robert Huntington. I decided it was time to go back to Washington to catch up on the investigation and to talk to the lady in black.

I called Detective Marshall's office again and finally was able to talk to his partner. She told me it had been determined that the lady in black was Linda Olivia, an intern for Congressman Manning. She filled me in on everything she knew about her. A student at George Washington University, she was the eldest daughter of one of Congressman Manning's best contributors, and had gotten the job as a favor to her father. She was also gay although neither the Congressman nor her father knew it. I wondered how they acquired that bit of information, but then realized they must have had her under surveillance.

During the flight to Washington, I thought about Linda Olivia and wondered why she had slipped me the piece of paper with the address of the warehouse. She apparently didn't agree with Congressman Manning's circumvention of Congress' dictate not to sell arms to Iran in exchange for the release of hostages. There had been congressional hearings going on for months about those illegal exchanges and whether or not President Reagan knew about them. I was sure he did. It was a noble gesture for Poindexter and Oliver North to take the fall, but how could the President not know something like this was going on?

I put aside that question and began to think of how to get Olivia alone so I could talk to her. She could get into serious trouble if anyone saw us together. Then I got an idea. While I had been sitting around the police station on my last visit to DC, I managed to locate Nicole. She was still practicing massage therapy, but for another doctor. Unfortunately, I hadn't had time to visit her as the FBI made me stick around their offices. We hadn't spoken in several years and I was curious anyway as to what was going on in her life. I thought while I was in town I'd pay her a surprise visit—maybe get a massage. The memory of the last one still lingered after all these years. And she could be the perfect lure to get Olivia alone.

Detective Marshall agreed to pick me up at the airport and he was there at baggage check-in when I arrived. We shook hands.

"Stan, how are you?" he asked.

"Not too bad, yourself?"

"Still kicking," he said giving me a hard look. "So, you can't leave this thing alone?"

"No. I've got to get to the bottom of it. I can't just let a client disappear the way Huntington did and then just blow it off. As far as I know Huntington didn't have any family, so if I don't follow through on this, who will?"

"Well, the FBI is actually glad you came back. They want in on your interview with the lady in black."

"They haven't talked to her yet?"

"They have but she won't acknowledge that she gave you the information on the warehouse."

"Really. So, what do they want me to do?"

"They think she might talk to you so they want you to wear a wire when you meet her."

"No. No way. I'll be happy to pass on any information I get that might help them find Huntington, but I'm not going to do anything to get Ms. Olivia in trouble. If anyone sees us together she could end up in a coffin."

He shrugged. "I didn't figure you'd agree to it, but I told them I'd ask."

We left the terminal and got into the detective's car which he had parked at the curb just outside. He drove me to the Holiday Inn and I checked into my room. On the way, he told me how to find Ms. Olivia. She often went to lunch alone at a sidewalk café about a half mile from Capitol Hill. I was tired from my flight, so I turned in early and got a good night's sleep. The next morning, after breakfast, I took a cab to the Marcus Sports Medicine Clinic where Nicole worked as a therapist. On the brochure in the lobby they advertised a stress reduction massage for $50. I asked if Nicole was available. They said she was but I'd have to wait about twenty minutes for her to finish up with her last client.

While I was waiting, I read a *U.S. News and World Report* article on the banking and savings and loan crisis. In the article, it mentioned that several thrifts had gotten into trouble because of defaults on loans used to fund the Contra Rebels in Nicaragua. The article didn't detail how the loans worked or how the borrowers expected to repay them, but I suddenly realized why the money from the Continental Exporters' bank account was wired to Panama. It was headed for the Contra Rebels.

The receptionist called my name and escorted me to a treatment room. She told me to take a seat and that Nicole would be there momentarily. I waited anxiously to see Nicole's reaction. A moment later the door swung open and she stepped inside the room. She was wearing a white gown and looked very professional. The years had been good to her. She looked up and gave me a hard look.

"Stan?"

I smiled and replied, "You still remember me."

"What—" she said and we embraced. "What are you doing here?"

"Well, I was in town but I only had a couple hours free this morning so I figured I'd get a massage and we could catch up on old times."

She looked me over and smiled. "You haven't changed much."

"Nor you. Pretty as ever."

She blushed. "Well, take off your clothes and get on the table so we can get started. The clock is ticking."

I looked at her and our eyes met. "That's okay. We

can just talk. I've already paid for the treatment."

"You sure? You look a little stressed out."

"Two murder cases and a lost client will do that to you."

"Yes. I've read about you in the papers."

There was an awkward moment of silence and then I said, "I still remember the last massage you gave me."

She laughed and turned to a large cabinet. She opened it and said, "As I recall you slept through most of it." She pulled out a large towel and handed it to me. "Take off your clothes and lie down on the table."

I nodded and she left while I got undressed. A few moments later she returned and began the massage. I could hardly talk it felt so good. She still had those magical fingers.

"So, fill me in on what you've been up to these past few years," I asked.

"Oh, my. A lot has happened."

"I'm listening."

She dug her thumbs into the small of my back sending a chill through my body. I moaned.

"I married Lt. Hooper," she said.

I sighed. "You did?"

"Yes. I would have invited you to the wedding but I figured it would be awkward."

"True. But you should have anyway. Rebekah and I would have come."

"I know. . . . It didn't last long—twenty-eight months. I hated living on base. He didn't have much time for me either with all his responsibilities."

"That's too bad."

"It was for the best."

"Any children?"

"No."

"Have you remarried?"

"No. I'm dating a Doctor—a neurosurgeon."

"Wow. That sounds promising."

"Too bad you're not in town longer. I 'd love you to meet him. I've told him all about you."

I frowned. "Really? Why?"

"Because I love to tell people how I saved your ass. It makes great cocktail conversation."

I turned over and looked up at her. "Really? How'd you like to have another story to tell?"

Her eyes lit up and she smiled, "That would be great. What did you have in mind?"

I told her my plan. I could tell she was excited. She left while I got dressed and then returned to give me the spare key to her apartment. My heart was pounding when we embraced and said goodbye.

The meeting at the café wasn't until 1:00 p.m. so I went back to my hotel room to wait. When I checked at the front desk to see if there were any messages, the clerk told me I had a package waiting. He handed me the thick manila folder and I looked it over warily. When I got to my room, I opened it. Five large bundles of $100 bills fell out of the package. There was a note tucked into one of them. I pulled it out and opened it.

Mr. Turner,

Thank you for your assistance in getting my checking account released at Metroplex Savings and Loan. You did a fine job and I've enclosed your fee plus a nice bonus for caring about my welfare. Now return to Dallas and forget you ever heard about me or Continental Exporters. Your services are no longer needed.

Sincerely,

Robert Huntington

The letter shook me up. I wondered if it really came from Robert Huntington. There was no way I could verify its authenticity. If Huntington was okay, and I had been discharged, I was duty bound to follow his instructions and go home. But what if this was simply someone's attempt to buy me off. I counted the money—$25,000.

After contemplating this development for a while, I called Detective Marshall. He told me to put the note in an envelope and leave it for him at the front desk. He'd have it picked up and analyzed by the FBI while I was meeting with Olivia. If it turned out to be authentic, then I could assume Robert Huntington was okay and terminate my investigation.

I got a cab and gave them Nicole's address. Twenty minutes later I was fumbling with the lock at her front door. I felt strange walking into her apartment. My heart was pounding again and I was in the midst of an adrenalin high. Nicole had always had that effect on me and each time we were together it took all my will power to resist her.

There was an antique clock ticking on a table next to the front door. I hated loud clocks as they seemed to make time slow down. I wondered what Nicole was doing and how long it would be until she arrived. I walked slowly around the apartment looking at her things, trying to get a feel for her life. I thought of Lt. Hooper and what a fool he was for letting her get away.

I stopped and closed my eyes. The door opened. She flew into my arms. We kissed wildly and frantically. She pushed me back against the wall and started unbuckling my belt. I ripped off her blouse and took her breast in my mouth. A loud knock at the door woke me from my daydream. I blinked and then ran to the front door. Nicole and Olivia rushed in. I closed the door.

"Did anyone follow you?" I asked.

"No. I don't think so," Nicole said.

Olivia looked at me and I smiled. "I wondered if I'd ever meet you," Olivia said.

"You didn't mind the intrigue," I asked.

"No, that was clever getting Nicole to pick me up. That was quite a kiss for a straight girl."

I looked at Nicole and said, "She's quite an actress. I've told her she should get a job on Broadway."

"No. I think I'd like to come work for you, Stan," Nicole said. "You live an exciting life."

I shrugged. "Well, we don't have much time so you better tell me what's going on, Olivia."

"What do you mean?"

"Well, you stuffed the address of the Continental Exporter's warehouse in my pocket, so you must have done that for a reason."

She sighed. "Right. About a year ago I went to work for Congressman Manning. He is a far-right wing Republican and I wouldn't have ever dreamed of working for him had my dad not insisted on it. About six months ago I discovered that he was masterminding clandestine aid to Iran through an organization set up by the CIA, Continental Exporters."

"Continental Exporters is operated by the CIA?" I asked.

"It's a front set up by several ex-naval officers for the CIA to sell arms to Iran. Your client, Robert Huntington, handled U.S. operations and the other officer handled delivery to Iran."

"Who was the other officer?"

"I'm not sure but he's referred to as Palmer."

"Palmer? Luther Palmer?"

"Yes, that sounds right. Anyway, Congress voted against providing arms to Iran and I couldn't sit idly by and watch a U.S. Congressman unilaterally defy Congress and alter U.S. foreign policy."

"So, why not cooperate with the FBI?"

"I don't want anyone to know I'm involved, particularly my father. He'd have a stroke if he found out what I was doing."

"Right."

"Besides, if I cooperated with the FBI the word will get out that I'm a snitch and I could end up in an ally with a bullet in my head."

"You think the Congressman would have you killed?"

"Yes, if there is one thing I have learned while working for him is that he won't let anything or anybody interfere with his agenda. He believes he's doing God's work by funneling money to the Contra Rebels."

"So, why give me the information?"

"You had a good reason to investigate what's going on because of your missing client. If you discovered something, nobody would expect that I was involved."

That was clever thinking on Olivia's part and lucky for me. Now I had an inside source that could lead me to the truth. We talked about a half hour until I looked at my watch and saw that it was nearly time to take Olivia back to the café.

"So, do you have any idea what happened to Robert Huntington?"

"Manning got very angry at him for letting the IRS tie up the contra money. I think he gave him a deadline for getting the money released or he'd have to relieve him of his duties. When the deadline passed, he sent some men to Dallas to replace him."

"Do you have any idea where they took him, or what they did to him?"

"No. I just overheard him talking to someone on the phone about going to Dallas and hiring a plumber to unclog a drain."

"Are you sure they were talking about Huntington and Metroplex Savings and Loan?"

"Yes, I heard enough bits and pieces to put it all together."

"Do they know that you are on to them?"

"I don't think so. I play the naive college student pretty well."

"So, you're an actress too," I said.

"Not as good as Nicole, I'm afraid."

"Speaking of acting," Nicole said. "I better get her back to the café. She's got to get back to work."

I looked at my watch and replied, "Right. You better go. One last question. Do you know the name of any of the men who were sent to Dallas?"

"He called one of them Skip. I remember that much. If I think of anything else, I'll let you know."

"How will you get the information to me?"

She looked at Nicole. "Through my new girlfriend."

Nicole blushed. "Right," I said. "Is that okay with you, Nicole?"

She nodded, "Like I said. I could use a little excitement in my life. A lesbian love affair is about as much excitement as a girl could ask for."

I laughed. "Well, you two have fun."

After the girls had left, I caught a cab back to my hotel and had lunch. Then I went downtown and acted like I was actually doing some investigating just in case I was being followed. Toward the end of the day I stopped by the FBI office and reported to the agent in charge what I had learned from Linda Olivia. He advised me the letter I had received was a forgery and hadn't been written by Huntington. Since the $25,000 was obviously a bribe to get me to back off the case, I turned it over to them hoping it would help lead them to the kidnappers. When I was done, Detective Marshall picked me up to take me to the airport.

"You know, Stan. You ought to step back from this case now. You've been a big help, but it's getting a little too dangerous for you to keep pushing this investigation. There's no way anybody can protect you."

"I know. Maybe I will."

"Particularly since they've given you money. If they think you've rejected their bribe they'll have no choice but to do you bodily harm or even kill you."

"But if I don't keep pushing, will they ever find Huntington?"

"Why do you care about Huntington? He's a grown man. He knew he was playing a dangerous game. He knew what he was doing was illegal. He's not some innocent victim here."

"I'm not so sure about that. If the CIA set him up in business, he may have thought he was serving his country. At least that's the impression I got from the time I spent with him."

Marshall sighed. "You could be right. But, either way, you need to leave it the professionals. You don't even carry a gun."

I laughed. "Yeah, if I carried a gun then I would definitely be in great peril."

On the flight home, I thought about Huntington and wondered if he was patriot or conspirator. Either way I didn't know of anything else I could do for him, so I decided to take Marshall's advice and step back. I certainly had plenty of other things to do. After my plane landed at DFW Airport, I got my luggage and walked to where I remembered having parked my car. Just as I got within a few yards of it, there was a shot and the windshield shattered. I turned away from my car to avoid the flying glass. Behind me there was an explosion that thrust me into the air. It felt like I'd been hit by a thousand bullets. I came down hard on top of a big Cadillac, rolled three times, and fell to the ground.

25

Phil

While Stan was in Washington, Rebekah called me to congratulate me about the wedding. She was very excited that I was getting married, and said she wanted to throw me a shower. Her enthusiasm dampened my spirits as it made me think of losing Stan forever. I wanted to kick myself for feeling that way. I had to get over Stan and focus on Bart. He was handsome, smart, loyal—and he loved me. Why couldn't I love him the same way he loved me? I would, in time, I told myself.

I was upset that Stan had gone off to Washington again. It didn't make sense that he was spending so much time trying to find Robert Huntington. Why in the hell did he care what happened to him? He hardly knew him and the bastard hadn't even given us a retainer. All this work was probably being done pro bono. I couldn't understand Stan sometimes, why he acted the way he did. Deep down, though, what was really nagging at me was fear—fear that he wouldn't come back to me. After his kidnaping in Ecuador, I worried constantly about him. I couldn't lose him.

The wedding planner had called that morning and wanted to have lunch with Bart and me so we could talk about the wedding and make some decisions. Although I was depressed I agreed and called Bart to see if he could make it. He said he'd juggle his schedule so he could fit it in. After lunch, I went back out to the Baker's condo to see if I could find Amanda Black's mysterious suitor. He was my best hope for a viable suspect in Don and Amanda's murder. I prayed he wouldn't have an alibi. I described him to the manager and told her I thought his name was Phil. She looked through the owner's roster and found him—Phillip F. Smart."

Phil reminded me of a weasel—short, intense, and annoying. I couldn't imagine Amanda Black going for this guy. There had to be money involved. It surprised me that he was home since it was in the middle of a work day. He checked me out and then smiled and said, "Hello."

I introduced myself and asked if I could have a moment of his time. He nodded and backed away to let me in. He motioned toward a big stuffed chair. The apartment was nicely decorated but dirty and cluttered. I sat down and he took a seat on the sofa.

"So, what's this about?" He asked.

"Amanda Black."

"Oh, that girl who was murdered?"

"Yes. Did you know her?"

"Ah. . . . Well. . . . Not really."

I frowned. "Hmm. I thought you two dated."

"Oh. . . . Well. That's ancient history."

"How did you two meet?"

"At the pool. I hang out there a lot, you know. I try to do twenty laps a day to keep fit."

"I see."

I could see Phil hanging out at the pool gawking at all the women sun bathing. I made a mental note to check to see if he had a criminal record—a sex offender perhaps.

"So, were you home the day she was murdered?"

He looked away like the answer was eluding him. "Ah, well . . . maybe."

"What kind of work do you do?"

"Consulting."

"Consulting? What kind of consulting?"

"Computer chip design. I do contract work for TI."

"Oh. I see. So, you work out of your home?"

"Yes, it's all computer work. Sometimes I work at home, sometimes at the TI plant in Lewisville."

"Did you see anything unusual the day Don and Amanda were murdered?"

He squinted like answering the question was painful to him. "No, not really."

"Did you see Amanda that day?"

"No," he said emphatically."

"Were you alone the night she was murdered?"

"Yes. There was a football game on TV that night. I worked on a project until the game started, fixed me something to eat, and watched it until it was over. Then I went to bed."

"When was it over?"

"About 11:00 p.m."

"So, can you think of anything that might help me figure out who murdered Amanda?"

He thought for a moment and replied, "No. Not really." He swallowed hard. "I've seen your client around here though, many times. He and Amanda had a thing going for quite a while, you know. He didn't like it when his father-in-law started doing her."

"Doing her?"

He shook his head. "Screwing her. You know what I mean. The bastard."

"You're right. I've heard that too. Did Amanda ever talk about Jimmy?"

"Sure, she liked him, but for her it was all about money. Jimmy couldn't compete with Don. He controlled all the money. The bastard."

"So, if Jimmy liked Amanda, why would he kill her?"

He shrugged. "Oh, I don't know. Maybe he wanted to punish both of them for betraying him. The bastard."

"What about you, Phil? Did you want to punish them for betraying you?"

Phil's face tightened. "Me? No. No way."

"You sure?" I asked. "You kill three birds with one stone—Don and Amanda with a knife and Jimmy by lethal injection."

He stood up. "I think this conversation is over," he said. "I've told you everything I know."

I smiled and stood up. "Yes, you have and I appreciate your cooperation."

Phil escorted me out and slammed the door behind me. I laughed inside as I walked back to my car. Even if Phil wasn't the killer, he was the perfect patsy for the ill deed. Any jury would relish the opportunity to nail a jerk like him. I went away a happy woman. Phil had made my day.

26

Tears

Any joy I had been feeling from finding my first real suspect in Don and Amanda's murder quickly evaporated when I heard the news on the radio of a car bomb explosion at DFW Airport. A horrible feeling came over me as I knew Stan was due in from Washington about the time of the explosion. I called Jodie at the office to see if she had heard from him. She hadn't. She told me she'd call me the moment she heard from him. It was only twenty minutes to DFW Airport, so I decided to drive out that way and see what I could find out.

Traffic was snarled going into Terminal A so I drove to Terminal B and took the tram around to Terminal A. There were police and fire personnel everywhere and a good size group of media people was milling around just outside the police perimeter. I walked around the reporters to get a look at the smoking car. My heart sank as I saw Stan's yellow Corvette still smoldering.

There was an ambulance just inside the perimeter so I ducked under the tape and headed for it. A police office ran over and tried to stop me. I ignored him and went straight up to one of the paramedics.

"Sir, what happened to the driver?"

The police officer put his arm on my shoulder and said, "Ma'am. You can't be here."

"That's my partner's car—is he okay?" I asked continuing to ignore the police officer."

"He was still alive when they took him away."

"Where did they take him?"

"Harris Methodist Hospital just up Highway 121 a ways," he said pointing west.

I turned and walked quickly back to the tram. As I was walking, I noticed a well-dressed man watching me. He turned away when I made eye contact with him. As I neared the tram, I looked back and he was watching me again. It occurred to me that this man may have been involved in the bombing and was there to enjoy the chaos he had created. I took the tram one stop and then walked back to observe him. After watching the scene for another ten minutes he went back to his car and left. I noted the make of his car and license number.

It took me about twenty more minutes to get to the hospital. Stan was in the emergency room. I talked to one of the doctors and he said he had a pretty serious concussion and some broken ribs. They were worried about brain damage. About an hour later Rebekah showed up with the kids and her mother and father. I waited with them for several hours. They eventually moved Stan to the ICU. Bart joined the group and we all waited until 11:00 p.m. There was no change and the doctor said he didn't expect anything to happen that night, so everyone left except Rebekah. She wouldn't leave although her mother and father tried to persuade her to. As Bart and I were leaving we were intercepted by a trio of reporters and a cameraman.

"Ms. Waters," A reporter said. "Who do you think tried to kill your partner?"

I shrugged. "I have no idea."

"What's his condition?" another reporter asked.

"He's stable. We're optimistic that he'll be all right."

"Do you think the bombing had anything to do with Jimmy Bennett's trial?" the first reporter asked.

"No, I don't think so," I replied.

"What was your partner working on?" the second reporter asked.

Bart pulled me through the group of reporters and we exited into the parking lot. We made a hasty walk to our cars. Back at home we relaxed and Bart mixed us each a drink. We were exhausted but needed to unwind and sort things out before we went to bed.

"Who do you think would do something like this?" Bart asked.

"I don't know. It's got to be someone connected to Congressman Manning and Continental Exporters. That's what Stan's been investigating in Washington. He's working with the local police and the FBI."

"You'd think they'd provide him a little protection," Bart said.

"I know. Maybe I should call Detective Besch and let him know what happened. . . . Oh, gosh. I forgot about the man in the suit."

"What man?"

"I saw someone suspicious at the airport and I took down his license number."

"Really? Yeah, you better call him."

I went to the telephone and called Detective Besch's

pager number. A few moments later the phone rang and I picked it up. He had heard about the car bomb and asked me how Stan was doing. I told him what I knew and then told him about the man in the suit and gave him the car make and license number. He said he'd get right on it.

That night I couldn't sleep. I tossed and turned thinking about Stan—wondering if he would be okay. Bart wasn't sleeping too well either. I wondered what was going through his mind. Did he know I was terrified that Stan wouldn't make it? I got up around 3:00 a.m. and called the hospital. The nurse on duty said there was no change. On the way back to bed, I ran into Bart.

"Can't sleep?"

"No. I called the hospital. No change."

"Hmm. Want something to eat?"

"Okay," I said.

Bart turned and headed for the kitchen. I followed him and took a seat at the kitchen table. He made a couple sandwiches and got us both a glass of milk. We ate quietly but I could feel Bart's mind whirling. Was he wondering if I'd be as upset if he were in the hospital? Suddenly I started bawling and tears began flowing down my cheek. Bart came over to me, put his arm around me, and hugged me tightly.

"He's gonna be okay, Paula. Don't worry. He'll be okay."

27

The Gates of Heaven

There was a dense fog all around me. I could see the sun ahead through the fog. It was drawing me toward it. Then I saw a woman on the side of the road in front of an easel painting a portrait. She had long dark hair. She turned and looked at me. I didn't recognize her at first but she looked familiar—such beautiful lips. It had been so long since I'd seen lips like those. Then I recognized her—it was Rita. She was staring at me, measuring me, like I was an inanimate object. I walked over to her and looked at her painting. I saw myself—a magnificent portrait of me in a full dress Marine Corps uniform.

She said, "So soon. I thought my wait would be much longer." A tear flowed down her cheek.

"Rita? Is that you?"

She stood up and embraced me. "Yes, my love. I've been here waiting for you to join me. I'm so glad you finally made it."

"Where are we?"

"We are at the gates of heaven. They wouldn't let me in without you."

"Why? Why wouldn't they let you in?"

"I committed a mortal sin when I took my life. But since

I did it for you, they said I could wait here for you and that—well, maybe, maybe we could go in together."

"Maybe?"

"Yes, they said we would be judged together and if we met God's test, we'd be admitted through the gates."

"And if we didn't?"

Her eyes suddenly turned a brilliant red and her skin began to disintegrate before my eyes. I let her go and stumbled back as she turned into a hideous monster.

"We would burn in hell, together!" the monster screamed.

"No! Get away!" I moaned as I sat up in my hospital bed.

Rebekah nearly jumped out of her skin. "Stan, Stan. It's okay," she said as she embraced me. "Nurse! Nurse!"

"Rebekah?" I began to cry and shake as I embraced her. "What happened to me? Where am I?"

"You're in the hospital, honey. There was an explosion. You nearly died."

Sharp pain ripped through me. I gasped.

"Nurse!" Rebekah yelled. A nurse came running in the room. "He woke up. He's in pain. Tell the doctor."

"Yes, ma'am," she said and ran out of the room.

"You've got some broken ribs and a nice concussion. You've been unconscious for nearly ten hours."

Rebekah laid me back in my bed. The pain had subsided, so I was able to talk.

"Am I going to be okay?" I asked.

"Yes, now that you're awake. They were worried about the concussion. There could have been brain damage, but you seem to be lucid. How do you feel?"

"Tired. I'm so tired."

"It's the pain pills. Rib injuries are very painful, so they've kept you pretty heavily medicated."

"Where are the kids?"

"They're in the waiting room. I'll go get them."

"Good. I want to see them."

The doctor walked in as Rebekah was leaving. He smiled at me.

"Well, you finally woke up. How do you feel?" he asked.

I shrugged. "Glad to be alive."

He nodded, then poked around my face and shone a small flashlight in my eyes. After making a few notations on my chart he got up and said, "Your eyes look clear. Do you remember what happened to you?"

I thought back a moment and replied, "The last thing I remember was falling on top of a car—it was black, I think. Then the lights went out."

"Before that," a voice said from behind the doctor. It was Detective Besch. He walked up next to the doctor. "What made you run?"

"The windshield exploded just before I got to the car," I replied. "I just naturally turned away and started to run for cover."

"Yes, it appears someone shot out the windshield. The bomb was a very sophisticated device triggered by a motion detector. We found remnants of it at the crime scene. Whoever shot out the windshield of your car saved your life. Did you see anyone?"

"No. . . . Who would have been capable of planting that type of bomb?"

"The mob perhaps—more likely the military or the CIA.

"Oh, God. I shouldn't have given the FBI the money."

"You're right. When you went to the FBI, whoever was behind this knew you weren't playing ball."

"Wonderful. Now what do I do?"

The door flew open and Marcia ran up to me. She threw her arms around me and began crying hard. "Daddy. Why did they try to kill you?"

Tears began flowing out of my eyes. Peter squeezed in and put his arms around me, too. Everyone was crying. Rebekah said, "Kids. One at a time. Daddy can't hug you all at once." Reggi grabbed Peter by the shoulder and pulled him away.

"It's okay," I said. "It's okay."

Detective Besch and the doctor left as the room wasn't big enough for everyone. Besch said he'd come by the next day to see me. The doctor told Rebekah not to stay too long as I needed rest. After the kids had calmed down, I tried to explain to them why someone wanted to kill me. Reggie and Mark seemed to understand, but Marcia and Peter just shook their heads. I tried to change the subject.

"So, my Corvette's toast, huh?"

"Yes, I'm afraid you're going to have to get a new car."

"I wonder if the insurance will pay for it?"

"I don't know," Rebekah said.

"What kind of car are you going to get," Reggie asked.

"I don't know. Maybe a 300ZX."

"Oh, that would be cool!" Mark said. "Have you seen the control panel in those suckers? It looks like you're in a space ship."

"Yeah, it is pretty neat, isn't it?"

"Can I drive it?" Reggie asked.

"Hmm," I moaned. "I haven't even got it yet."

Rebekah stood up and said, "Okay, it's time to let Daddy rest. I'm going to take you kids home. Grandma and Grandpa want to visit him for a minute before we leave." Rebekah looked at me and said, "I didn't call your mother. I was afraid she'd jump on a plane and fly out here. It would have been—"

"It's okay," I said. "You had your hands full. I understand."

After I had visited briefly with Rebekah's parents, she left and I thanked God that I had survived. I wondered if I had done the right thing in trying to find Huntington. I could have been killed and my children left fatherless. I was torn between my professional duty to my client and my profound desire to stay alive. Should I give up my search for Huntington? That would be the safe thing to do, yet did I have that choice? My heart told me no. I couldn't let my enemies deter me from doing what was right.

28

The Orderly

The next morning, I got up early and went to the hospital. It was a long drive and the rush hour traffic was horrible. The trip was worth it though since I found out Stan had awakened and seemed to be okay. The nurse told me that he was visiting with Rebekah and the kids and that I could see him when they were finished. I took a seat in the waiting room and started flipping through a magazine. As I was reading an article on wedding decorations an orderly walked in, looked around, and then left. A few moments later Rebekah and the kids came in the waiting room.

"Paula," Rebekah said.

"Hi. I heard Stan is awake."

"Yes, isn't that wonderful?"

"Oh, my God, yes. We were all so worried about him."

"Well, I'm glad you're here. I need to take the kids home. They've got to go to school and I hate Stan to be alone. It will just take me about an hour or so."

"No problem. I can stay until you get back."

"Great, I really appreciate it."

We talked for a few more minutes and then I went to Stan's room. It startled me to see a policeman on duty just outside. There hadn't been one there the previous evening. I presumed Besch was responsible for this extra precaution and I was grateful. As I stepped in the room Stan smiled.

"Paula. Come in and sit down. Rebekah and kids just left."

"I know. I talked to them. How are you feeling?"

"Not too bad. Just a little sore and groggy from the meds."

I shook my head. "I can't believe this happened."

Stan shrugged. "Well, I guess I halfway expected something."

"It's a good thing somebody blew out your windshield when they did."

"Yeah, it must have been my guardian angel."

"Who could it have been, you think?"

Stan shrugged. "I know it sounds bizarre, but people had been following me in DC. Maybe someone who was following me saw someone else plant the bomb in my car."

"That is bizarre. But I'd like to thank whoever it was," I said.

"Who do you think were following you in DC?"

"I don't know, but they picked me up at the airport and stayed on me like glue."

Stan filled me in on his adventures in DC. I couldn't believe he'd enlisted an old flame to help out. I'd heard about Nicole. He claimed not to have had sex with her, but I wasn't so sure about that. Why had she been so eager to help him prove his innocence unless she was more than a friend? And why would she drop everything to help him now? A tinge of jealousy came over me. He was like a damn sailor with a girl in every port.

He said, "So, I should be out of here in a couple days

the doctor says."

"Good. Jodie and I miss you."

He smiled. "Anything new with you?"

"Yes, I've been dying to tell you. I found us a great suspect in the Don Baker and Amanda Black murders."

"You're kidding? Who?"

I told him about Philip Smart and his infatuation with Amanda Black. Then I filled him in on the other developments in the case. He listened intently but he was starting to look tired so I figured it was time to leave.

"Listen. I'm going to go wait for Rebekah in the waiting room. You need to get some rest."

He didn't argue—just nodded struggling to keep his eyes open.

"Thanks for stopping by. I really appreciate it. I think I *will* get a little shut eye now. These drugs really make me sleepy."

As I was leaving the ward, I noticed the same orderly that I had seen earlier. He was standing in front of the drinking fountain next to a cart full of medications. He was looking at me but when our eyes met he turned away. There was something about him that seemed strange but I couldn't figure it out. I continued on to the waiting room and saw Detective Besch and a man coming toward me.

"Detective Besch," I called out.

"Hi. Paula. This is Agent Roger Benson with the FBI."

I extended my hand and said, "Nice to meet you."

We shook hands and he said, "The pleasure's mine. I'm glad to finally meet you. I've read a lot about you in the newspaper."

"Really. Are you from around here?"

"Memphis is my home, but I'm on temporary duty here in Dallas."

"So, what brings you to Methodist Hospital?"

"Your telephone call last night," Besch said.

"Did you find the car?"

"Yes, that's why we're here. It's right here in the hospital parking lot."

"What! That means the killer is in the hospital?"

"Shhh!" Besch said. "Yes, the killer is somewhere on the hospital grounds. He probably doesn't realize you followed him to his car last night and got his license number. I'd bet he's just waiting for the right moment to finish-off Stan."

"Oh, shit. The orderly—he's the assassin."

I turned and rushed back toward Stan's room. Besch and Benson started chasing after me. I pushed open the big swinging door and looked at the spot I'd last seen the orderly. He wasn't there. Besch and Benson came running up behind me.

"What did he look like?" Besch asked.

"He was short, medium build, and salt and pepper hair—Greek or Italian maybe. He had on a green hospital uniform. We better check on Stan."

We all started running down the hall toward Stan's room. As we turned the corner, my heart nearly stopped. The guard who had been standing in front of Stan's room was gone. We rushed over to the door. Benson and Besch pulled out their revolvers and prepared to enter the room. Benson gave the signal and they both burst in ready to do battle.

Stan was asleep and the orderly was preparing to

inject something into his arm with a long needle. When he saw the two officers, he grabbed Stan's shoulder and put a gun to his head. Stan woke up abruptly and tried to move away, but the man put his arm around his neck and got him a choke hold.

"You move and he's a dead man."

"Hold on now," Besch said. "It's all over. There's no way out of here. Just drop your weapon."

The orderly pulled Stan backward and said, "Get up."

Stan struggled to his feet the best he could with his neck in a choke hold. He screamed when the IV needle was jerked from his arm. The man pulled him up straight and led him slowly right at us.

"Move over to the right and let me through or Turner's gonna get a bullet in his head."

I moved back outside and Benson and Besch moved over as they were told. Once outside the room, the man walked backward toward the stairs still holding the gun at Stan's head. When he got to the stairwell, he lowered the gun to open the door. Kicking the door open he looked up at Benson and then at Besch who had their guns raised. I feared he was about to blow Stan's brains out. If he had tried, he would have died too. I guess he knew that because he shoved Stan out of his way and started hurdling himself down the stairwell.

Benson went after him and Besch and I went to the elevator. Besch pushed the button. Ten seconds later it opened and we got in. The ride to the bottom seemed like it took forever. As we got out of the elevator, I noticed the stairwell door opening on the ground floor. The orderly flew out and ran toward the front door. Besch spotted him and gave chase. He tackled him before he made it to the door. They scuffled for a moment until Benson showed up and slammed the orderly to the ground. Besch grabbed a pair of cuffs and slapped them around the man's wrists.

Knowing the assassin was safely in custody I took the next elevator upstairs to check on Stan. A nurse was escorting him back to his room. He was shaken but not hurt. They found the police officer who had been guarding Stan in a closet. He'd been knocked out but was otherwise okay. The assassin had obviously hoped to slip in and out unnoticed and be miles away before anyone noticed Stan was dead.

29

The Ludinburg Collection

It took a few weeks before I was able to get back to the office and tackle the mounds of work that had stacked up. Other than a few sore ribs and bruises, I was okay. A high-priced defense attorney arrived on the scene immediately after the assassin's attempt on my life, so the police weren't able to determine who was behind the bombing of my car. They did find some interesting evidence in the assassin's apartment though—a pocket calendar with several pages of notes and information about Robert Huntington. Unfortunately, I hadn't been allowed to see the calendar nor had I been briefed by the FBI on their progress, if any, at finding Huntington. Since there was nothing more for me to do in that regard, I turned my attention back to Lottie West's estate.

Luther Zimmerman refused to see me so I asked Detective Besch to help me out. We arrived at his office in North Dallas about 10:30 a.m. His secretary said he was in a meeting and couldn't be disturbed. Detective Besch flashed his badge and suggested he may want to end his meeting early. The receptionist reluctantly left to give him the message. A few moments later we were invited into a conference room and told Mr. Zimmerman would be there shortly.

A tall, stout, and nearly bald man walked in the room. He stood erect with a grim face and asked, "What do you want?"

Besch replied, "You're Mr. Zimmerman?"

"Yes," Zimmerman replied.

Besch identified himself, showed Zimmerman his badge, and told him he needed to ask him some questions.

"What's this about?" Zimmerman asked.

"Does the name William West mean anything to you?"

Zimmerman shook his head. "No. Can't say that it does."

"Come on Mr. Zimmerman. We know you two did business together."

"I do business with a lot of people. I can't remember every one of them."

"Oh, this one you'd remember," I interjected. "He showed you a picture of the Ludinburg Collection."

Zimmerman shrugged. "I don't remember that."

"You know," Besch said. "Playing dumb might buy you some time, but if I find out you've been lying to me, I'm gonna be mighty pissed off."

Zimmerman looked at him, grinned, and replied, "So, what are you gonna do, charge me with having a bad memory?"

Besch took a deep breath, "No. I can be more creative than that," he said, "how about obstruction of justice? Or, let's see, I could see to it that an investigation was started into every art deal you've made in the last ten years. I bet that would be very revealing."

Zimmerman's grin disappeared. "Okay, relax. Maybe I have a vague recollection of Mr. West. It's coming back to me now. Yeah, I think he sold me a couple pieces he had inherited from his father."

"A couple pieces? How about the entire Ludinburg Collection?" I asked.

"No," he said emphatically, "just a chalice and a reliquary, that was it."

"Mr. Zimmerman, we have no interest at this time in prosecuting you for any crimes you may have committed while dealing in this stolen property, but if you don't cooperate, that posture will change, I promise you."

Zimmerman sighed. "I'm telling you the truth. Those two pieces were the only ones I ever saw."

"How much did you pay for them?"

"Two hundred and fifty thousand dollars each. He wanted three million for the entire collection, but I needed time to line up buyers. I told him we'd have to take it slow and move a few pieces at a time."

"So, what happened to the rest of the collection?"

"I don't know. I couldn't get anyone to commit enough money to buy the rest of it. A German organization contacted me and offered to pay a million dollars but wouldn't pay any more."

"So, what did you do with the two pieces you bought?"

"I sold them to a dealer in New York."

"What was the dealer's name?"

"I don't remember."

"You don't remember? Don't you have a record?"

He snickered, "I don't keep records of transactions like that."

"How much did you get for them?"

"Is that relevant to anything?" Zimmerman asked.

"Yes," Besch said. "And I'm getting tired of having to pry every little piece of information out of you. You better start cooperating."

He shook his head and replied, "Okay, seven hundred and fifty thousand."

"So, you made a quick $250,000?" Besch said.

"Well, that's how this business works."

"Any idea what happened to the rest of the collection?"

"No. Like I said, after a while I gave up trying to acquire it. West wanted too much money."

"Where did he keep the collection?"

"I don't know. He brought me the two pieces I purchased. I seem to recall him mentioning a safety deposit box."

"Did he mention where it was located?"

"Nope. Can't help you there."

Besch told him about Lottie West's murder and the possibility that the thief might have found some of the treasure in her home. He asked him where he was on the day of the murder. Zimmerman couldn't remember. Besch suggested he give it some thought and come up with an alibi or Besch would have to consider him a suspect.

"I doubt she'd keep it in her home. It would be way too risky," Zimmerman said. "Lottie wasn't stupid. She knew the value of the artifacts."

"You knew Lottie?"

"I met her a few times. William talked a lot about her too. She ruled the roost."

"You mean, she was a willing participant in the sale of the collection?"

"Yes, she desperately wanted to get rid of the stuff. She put a lot of pressure on William to dispose of it."

"Why?" Besch asked.

"I don't know. Maybe she wanted the money. The treasure was worthless to her. She couldn't even show it to anyone for fear they'd turn William and her in."

We left Zimmerman's feeling like we'd only heard part of the story. He was a very smart man and obviously knew a lot more than he was letting on. Besch said he was putting Zimmerman at the top of his list of suspects. He asked me to check around Lottie's neighborhood and see if anyone had seen Zimmerman hanging around there. I picked up a brochure on the way out of his office. It had his picture on it.

The next day I went back to Lottie's place. I knocked on all the neighbors' doors and asked if they had seen Zimmerman around the neighborhood in the last few months. Nobody had. I also showed them photos of James, Loretta and Otto Barringer. When I showed Otto Barringer's photo to Martha Green in the house across the street, she remembered him.

"He's been around here. I've seen him before."

"Really? Can you remember when and where?" I asked.

"Let me think," she said. "He mowed my neighbor's lawn once."

"Really? How long ago?"

"A month or two ago?"

"Did you talk to him?"

"Yes. When he was done, I went over to ask him if he

was available to do my yard."

"What did say?"

"He said he didn't have his appointment book but that he'd stop by to set something up the following week. But he never came by again."

"Was your neighbor home while he was working?"

"No, she was out of town."

"Did you ever talk to her about this guy?"

"No."

"What's your neighbor's name?" I asked.

"Mabel Riddle."

After thanking Mrs. Green for her help, I went next door to see Mrs. Riddle. I suspected she wouldn't know Otto Barringer and I was right. She wondered who had mowed her yard. It was clear Otto Barringer had not been candid with us. Was he Lottie's killer? He seemed to have a keen interest in her. I called Besch and told him what I had learned. He said he'd find Otto and haul him in for further questioning.

30

Pool Man

It was hard to get back on the investigation of Baker's murder after Stan had narrowly escaped death. I was scared. True they'd caught the assassin but whoever had hired him could hire someone else. Was it Congressman Manning? Would a U.S. Congressman hire a hit man? I cursed the day Huntington had stepped into his office. While I was worrying, the telephone rang. It was Jimmy Bennett.

"Jimmy. How are you feeling?"

"Better. Betty told me you rescued me from breaking my bail. I don't remember any of it."

"You don't remember heading off to Oklahoma?"

"No. I remember getting depressed and smoking a joint. Betty was out with the kids at some kind of school event, so I went to a bar just to have a drink. I met someone there, I think. I don't remember who it was but they must have had some dope."

"Well, you've got to stay off that stuff while this trial is going on. If the cops catch you snortin' coke, they'll arrest you and you may never get out of jail."

"God. You can't let that happen."

"Hey. It's not up to me. You're the one that's got to keep clear of trouble."

"Okay. So, how is my defense coming?" Jimmy asked.

"Well, it's starting to take shape, which is good since your trial is less than ninety days away."

"Yeah, I know. That's why I asked."

"I've found several other people with motive and opportunity to kill your father-in-law."

"Good. God knows he had lots of enemies."

I filled Jimmy in on where I was on the investigation. He seemed relieved that things were starting to turn a little brighter. He had obviously been depressed and I assumed that was why he had turned to cocaine. I prayed he could resist that temptation in the future or we were in for some serious trouble.

"If I can help you in any way, let me know," Jimmy said.

"I will. Just promise me you'll stay clean and won't do any traveling."

"I promise. . . . And thanks, Paula, for all you're doing."

Hearing from Jimmy got me pumped up again so I started flipping through my notes. Who was the dark-skinned man that Amanda's friend saw walk by her window the night Don and Amanda were murdered? What did she mean by dark skinned—Hispanic, Black? The manager had mentioned that there was a pool maintenance man working on the deck the day of the murder. It occurred to me that I should track him down. He might be the dark stranger. If someone did want to kill Don and Amanda, using the cover of a workman would be quite easy and very effective.

I called the manager and she gave me the name of the pool maintenance company and the contact person's name and telephone number. The contact person was the office manager, Ruth Wixon. I dialed the number and got her on the line. After introducing myself, I asked her who was out at the pool that day.

"I don't show any record of us doing work out there on that day," she said.

"Really?" I replied. "The manager said there was someone there all day working on the deck."

"We have no record of it."

"A handsome, muscular—perhaps Italian, Greek, or Spanish."

"Doesn't ring a bell," she said. "Most of our workers are white or Mexican."

"He could have been Hispanic," I said.

"Like I said, none of our guys were out there that day."

After thanking her I decided to go out to the Baker condo and talk to the manager again. I had to find out more about this unauthorized pool man. Maybe there would be other owners who saw him and could help me identify him. If this were the man who Sylvia Stock saw walk by her window, it could well be the real killer. About an hour later I was at the pool talking to a group of girls sunbathing. I identified myself and told them I was investigating the Don Baker and Amanda Black murders.

"Were any of you here the day of the murder?" I asked.

"Yes, we all were," the short brunette said.

"The manager tells me there was a maintenance man working here that day. Do any of you remember him?"

Their eyes lit up and the short brunette said, "How could you forget someone like that. He was a hunk—tall, nice tan, big muscles—must have worked out a lot."

"Have you seen him around here before?"

"No. That was the first time. He's been back, though."

"Really? When?"

"I saw him the day before yesterday in the parking lot."

"What was he doing?"

"Just sitting in his car. It looked like he was waiting for somebody."

"What kind of car?"

"A nice car—a red Mazda RX7 convertible."

"Did you talk to him?"

"No. I was going to but when he saw me looking at him he got out and walked in the opposite direction."

"How was he dressed?"

"The first time he wore work clothes but the last time he was dressed like a cowboy. He had on suede cowboy boots, blue jeans, a leather belt with a silver belt buckle, and a big straw cowboy hat."

"Did you see the person he was meeting?"

"Later on I saw him with an older woman. I figured it must be his mother. Maybe she lives here."

"But he was working on the deck the first time you saw him?"

"Yeah, he had a bunch of tools and was mixing cement in a wheelbarrow."

"Did this man have a dark complexion?"

"Yeah, he looked like he was part Mexican or Indian."

One of the other girls who was blonde and a bit taller said, "No, he was Spanish."

The short blonde shrugged. "Hell, who knows where he came from. All I know is I'd like to wake up next to him some morning."

The girls giggled. There was no doubt in my mind that the pool man was, at least, involved in Don and Amanda's death somehow. He was on the premises under false pretenses. He met the description of the man seen walking up to Don and Amanda's door just before the murder. Somehow, I had to figure out his identity for only then could I determine if he had motive and opportunity. I racked my brain trying to figure out a way to find him, but nothing jumped out at me. I'd just have to be patient and wait for him to show his face.

31

Lottie's Killer

Tex called to tell me he'd been sued by Metroplex Savings and Loan. I told him to bring me the citation and we could talk about his options. Before he arrived, I got on the telephone with Jimmy Bennett. I hadn't discussed our potential conflict of interest and wanted to get that over with before Tex arrived. I asked Jodie to get him on the line. Her voice came over the intercom advising me that he was on line two.

"Jimmy, how are you feeling?"

"A little better, but it's hard to cope with the damn press stalking me wherever I go. They won't leave me alone."

"How did you lose them the other night?"

"I had to sneak out of the office down the back stairway and walk through the alley to get back to the parking garage. What a pain in the ass that was."

"Well, it worked. Lucky for you they didn't see you leave with your bags packed."

"Right."

"Hey. Listen. I need to talk to you about something."

"What's up?"

"You know one of our long-time clients is Tex Weller."

"I've heard that name. Should I know him?"

"He went to your wedding—one of Don's friends and a customer at Metroplex."

"Oh, right. He owns all those health stores."

"Right, and they were financed by Metroplex."

"Okay."

"Well, he took a big hit on Black Monday and Metroplex responded with a big margin call."

"Oh, God. That's why I don't invest in the market—it's hard to predict what a bunch of tight ass Yankees will do on any given day. I like a nice piece of real estate that's guaranteed to appreciate ten or 20 percent every year."

"I agree with that. Anyway, he was pretty upset and sent a nasty letter to your father-in-law. Technically the margin call gave him motive to kill Don. I don't think he did, but it creates a conflict of interest for us."

"What do you mean?"

"I mean to properly defend you, we should be looking at Tex from all angles to see if he might possibly be responsible for Don's death. The problem is, he's a friend and it's hard for me to conceive of him being a killer. I can't be very objective on that subject."

"He's not Paula's friend though, right?"

"No. She doesn't like him much, actually."

"Well, then I'm not worried."

"Still, technically we shouldn't represent you. Your life's on the line and you should have impartial counsel."

"Ah. That's bullshit. You're gonna do the best you can, right?"

"Sure. But–"

"Then don't sweat it."

"You sure? I'll have to have you sign a waiver."

"Whatever."

It was a great relief that Jimmy hadn't fired us. Paula would have had a stroke had she been booted off the case. I went into her office and gave her the good news. She was elated, of course. I cautioned her not to write off Tex as a suspect. We had a duty to check him out thoroughly. She said she'd hire an independent private investigator just to remove any question of our diligence in that regard. When I got back to my office, Jodie informed me that Tex had arrived. She escorted him into my office. He was in a somber mood.

"Let me see the paper," I said.

He handed me the citation. He'd been sued in the 101st District Court of Dallas County for $343,000, plus interest at 18% per annum, and attorney's fees of $75,000. They were also asking the court to compel Tex to assemble all the property that collateralized the loan and turn it over to an auctioneer to be sold to reduce the balance on the note.

"This is so humiliating. The dirty bastards are trying to put me out of business and I've never even been late on a payment. Can't you do something about this?"

"Yes, let's just file a Chapter 11. That will stop them in their tracks."

"Yeah, but I hate to file bankruptcy," Tex moaned.

"Well, it's that or give 'em the keys to all your stores."

"I wish Don Baker were alive so I could have the pleasure of killing him myself."

"Don't talk like that. If we file right away, there won't be any disruption in your business. The lawsuit will be dead in the water and we'll have six months or better to get it approved and implemented. During that time, you may not even have to pay Metroplex a dime."

"I don't have to pay Metroplex anything?"

"Maybe a little—adequate protection payments they call it. Basically, it's just interest on what you owe them."

"Okay, Stan—you're the boss. If that's my only alternative."

"I think it is."

For the next four hours, we worked on Tex's chapter 11 bankruptcy. We had to file it the next morning to stop the bank from seizing any property that Tex needed to operate his stores. When we were done, he left with a long list of information that he needed to collect and bring back to me. In the meantime, Jodie worked hard to get his schedules typed up and ready for filing the next morning. While I was working, I got a call from Detective Besch. He wanted me to come in and observe him question Otto Barringer. I needed a break, so I said I'd be right over.

It was rush hour when I got onto Central Expressway so the drive over to police headquarters was very slow. A young dispatcher was waiting for me when I walked in. She escorted me to the interrogation room where Besch was waiting. Otto looked very nervous sitting at the small table in the big, otherwise empty room. I figured he must have been pretty shaken up when he was invited to police headquarters. I wondered why he didn't have an attorney. He had to realize he was a major suspect now in Lottie West's murder. Besch read him his rights again. He said he understood them.

"Mr. Barringer," Besch said. "I brought you down here because there are some discrepancies in your story."

"What do you mean?"

"You told us you didn't have any kind of relationship with Lottie West, yet we have witnesses who saw you working across the street from her house just a week before she was murdered. What were you doing there?"

"Ah. Well, I do odd jobs around town for people sometimes. I didn't know Lottie lived in that neighborhood."

Besch looked up at the two-way mirror and shook his head. "Do you really expect us to believe that, Otto? Come on, we've talked to Mrs. Riddle. You weren't even hired to mow her yard. She doesn't even know you."

"Sure, I was. I talked to somebody there and—"

"Quit lying," Besch said sternly. "You were there casing out Lottie's place so you could steal her art collection."

"What. I don't know anything about her art collection."

"The hell you don't. You knew her husband had stolen it from Germany after the war. Your sister told me all about it. You knew it was priceless, so you made sure you had access to her house so you could steal it."

"That's not true. I wouldn't do that."

"It was pretty clever filling the house up with gas so Lottie and the dogs would pass out and make it easy for you to steal everything."

Otto shook his head. "You've got this all wrong. I didn't know anything about Lottie's art collection for godsakes."

"Where did you learn to handle natural gas? Did you ever work for the gas company?"

Otto's face turned a shade whiter. "Well, a few years back I did."

"You bet you did. I checked it out. You worked for

Lone Star Gas for over three years. I bet it was a breeze rigging the line so it would fill up the house with gas."

"I didn't do that," Otto muttered.

"Did you go in with a gas mask when you looted the place?"

"Lottie didn't keep them in her house."

"How do you know what was in her house if you've never been in there?"

"Ah, come on. You know what I mean—she wouldn't keep any art treasures in her home. Uncle Bill kept them in a safety deposit box somewhere."

"Uncle Bill?"

"That's what I called him before he died."

"So, you had more of a relationship with Aunt Lottie and Uncle Bill than you've led us to believe."

"I saw them a couple of times over the years."

"You know you should have worn gloves, Otto. You left some fingerprints in the house."

Otto was speechless. He just looked at Besch with his mouth open. "That's not true," he finally said.

"Oh, you wore gloves?"

"No, I mean—I didn't wear gloves 'cause I didn't go in her damn house. You're trying to confuse me."

"Well, it would be a lot less confusing for us all if you just tell the truth."

"I am telling you the truth. I don't know anything about Lottie's death."

"Yeah, right," Besch replied.

Besch left the interview room and joined me at the window. Otto was running his hands through his hair nervously. Besch had shaken him but hadn't broken him yet. Besch took a deep breath.

"So, what do you think, Stan?"

"He's acting like he's guilty. He's obviously not telling you everything he knows. Did you really find his fingerprints inside the house?"

"Not inside. We found a print on the door knob of the front door."

"Hmm. That proves he was there. Are you going to charge him?"

"Not quite yet. First, I want to search his house. I should have a warrant here in a minute. As soon as it comes in we can take a ride out to his place and see if he has any art treasures stashed away."

"I doubt he'd keep them at his house."

"Yeah, well you never know. Otto's probably not the brightest kid on the block."

When the warrant came in we took Besch's unmarked Crown Victoria to Barringer's house. The place was already being searched by several officers. The three-bedroom apartment was nicely decorated. Judging by a group of photographs on the TV, Otto had an eight or nine-year-old daughter and a teenage son. One of the bedrooms had been converted to a study and was richly decorated with World War II memorabilia. Besch looked around and then shook his head.

"These aren't art treasures but Otto certainly is into World War II."

"Yes, I get the impression the whole family has been obsessed by West's art theft. It's torn apart the entire family."

"I wonder why that is?" Besch asked. "A lot of families

have members who have turned to crime, but the rest of the family usually copes with the situation. Why has this family been so affected by William West's crime?"

"Perhaps it's because of the great value of the Ludinburg Collection," I suggested.

"Or the high-profile nature of the theft. Either way this family has been hiding a big secret for over forty years. I guess that's a lot of guilt to live with."

As we were talking, an officer came in the room and reported they'd found something in the basement. We immediately followed the officer into a hallway that led to a stairway down to the basement. Two crime scene investigators were knelling over some tools, hoses, and other equipment.

"What did you find?" Besch asked.

One of them said, "A tool box."

Besch squinted. "Just a tool box?"

The man closed the box and on its lid was a label that said property of Lone Star Gas.

"He kept his tool box," I said.

"It appears so," Besch replied. "I wonder if he used any of those tools to pipe natural gas into Lottie's place?"

"Take all this to the lab," Besch told the investigators. Let's see if we can somehow prove Otto was at Lottie's place on the day of the murder."

On the way back upstairs, another investigator called out to Besch. Besch quickened his pace and headed to where the investigator was going through a freezer. The investigator pointed to a box of labeled Black Angus Beef. Besch opened the box and discovered it was full of neatly stacked, very cold cash—hundred-dollar bills to be exact. I made a quick mental calculation as Besch looked through the box. There were eight rows across, six rows down, and six deep—$288,000.

Besch looked up at me and smiled. "Well, this ought to make the DA happy. It appears Otto was able to unload the art treasures pretty fast."

"I guess so," I said, although I wasn't ready to draw the same conclusion that Besch had drawn. If he only got $288,000 for the art treasures, he'd only been paid pennies on the dollar. I suspected there was more to this than met the eye. Later that day Otto Barringer was charged with the murder of Lottie West. I had no doubt that he was the murderer and would be convicted, but I knew there were more family secrets to be discovered and I was determined to discover them.

32

Presumed Dead

With Barringer behind bars I started to wonder about my would-be assassin. I hadn't heard anything since his arrest and I was curious as to what the FBI was doing with him. I had asked Besch about it, but he said he knew as little about it as I did. I decided to call Agent Roger Benson and find out what was going on.

"Stan, how are you feeling?"

"Good. The first few weeks were painful, so they kept me doped up. I've pretty much recovered now except for a little lingering soreness in my ribs."

"You were lucky Mr. Z didn't stick you with that needle or you wouldn't be feeling anything."

"Mr. Z?"

"Yes, your assailant was Sean Anthony Zehpopolis—Mr. Z to his friends."

"What is he some kind of a hit man?"

"Ordinarily he's hired just to scare people. I'm surprised they hired him to do a hit. I guess they didn't think you'd be much of a challenge."

"Ordinarily I wouldn't have been. I guess someone upstairs is watching out for me."

"Lucky for you."

"So, what's Mr. Z's status? Has he been charged yet? Do I need to sign a complaint or something?"

Benson didn't respond. I could hear papers shuffling in the background. I said, "Where do you have him locked up?"

"Listen, Stan. I've got some bad news?"

"Bad news? What do you mean?"

"He's not in custody."

"What? You let him go? He tried to kill me."

"It was some kind of administrative snafu in the U.S. Marshall's office. Benson managed to switch identifications with another inmate who was being released. They didn't discover the error until several hours after Benson had hit the street. There's an all-points bulletin out for him. It shouldn't be long before he's back in custody."

The news that Mr. Z was out on the street made me livid. How could a penal institution of all things be guilty of such gross negligence. If Benson had been hired to kill me, what would prevent him from finishing the job now that he was free again.

"What about me and my family? What if he's still after us?"

"I don't think you have to worry about him now. He's a wanted man and will probably get out of the country just as fast as he can."

"What if he doesn't?"

Benson was silent. I could hear him breathing.

"What about Huntington? Did Mr. Z kill him?"

"It appears that way, although we haven't found a body. He had a lot of information about him in a notepad he was carrying. He was obviously looking for him."

"What else was in the notepad? Were there any other

leads in it?"

"All his notations were abbreviations or some kind of code he used. It's pretty meaningless to us."

"I thought you guys could crack any kind of code? I can't believe you can't figure out this guy's pocket calendar."

"It's his own code and probably isn't based on logic."

"So that's it? You're at a dead-end?" I asked.

"No, like I said. We've got an intense search going on for Mr. Z. We'll find him, if he hasn't left the country."

Benson's assurances didn't give me much hope. It appeared Mr. Z had outsmarted the FBI. If he was that good he might not be running at all. He might be lurking around the next corner ready to unleash an attack on me. In fact, I figured he was probably very upset that he'd tried to kill me twice and failed. Now it would be a matter of principle—a matter of pride that he finishes the job.

Although I hated guns, the thought occurred to me that I should get one just in case. Since I didn't know much about them, I asked Detective Besch to help me pick one out. He agreed and offered to show me how to use it too. I didn't relish the idea of carrying a gun around all day. It would be cumbersome and annoying, but it appeared I had no choice.

Another problem was Rebekah. I didn't dare tell her what was going on as she was a worrier and wouldn't sleep at night if she knew I was running around with a concealed weapon. I prayed the FBI would find Mr. Z immediately so I didn't have to take this drastic action.

Besch picked me up and we went to a gun dealer frequented by many Dallas police officers. After looking at dozens of different possibilities, I settled on a small caliber

Bareta that I could strap around my ankle. I figured this would be the least conspicuous place to carry it. After I finished all the paperwork to make carrying it legal, we went to the police target range to try it out.

It was kind of fun firing it, but I couldn't imagine pointing it a person and pulling the trigger. Besch assured me if I was being attacked I'd find the courage to do it. I hoped he was right. After a couple hours, Besch said we'd done enough for one day and offered to buy me a drink at a local bar. Although I didn't hang out at bars too often, I felt obliged to have a drink with him since he'd taken the time to help me out. When we arrived, Besch went straight to the bartender and ordered a Scotch on the rocks. I ordered a beer.

"Well, I hope you never have to use it, Stan."

"You and me both."

"It's a good little piece, though. I guarantee it will stop Mr. Z in his tracks if you hit him."

"If I even see him coming," I said.

Besch told me I needed a few more sessions at the range before I'd be competent to use my new weapon. He talked to the officer in charge and arranged for me to come back and get more training. He also promised to have extra patrols around my house and our office for the next few weeks. He said he'd give all his officers a description of Mr. Z and if anyone saw him they'd report it immediately. Besch seemed genuinely concerned about my safety and for that I was grateful. After drinking a second beer, I thanked him and headed home. Now all I had to do was figure out how to hide the gun from Rebekah.

33

From Bad to Hopeless

It was February before I knew it—less than sixty days to Jimmy's trial. Unfortunately, I still hadn't been able to identify the pool man. All the leads that I had developed led nowhere. My best shot at creating reasonable doubt was Amanda's wannabe boyfriend, Phil Smart. He lived on the premises, had a crush on Amanda, and hated Don Baker. The fact he didn't have an alibi and acted like a jerk was a bonus. In my heart, though, I was worried about selling him as the killer to the jury. It was a big gamble.

While I continued to look for the illusive pool man, I decided it was time to develop my attack on the prosecution's case against Jimmy. It was about time to have a serious talk with the prosecuting attorney. The last time I had talked to him I was pissed off that the police were interrogating Jimmy without my presence. Wilkerson probably wouldn't be happy to hear from me but I had no choice but to initiate contact. I called the DA's office and asked for him. He was out so I left a message. Later that day he returned my call.

"You called," he said cooly.

"Right. Our trial date is fast approaching and I thought it was time for us to exchange witness lists and take a look at each other's evidence."

"Yeah. I suppose we gotta do it sometime."

"I think so."

"I'll get somebody working on it."

"I guess you know I used to work in your office."

"So, I've been told. What made you go to the dark side?"

"The dark side? Not everybody you indict is guilty."

"The vast majority are. You should have learned that when you worked in this office."

"Maybe so, but it doesn't change the fact that they're all innocent until proven guilty."

"Yeah, right. Is your guy interested in cutting a deal, or not? I might be willing to withdraw our request for the death penalty if he comes clean before I have to waste any more time on this case."

His words cut me like a switchblade. Anger swept over me. I hated Wilkerson's presumptive attitude. He was so sure Jimmy was guilty and that he would squash me like a bug at trial. My head began to throb as adrenalin flooded my system. *I'll show that son of a bitch!*

"Well, that's very generous of you, but he happens to be innocent, so I'm going to have to decline."

He laughed. "Suit yourself, just trying to simply your life. I'll see you tomorrow."

I slammed the phone down. Stan was walking by and heard me cursing. He rushed in.

"What's wrong?"

"I just got off the phone with Wilkerson. He's an asshole."

Stan smiled. "Got you riled up, did he?"

I nodded. "I don't know why. He just rubbed me the wrong way. He's offering to withdraw his request for the death penalty if Jimmy confesses."

"Hmm. Well, you've got to tell Jimmy about the offer. I don't think he'll go for it, but you've got to tell him."

"I know. I will."

"You getting nervous about the big trial?" Stan asked.

I shrugged and rubbed the back of my aching neck. "I guess so. Up until now it's just been a fuzzy thought in the back of my mind—kind of like my wedding. It didn't seem real. Today suddenly, reality hit me like a Freightliner—I'm going to have to try this case in a few weeks."

Stan chuckled and walked around behind me. I wondered what he was up to. He put his hands on my shoulders and said, "I think you need a massage. You look like you're in pain."

He waited for my response. My pulse quickened.

"Sure, that would be wonderful," I replied.

Stan's fingers sent a jolt of excitement through me I hadn't expected. My tense muscles relaxed as his fingers moved expertly over my neck and shoulders. I moaned. He stopped abruptly.

"Feeling better," he said and moved quickly away.

"Yes, but don't stop. That feels so good."

"Well, I probably shouldn't be—"

I smiled. "It's okay. I won't sue you for sexual harassment—that is, if you get back here and finish your work."

"I would, but Bart—he might not—"

"You let me worry about Bart," I said, enjoying the moment immensely.

Stan finished massaging my neck and then made a hasty retreat. In a heartbeat, he had totally changed my mood. How had he done that? Why did he have that affect on me? After contemplating that fact for a while, I decided I better cut short my psychoanalysis and get back to work.

The court had provided us a scheduling order that required us to exchange witness lists and evidence fifteen days before trial. I had only a few more days to comply with this order. I started outlining Wilkerson's case against Jimmy so I could figure out how to poke holes in it. I made a list of the facts that pointed to him as the killer.

1.   *Betty's unexpected divorce filing*
2.   *The argument on Saturday*
3.   *Jimmy's lack of an alibi*
4.   *Jimmy's use of cocaine and heavy drinking*
5.   *Jimmy's blackouts and memory loss*
6.   *Jimmy's temper*

Wilkerson would contend that Jimmy loved Betty and blamed the divorce on Don. The killing was an act of revenge and punishment for Don ruining Jimmy's life. Or he might say that Jimmy loved Amanda and killed both of them in a jealous rage. Or he could say it was a combination of both factors. With Don out of the way, all he had to do were patch things up with Betty and he'd control the entire Baker empire.

The thought that maybe the announcement of the divorce was done to provoke a confrontation between Don and Jimmy surfaced again. Betty certainly had much to gain by either one of them killing the other. No matter who survived such an encounter, they would be charged with murder leaving the Baker fortune to her and her mother. Since her mother didn't have the ability or desire to manage the family fortune, it would be left up to Betty. But would she kill her father? I could see her killing Amanda. That made sense, since Jimmy and Amanda had been lovers. Betty killing her father, though, just didn't feel right. Jimmy would never let me play that card anyway, for fear he'd lose Betty forever.

The next day I dropped by the DA's office and met with Wilkerson. I had gotten over my anger and tried to be civil with him. He gave me copies of several forensic reports. One of the reports indicated Jimmy's fingerprints had been found in the bedroom of the condo where the murder took place. That wasn't a big surprise since I knew he went there a lot. What I didn't expect was what Wilkerson claimed was the murder weapon—a hunting knife that he said belonged to Jimmy. Wilkerson claimed it had been found in a dumpster a half mile from the condo. I asked him how they figured it was Jimmy's and his reply was that, according to Margie Baker, Don had given it to him as a birthday present.

I left Wilkerson's office with a sinking feeling—I had stepped in a snake pit and didn't know how to extricate myself without suffering a lethal bite. When I got home, Bart was sitting on the sofa reading the newspaper. He got up when he saw me and we embraced. After he got us both a drink, we sat at the bar and talked. I told him about Jimmy's knife, the fingerprints, and the blood.

"The knife doesn't prove anything. If Jimmy did it, why would he use his own knife for godsakes? He's not that stupid. You can just say the killer wanted to make it look like Jimmy did it."

"Yeah, but if it was a crime of passion, which is the way Wilkerson will paint it, Jimmy wouldn't have necessarily thought it through. Or, if he was on one of his cocaine induced episodes, he might not have been lucid enough to worry about the ownership of the weapon he was going to use."

"So, either way it's all speculation. Use that angle. Wilkerson's got his theory and you've got your theory—both are plausible. The fact is you're both speculating and there is no proof as to what actually happened—no witnesses, hence, reasonable doubt."

"Thank you, honey, for trying to cheer me up. The truth is, and you know it, my case sucks."

Bart nodded. "Oh, well. You win some, you lose some."

"No. Damn it," I said, slamming my fist on the bar. "I can't lose this case! I won't lose this case!"

Bart grabbed my hand and squeezed it gently. "Come on, honey, relax. You'll figure something out. I know you will."

I smiled and pulled Bart over to me. We kissed. "So, let's get something to eat and then you can show me how to relax."

"That works for me," Bart replied.

After that I forgot about Jimmy Bennett, Rob Wilkerson, Stan Turner, Judge Wingate, and everyone else in my life. I thought only of my fiancé Bart Williams. I hadn't thought about it before, but my name would soon be changing to Paula Williams. Or should I leave it as Waters? I didn't want to hurt Bart's feelings by not taking his name, but I had created a reputation under the name of Paula Waters. I thought about that for a moment and then it occurred to me—I might *need* to change my name after Wilkerson got through with me.

34

More Media

The probate code only gave me ninety days to file an inventory of Lottie West's estate. Obviously, I was nowhere near knowing the extent of her assets, so I filed a motion for an extension of time to file it. The probate judge granted the motion extending the deadline sixty more days. That still wasn't much time, but I was grateful for a little breathing room. The question now was how I would discover the rest of Lottie's assets?

After drafting letters to all the major banks in the city asking them to search their records for accounts or safety deposit boxes in Lottie's name, I decided to contact the SPCA and advise them of their interest in the estate. I hadn't contacted them earlier because, if the bulk of Lottie's estate turned out to be stolen property or the proceeds of stolen property, it might all be forfeited. The local director was ecstatic over the news that they might be receiving upwards of half a million dollars. When I told her not to start counting the money yet, her mood changed.

"Well, I'm going to contact the Attorney General. That's our money and we need it. Do you know how many dogs and cats we get in here every week?"

She was right. I had forgotten about the fact that the

Attorney General of Texas was charged with the responsibility of representing charitable organizations. That's all I needed—more complications.

"Hey, I hope I can turn it over to you. I just wanted to warn you that until we know where the money came from, we can't distribute any of it. Besides, the police are holding a lot of it as evidence for now."

"How long until they release it?"

I gave her Detective Besch's telephone number and suggested she might want to talk to him about that since he was handling the investigation into Lottie's murder. She said she would. After I hung up, Jodie came in and advised me she had completed her research on the Ludinburg collection. I told her to sit down and tell me about it.

"Ludinburg is a small city of about 15,000 people in Saxony-Anhalt which in Central Germany. One of the oldest German cities, Ludinburg was fortified in 923 by Henry I. The castle, church, and convent were built from the 10th to the 14th century."

"What about the art treasures?" I asked.

"They belonged to the Lutheran Church and included a ninth-century illuminated Latin manuscript with jeweled encrusted cover; a printed manuscript with jeweled cover dating back to 1513; five crystal reliquary flasks with gilded and jeweled mounts; a small silver reliquary box; a carved ivory comb; and a reliquary casket decorated with jewels, gilt copper repousse plaques, and carved ivory inlays that belonged to Henry I, the First Saxon king who unified the German states in the early tenth century."

"So, did you talk to someone at the Ludinburg church?"

"No, they referred me to an investigator who had been looking for the treasure."

"What did he have to say?"

"He said that the search for the art treasures had ended years ago, but that if any of the treasures turned up to let him know. They are still offering a big reward for the return of the collection."

"Okay. Very interesting. Thanks."

Jodie nodded and left. Ten minutes later Jodie buzzed me on the intercom and said a reporter from the *New York Times* was on the phone. That surprised me because I didn't often get calls from out of state news organizations. Normally it was the Dallas Morning News or one of the local TV stations who called for information on cases we were handling. I took the call.

"Mr. Turner. This is Frank Beecham. I'm a freelance reporter on assignment for the New York Times."

"Oh. Hi. What can I do for you?"

"We just got a tip that you have found the Ludinburg Collection. Can you confirm that?"

"Not exactly," I said.

I told him about Lottie West and the possibility that her late husband might have acquired the collection while in Germany. I cautioned him that we hadn't found it yet and that it might have been stolen again by the person who killed Lottie West. He said he was getting on the next plane to Dallas.

"I should be there by this evening. I'd like to meet with you first thing in the morning. Please don't talk to any other reporters. This could be the biggest story of my career."

"How did you find out about it?" I asked.

"Your secretary called the Ludinburg Church and asked about the collection. I've got friends there who passed on the information to me. I have been working this story for years and this is the first lead we've had in a long time."

"Well. Like I said, we haven't found the collection yet. I just hope it's not a waste of your time coming all the way to Dallas."

"From what you've told me, this may be the closest we've ever come to finding the Ludinburg Collection. Believe me. This is an important development with potentially great historical significance."

"Okay. I'll be seeing you soon then."

"You bet, and thank you so much for giving me this story."

"No problem."

The next morning Frank Beecham was in my office bright and early along with Detective Besch. He was a stout man of medium height and spoke with a strong German accent. I figured he must have been born in Germany and immigrated to the United States. I told him everything I knew about Lottie and WilliamWest and the sale of two pieces from the Ludinburg Collection to Zimmerman.

"We knew the collection was here somewhere in Texas. When the two pieces showed up in New York, we were able to trace the purchase money to Dallas. I spent two months here trying to identify the recipient of the funds, but the money went through a couple dummy corporations."

"Who owned the corporations?" Besch asked

"They were formed by an attorney who refused to identify his clients."

"Couldn't the police or the FBI force him to identify

who they were?"

He shook his head. "They tried but when they finally got a court order compelling him to disclose their identity, he disappeared."

"What about his records, his staff—"

"He was a sole practitioner and every piece of paper in his office had been shredded by the time the police got there with a search warrant."

"Jesus," I said. "How frustrating that must have been."

"That's why I was so excited when I heard about your secretary's call."

We talked for another hour and both Besch and I promised him that we would do everything possible to find the Ludinburg Treasures. He thanked us and asked us to inform him immediately if there were any new developments. The next day Beecham's story came out in the New York Times. By noon Jodie was swamped with calls from reporters from all over the world.

Although all the media attention was exciting, it was a major distraction. Now suddenly, I was under great pressure to find the missing art treasures. Had this been the only case I had to worry about it wouldn't have been so bad. Unfortunately, I had fifty other cases to juggle and I needed to help Paula on the Jimmy Bennett case. I was getting a headache just thinking about it.

35

Lies

The investigative report on Tex Weller was sitting on my desk when I got to the office. I had hired Paul Thayer to do it and asked him to be very discreet as we didn't want Tex to know about it. The thrust of the investigation was to determine Tex's whereabouts on the day of the murder. I didn't really think Tex had anything to do with Don Baker's murder, but prudence dictated we make doubly sure he didn't.

The murders took place on Monday, October 19, 1987. Tex claimed to have been at home with his wife Sunday night watching the Cowboy game. In order to verify Tex's story, Paul had surreptitiously obtained telephone records, credit card receipts, and talked to neighbors. The telephone records showed only two incoming calls both before nine o'clock and no outgoing calls. The incoming calls lasted less than one minute indicating that they were answered by an answering machine. Interviews with neighbors provided no useful information. There was one disturbing credit card receipt, however. It was from a gas station in Grand Prairie where either Tex or Toni filled up their tank at 8:57 p.m.

It was clear Tex had lied to Stan about his activities the night of the murders. That didn't prove anything in particular but it did indicate Tex was hiding something. I decided I better discuss the matter with Stan. I went into his office and told him what I'd found out.

"You think Tex lied to me?" Stan asked.

"Obviously, unless they hired someone to go fill up their car with gas."

"Maybe one of them just ran out to get gas?"

"Then why didn't they tell you about it?"

"They probably forgot about it."

"Maybe, but my bet is they weren't home that night. You usually get gas on the way out or on the way home."

"So, what do you think I should do?"

"Talk to Toni and see if she verifies that she was with her husband that night," I said.

Stan took a deep breath. "I don't know. That will be a slap in the face."

"Better a slap in the face than a bullet in the head. If he's not telling us something, we better find out what it is."

Stan shook his head. "Okay, I'll talk to her."

It was awkward having Tex in trouble with Metroplex while I was defending Jimmy Bennett. I knew Stan was having trouble dealing with it, but I thought it better he talk to Toni than I. Toni didn't know me as well and might take offense at me suggesting that her husband might be a murderer. Stan had saved her husband's life, though, so she wouldn't take offense so quickly if Stan asked her about his alibi.

I went back to my office and starting thumbing through my to-do list. The trial was rapidly approaching so I started working on my voir dire questions for the jury. Being a high-profile case, it would be difficult to find jurors who hadn't heard about the case and already formed opinions as to Jimmy's guilt or innocence. Another consideration was that Metroplex Savings and Loan had hundreds of thousands of customers and many of them could easily show up in the jury pool. Their experience with Metroplex could cloud their objectivity. There were also issues with drinking, drug use, and capital punishment to complicate matters.

Several hours later I put away my voir dire outline and called Bart. I was too tired to cook so I suggested we go out and check out a few spots that had been suggested for our rehearsal dinner. Bart said that sounded good and he'd meet me at home at six. After I hung up, Stan came into my office.

"Toni said she had a book club meeting that night. She left at 6:30 p.m. and she thinks Tex went to a sports bar that night. Apparently, he goes there often to watch football games."

"Shit. That lying son of a bitch."

"Hang on," Stan said. "There might be some other explanation."

"If he was at a sports bar, he would have told you. He'd have an alibi. He obviously didn't go to the sports bar."

Stan shook his head dejectedly. "Let me talk to him. There must be some other explanation."

"Was Toni upset you asked her about Tex's whereabouts?" I asked.

"No, I blamed it on the DA. I told her the police would be snooping around checking out everyone's alibi for the DA and that she had better think back and figure out what she and Tex were doing at the time of the murders. She just blurted it out. Apparently, she and Tex hadn't talked about it."

"Good. I was worried she'd be upset with you."

"She'll be very upset if it turns out Tex was involved in the murders."

Stan left and I started packing up to go home. Over the last several hours I'd developed a severe headache and my stomach was in a knot. On the way out the door, I took three aspirins with a Coke chaser. Heavy traffic on Preston Road didn't improve matters. All I could think about was getting into a hot tub and relaxing a little before Bart got home. I was already a wreck and I still had two weeks until Jimmy's trial would begin.

When Bart got home, I was still in the tub. He came in and was amused to see me there. I started to explain but he gestured for me to shut up. He knelt down and started washing my back.

"Have a bad day, honey?"

He was a dream and I was so lucky to have him, yet I couldn't help comparing his back rub to the one Stan had just given me. I know it was terrible, but I couldn't help myself. Even immersed in as highly a conductive medium as water, the electricity just wasn't flowing. What was I going to do? I closed my eyes a moment trying hard to rid myself of the memory of Stan's gentle touch.

"Yes, more problems with Tex."

"Oh, no. I thought that issue had been put to bed."

"So, did I until I read Paul Thayer's surveillance report."

I briefed Bart on what I'd learned.

"Well, that doesn't prove anything."

"Except that he was lying."

"Maybe he has a girlfriend," Bart suggested.

"You think? An old guy like that?"

"Hey. There are a lot of young women out there looking for a sugar daddy. Tex would make a good one too—plenty of money and as gullible as he is. If a girl said she was in love with him, he'd probably believe it."

I thought about that a moment and hoped it was true. Not that I wanted to hurt Toni, but it would eliminate Tex as a suspect so I could get on with my murder trial without worrying about stepping on a landmine. I made a mental note to discuss that possibility with Stan.

An hour later Bart and I left to check out three spots as possible locations for our rehearsal dinner. The first was the Belo Mansion which had been converted into the headquarters of the Dallas Bar Association. It was elegant yet cozy and the food was excellent. Next, we went to the Mansion. We went to the bar and ordered drinks.

"Boy, this place is nice," Bart said.

"A little too high class maybe," I said. "We're not exactly high society."

"Well, circumstances change. We're moving up in the world—at least you are with your high-profile murder cases."

"Yeah, but you can't change who you are. I'm not comfortable here."

"Okay, then McDonald's it is."

I laughed. "That's not a bad idea. It would save us a bundle."

"So, Baby Doe's?"

"Yeah, it's where we decided to take the plunge. I like

the atmosphere and I feel comfortable there."

Bart took my hands. "Well, I want you to be happy so that will be fine."

I smiled and said, "Monique called and said she ordered the cake from Stein's and scheduled a bridal luncheon at the S & S Tea Room."

"That's nice."

"It's going to be a five-layer cake with lemon icing."

"Hmm. Sounds good."

"She's hired Gittings as our photographer."

"Gittings? I think I've heard of them."

"They're the best in Dallas."

Bart nodded like he was interested but I could tell wedding arrangements didn't excite him. When it came to weddings, it seemed men were just there for the ride. They'd just as soon go to a JP and have a cozy little ceremony in front of a couple of strangers and miss the hoopla of a formal wedding. I decided to change the subject.

"So, tell me about your day?" I said.

Bart looked at me and shrugged. "Ah. Just a typical day in court—a couple dope dealers pled out, a short shop lifting trial, and a bond hearing."

"Whose bond hearing?"

"Amy Garner, the assistant cashier at Metroplex Savings & Loan."

"What's she charged with?"

"Embezzlement. It seems she and a loan officer concocted a plan to give a loan to a dummy corporation, take the money for their own use, and then report that the corporation had gone out of business. If you looked in the file, it looked just like a typical loan default."

"Really? Wow. That's amazing," I said. "How much money?"

"Eighty grand."

"God. I can't believe they thought they could get away with something like that."

"Well, they almost did. If the bank examiners hadn't insisted the bank file suit against the corporation, they probably would have gotten away with it. Unfortunately, the law firm hired to collect the account discovered the corporation was just a shell."

"How stupid people can be," I said. "You'd think they'd take the money and run."

"I know. But most thieves think they are smarter than everyone else and will never get caught."

After having a few drinks we went to the dining room and had dinner. The food was great but I was glad we weren't going to have the rehearsal dinner there. My father wasn't rich and I knew the wedding tab was already over ten grand and climbing. I wanted to help out with the cost but he insisted I let him handle it. After dinner, we went to the bar where a band was playing and people were dancing. It was after eleven when we got home. All the dancing and drinking that night had taken its toll on us. When I finished in the bathroom and came to bed. Bart was fast asleep. I climbed into bed and put my arm around him. He'd make me happy. I knew he would.

36

The Affair

Within ten days of filing a chapter 11 a representative from the United States Trustee's office calls the debtor-in-possession and counsel in for a conference at their offices in the Earle Cabell Federal Building. Chapter 11 is rather complicated and the trustee wants to be sure everyone knows the rules and will comply with them. In this case Tex was the debtor-in-possession. What that term meant was that he was still operating his business despite the fact that he had filed bankruptcy. The meeting went well and after it was over I suggested we stop for a cup of coffee at the seventh-floor cafeteria.

"Can you get someone to help with that monthly operating report?" Tex asked. "I'm not a number cruncher."

"Sure. I know an accountant who can do it for you."

"Good. I hate accounting."

I laughed. "That's probably one reason you're down here today."

"Bullshit. I'm down here because of that mother—"

"Speaking of Don Baker. We may have a problem."

"What?"

"You told me you were home on Sunday night watching football when Don Baker was murdered, but Toni doesn't confirm that alibi."

"Shit. What did she tell you?"

"That you both went out that night alone. She thinks you went to a sports bar."

"Good. That's where I went—Gameday Sports Bar & Grille. You know, the one on Main Street in Grand Prairie."

"Good. Then you'll have lots of witnesses who can confirm your alibi."

Tex looked away and swallowed hard. "Well, I don't know. I may not have talked to anyone."

"Damn it, Tex. Quit playing games."

"Okay. Okay. You got me," he said looking like a wounded puppy. "I wasn't at the sports bar. So now what?"

"How about the truth. It's attorney-client privileged. I won't tell a soul what you tell me."

Tex rotated his head from side to side nervously. He took a deep breath.

"Come on, Tex. Spit it out. I need to know."

He looked me in the eyes. "She came on to me. I was just sitting there watching the Cowboys get slaughtered by Oakland."

Paula was right, he was screwing around on Toni. I was relieved but also shocked by this revelation. Tex and Toni seemed so happy, but I certainly could appreciate the difficulty in resisting temptation. I smiled sympathetically.

"Who was she?"

"A college girl from UT Arlington. We started talking and one thing led to another."

"Why would a college girl be interested in—?"

"A man of my maturity," Tex replied, smiling.

"Yes, an old fart like you."

"She was complaining about her boyfriend—you know— ejaculating early."

"What! You meet a girl and suddenly start talking about her sex life?"

"Hey. The Cowboys were losing. What else was there to talk about."

I shook my head and chuckled. I couldn't believe what I was hearing.

"So, I told her that wouldn't be a problem with me. She could ride me all night long and I'd hold it in."

"Okay. I don't need to hear anymore. Just give me her name and number."

"Why? You want a piece of the action? I don't know—"

"No, I need to verify your alibi, you idiot."

Tex shrugged. "Oh. . . . You're not going to tell Toni, are you?"

"No. Your dirty little secret is safe with me."

"Good. A man of my age doesn't get this kind of opportunity too often. I don't want you—"

"You're still seeing her?"

He gave me a blank look.

"Tex, you're thirty years older than she is. She's got to have some ulterior motive for having a relationship with you. Does she know you're in bankruptcy or have you been feeding her a line about the millions of dollars you have?"

"She's not after my money. Anyway, I'd still have a million dollars had it not been for that sleazy bastard, Don Baker."

"Okay, I think this is where this conversation started. Let's get out of here," I said, feeling a little nauseous.

When I got back to the office, I told Paula the good

news. She was very much relieved and not at all surprised by Tex's wayward ways. In fact, she rubbed in the fact that she had warned me about Tex's lack of moral fiber. After talking to Paula, I went back to my office to face the mail and a pile of telephone messages that would have fueled a good size campfire. As I was rummaging through them, Jodie told me there was a telephone call for me. She said it sounded like Mo, my friend at the CIA.

"Are you okay?" he asked. "I've been worried about you."

"I'm fine."

"Listen. I just wanted to let you know that Robert is alive. He's here with me right now. He's fine and Luther Palmer is with us too. You don't have to worry about them anymore."

"But Robert was kidnapped? I saw his place. It looked like he was forcibly taken away."

"No, he just left in a hurry. He had to be extracted quickly."

"Why?"

"It's a long story and I can't talk much about it by telephone. You just have to trust me."

"Where are you?"

"I can't say. We're about to board an airplane. I just wanted you to know they were both okay and ask you to end your search for them."

"Okay. Where are you going?"

"Like I said. I can't say. Just forget about us. You did your job. I'm sorry they tried to kill you. I was able to protect you this time, but I won't be around the next time."

"Who's they?"

"The people who don't want the truth to be known."

"What truth?"

"If you look in your right coat pocket of your tan sport coat you'll find a key. Robert slipped it there when you weren't looking. It's a lockbox at DFW. We've left you something for your time and trouble. Don't give it to the FBI this time. I've got to hang up now in case they've got your line tapped. Read the newspaper and you'll probably be able to figure what's been happening. . . . Oh, by the way. Robert is the one who got the money out of the Metroplex account, thanks to you. You're a good attorney."

"What about Congressman Manning?"

"He's a friend. Leave him alone and stay away from Washington."

"Ooookay, but what do I tell the FBI?"

"Nothing. Don't mention this phone call. Just forget you ever met Robert Huntington. I'm serious. If you keep pushing this investigation, they'll kill you."

The phone went dead. I held it a moment in shock and then slowly hung it up. *Was this for real? What did he mean he was able to protect me? Why do they want to kill me?* Then I thought about the window shattering just before the car exploded. That was odd. Mo must have known the car was rigged to explode, so he shot out the window to warn me and to prematurely trigger the explosion. He had saved my life. As I was playing the conversation back in my head, I remembered Mo's mention of a key. My brown sports coat was at home. I'd have run home before I went to DFW.

37

Reconciliation

After finishing preparations for picking a jury I started concentrating on my trial outline and witness list. As I listed all the names of potential witnesses, I started thinking about the difficult question as to whether Jimmy Bennett should testify or not. He was a likeable guy but there was so much circumstantial evidence against him I knew Wilkerson would just love to shove all of it down his throat. After imagining that scenario in my mind awhile, I decided it wouldn't be wise to give him that opportunity.

As I was planning my defense strategy, I thought about Betty. As Jimmy's spouse, she couldn't be forced to testify but she could testify if she wanted to. If she did testify, her testimony would be critical. I knew Betty said she didn't think her husband had killed Don and Amanda, but I was worried about Wilkerson distorting her testimony and playing up the divorce. I decided to call her and see if her attitude had changed at all since I had last talked to her. I needed to know if she was going to testify. She answered on the second ring and asked me about the wedding. I gave her a brief progress report and then asked her if she'd been keeping in touch with Jimmy?

"Yes, I saw him this morning."

"Oh, really. Did he come by?"

"No, he's staying here now."

"He is? How come?"

"We're back together."

"Back together? That's wonderful news. What happened?"

"I don't know. After that last cocaine episode, I figured I'd better keep a close eye on him—at least until after the trial."

"Un huh."

"So, we've been spending a lot of time together. He feels really bad about the way he's been treating me and the kids and has begged me for a second chance."

"Is that right?"

"He's a changed man. I know this might sound terrible, but I think with daddy gone, our marriage might have a chance."

"So, is the divorce off?"

"For now. We'll see how it goes. I didn't really want a divorce. I just felt like I didn't have a choice. Now things are different. He needs me."

"That's great. I'm so happy for you."

"So, how are things going with the investigation? Are you going to be able to get Jimmy off? Please tell me you've got some new suspects."

"We have a lot of suspects, but we can't prove someone else did it yet."

"Keep trying. You've got to get Jimmy off."

"I'll try my best. A lot will depend on you, though."

"What do you mean?"

"Well, Wilkerson is sure to call you as a witness. If you didn't testify that would be great. If you do testify, Wilkerson is likely to twist your testimony to help him convict Jimmy."

"I won't testify then."

"Good. I would like you there at Jimmy's side, though, during the trial. "

"I'll be there, don't worry. And if Wilkerson somehow gets me on the stand thinking I'll help convict Jimmy, he'll regret it."

Betty's announcement that the divorce was off was the best news I heard in weeks. It was important that the jury like Jimmy and the fact that he and Betty were trying to reconcile and overcome their problems would help a lot. There would no doubt be jurors who had faced similar marital problems and would sympathize with them. I was in such a good mood after talking to Betty, I decided to do something I had been putting off for weeks—talking to Speaker Potts and Congressman Manning.

Speaker Potts's district encompassed west Arlington and southeast Ft. Worth. Luckily the Texas State Legislature wasn't in session so he was at his home office. The office was located in Arlington on Cooper Street near the University of Texas at Arlington. His appointment's secretary squeezed me in his last open slot late that afternoon. She warned me he'd only have fifteen minutes. I arrived a few minutes early and flipped open a Good Housekeeping magazine while I waited. I was reading an article on making holiday table decorations when the receptionist advised me that he was ready to see me.

The office was ornately decorated in military memorabilia. From a quick inventory of the room I surmised the Speaker was a Vietnam vet—a retired colonel according to a notation on a photo of he and President Reagan. He smiled amicably and invited me to sit down.

"I really appreciate you seeing me on such short notice," I said.

"Well, I'm glad I was able to squeeze you in. I understand Jimmy's trial is coming up in a couple of weeks."

"Yes, time has really flown by and I still have so much to do."

"So, how can I help you?"

"Well, I've been informed that you and Don Baker were friends and business partners."

"Yes, that's correct. I've known Don for years. We've been partners in several ventures."

"I'm interested in the most recent one. According to the loan file at Metroplex Savings, a note became delinquent and had to be written off."

The Speaker shook his head. "Yes, that's true. What can I say? We really miscalculated the market and underestimated our competition. We tried everything to increase demand, cut our expenses, you know, but—"

"What kind of business was it? According to the records it was a corporation called United Recycling Corporation."

"Right. Its primary business was plastic recycling."

I nodded. "Hmm. So where was your recycling plant?"

"We contracted it out?"

"What do you mean?"

"We were a collector of used plastic which we in turn sold to another recycling company."

"I see. So, you didn't have any assets?"

"Just cash and receivables."

"How long were you in business?"

"I'm afraid we didn't last eighteen months."

"Who owned the company?"

"Myself, Don, and several other investors."

"Was Congressman Manning one of them?"

He nodded. "Yes, but I expect you knew that."

I smiled. "Yes, I just wanted to confirm it. . . . How much did you all invest?"

"Is this really relevant to your inquiry, Miss Waters?"

"I'm afraid it is. I'm having to check all the loans that Don called. There is a strong possibility that someone whose loan was called was angry enough to kill him."

"You're not suggesting—?"

"No. No. I just have to be thorough. I can't play favorites, particularly since you're a public figure. I have to treat you just like all the other suspects."

"Right."

"So, wasn't it embarrassing to Don to have your loan called?"

"I suspect it was, but there wasn't much that could be done about it."

"Did you and Congressman Manning personally guarantee the loan?"

"No. We did not."

"Isn't it unusual for a financial institution to loan money to a startup company and not require personal guarantees from the principals?"

"No. I never personally guarantee my investments. Don didn't require it."

"Did the OTS question your loan at all?"

Speaker Potts looked at his watch. "Ah, I'm sorry, Miss Waters. I'm afraid our time is up. I've got a meeting with a big contributor in two minutes. If you have any other questions, please feel free to submit them to my assistant and I'll try to answer them as soon as possible."

He stood up. I closed my notebook, put it in my purse, and reluctantly got up.

"It's been so nice to meet you," Speaker Potts said.

I smiled and we shook hands. "Thank you, Mr. Speaker."

As I was leaving, I noticed a man in an expensive suit in the reception area looking at me. He turned away when we made eye contact. An uneasy feeling came over me as I made my way to my car. As I was pulling out of the parking garage, I noticed the man in the expensive suit and Speaker Potts rush out and get into a blue Mercedes. I was probably being paranoid, but I got the feeling the man in the expensive suit was there to size me up. If I was right then wherever they were going had something to do with Metroplex Savings and Loan and, perhaps, Don's murder. I decided to follow them.

Up ahead I saw a gas station. I turned in and pulled up to a telephone booth and pretended to be searching my purse for a telephone number. When the blue Mercedes went by, I took up the chase. They drove South on Cooper to Interstate 20 and took the eastbound on-ramp. I followed them at a safe distance for several miles until they got off the freeway. It was soon clear where they were headed—the Dallas Naval Air Station. Unfortunately, I couldn't follow them onto the base. As I watched them drive through the gate, I took down the license plate number.

38

The Lockbox

Rebekah insisted she go with me to the airport. I didn't resist as I was anxious to get going. It was early afternoon and it was a forty-five-minute drive to DFW from our home. As we were driving, I gave her a word by word account of my conversation with Mo. It sounded even more bizarre when I repeated it.

"Why would someone want you dead?" Rebekah asked.

"I don't know. I'm supposed to read the newspaper to figure it out."

"The newspaper. What's in the newspaper?"

"It's got to be something to do with Iran-Contra hearings."

"Oh, I've been watching them on TV. What did Huntington have to do with them?"

"I'm not sure. It appears he was selling arms to Iran. Luther Palmer was in on the deal too. Huntington told me Palmer was in Beijing but he must have been in Iran."

"So, maybe Huntington knew too much," Rebekah suggested.

I nodded. "I think you're right. Maybe the CIA needed to get rid of him so that he couldn't testify."

"And that's why they want to get rid of you. They're

afraid Huntington might have told you something."

"He didn't tell me squat."

"But they don't know that. I'm so worried. What if they try to kill you again. What if there is a bomb in the locker at the airport."

"No. I can trust Mo."

"I don't know. Maybe you should call Detective Besch."

"No, Mo said explicitly not to tell anyone about the call."

"But there may be a bomb in there!"

"I don't think so. I think Mo was just warning me to back off for my own safety."

"Stan. You can't open that locker," Rebekah pleaded.

"It's okay. I think it's just some money."

"But can you take it?"

"I don't know. It's not like I did something illegal."

"But you might be participating in something illegal and not even know it."

"Then, I lack mens rea."

"Mens what?"

"Intent. I don't have any criminal intent."

"Let's just turn around and go home."

"No, we've come this far. Let's just see what's in the locker."

Traffic was light at DFW and it didn't take us long to get to Gate 22 in Terminal A. Rebekah continued to try to persuade me to call Detective Besch but my gut feeling told me it was okay. Rebekah refused to follow me to the locker. She stayed thirty yards away when I opened it. When I looked over at her, she was biting her fingernails.

Sweat was beading on my forehead as I placed the key in the lock. I held my breath and started to turn it.

"No, don't!" Rebekah screamed.

I looked over my shoulder and Rebekah was running toward me. The lady next to me turned quickly and looked at Rebekah like she was crazy. I turned the key, opened the locker, and pulled out a small navy-blue sports bag. I looked around and saw that people were staring at us. I took Rebekah's hand and walked a little way away.

"I should have left you at home," I said.

We found two seats off in a corner and I opened the bag.

"It looks to be about a hundred grand in cash," I said.

"A hundred thousand dollars?"

"That's just a rough estimate."

"But why so much?"

"I don't know. I guess they really want me to keep my mouth shut.'

"What are you going to do?"

"Put this in a safety deposit box for safe keeping, I guess, until I can sort things out."

On the way home Rebekah was very quiet. I felt bad about what had happened and having put her through so much trauma. I prayed I'd never hear from Robert Huntington or the CIA again. I took her hand and squeezed it gently.

"I'm sorry, honey. I should have just left the money in the locker."

She looked away. There was a moment of silence. Then she said firmly, "No. You're right. You couldn't have done that. They blew up your car and almost got you killed for godsakes. You deserve that money."

I smiled and replied, "Okay, then. We'll keep it. I was worried about how I was going to pay for my new 300ZX. Now I can pay cash for it."

"That's fine, but we need to put the rest of it in the kid's college fund."

I laughed. "What college fund?"

"Exactly. We need to start a college fund."

"Fine with me. That will be one less problem we'll have to worry about."

She took a deep breath and laid her head on my shoulder. I put my arm around her without taking my eyes off the road. She sighed and said, "Promise me all the excitement is over?"

I squeezed her and said, "Everything is going to be fine, honey. Don't worry."

As we continued down the road, I prayed my optimism would prove to be well founded. Deep down, however, I wasn't so sure. If we continued our investigation of Congressman Manning and Speaker Potts, we'd soon have to deal with a whole new set of enemies.

39
Shell Game

Stan told me about his adventure at DFW over a cup of coffee. I told him I was going to call Derek Donner and have him come write a big insurance policy on his life. Stan thought that was a good idea. I told him I was joking but he said he was serious. He thought key man insurance made a lot of sense. After hearing his exploits, I told him about my meeting with Speaker Potts. While we were talking, Jodie interrupted to tell us she'd checked the license number I had copied down the night before. The car belonged to Mint, Ltd. A check with the Secretary of State revealed that Horace Manning was a limited partner of Mint, Ltd.

After talking about this latest information, we decided we had to look into United Recycling and have Paul Thayer try to figure out who Manning and Potts were visiting at the Dallas Naval Air Station. Since time was running out, we had Jodie contact a legal research firm in Austin to have someone go over to the Secretary of State's office to check out what they could on United Recycling.

Several hours later we had our report. The registered agent was a Simon Trueblood of Austin, Texas and the sole officer of the company was none other than Don Baker. I called Jimmy and asked him if he knew Trueblood. He advised me that he did and that Trueblood was Speaker Pott's attorney. I asked him if he'd ever heard of United Recycling and he said he had heard the name mentioned, but that was it.

The physical address of United Recycling according to the Secretary of State's file was on Mockingbird Lane south of R.L. Thornton Freeway. I decided to drive over there and check out the facility. The address was in a warehouse district and when I got there, I found a chain link fence surrounding the building. Unfortunately, it was padlocked but there was a realtor's sign on the fence, so I copied the number and called it when I got back to the office.

A young lady answered and I inquired about the availability of the property. In our conversation, I asked about the previous tenant. She confirmed that United Recycling had leased the place for a year, but to her knowledge hadn't conducted much business there.

"Yes, it was very strange. They paid their deposit and a year's rent but never moved anything in the place. There was a caretaker who came and occupied one small office. He did a little shipping and receiving, but there were rarely any cars in the parking lot."

"Did you ever ask them about the lack of activity?" I asked.

"No, the rent was paid so it wasn't any of my business."

"Who handled the lease negotiations?"

"A realtor, Bass Realty. Roger Bass was their agent. He contacted me and said he had a client who wanted to lease the warehouse. I was happy about it because there was a glut of warehouse space and it had been vacant for some time."

"Did you ever meet the tenants?"

"No, the agent got the lease signed and collected the rent. I never really had any dealings with them."

After hanging up with the realtor, I called Bass Realty and talked to Roger Bass. He confirmed that he had been hired to find warehouse space for a recycling operation. He said his contact was Simon Trueblood. I asked him about the fact that no recycling ever took place on the premises. He said Trueblood informed him that the company's financing fell through and asked him to try to sublease it, but with the market so bad he wasn't able to do it.

It wasn't until the following day that we heard back from Paul Thayer. He had done background checks on Congressman Manning and Speaker Potts. It seems they both had served in the Naval Air Force from 1964 to 1970 and were assigned to the same aircraft carrier during the Vietnam War. Thayer checked the roster of officers assigned to the Dallas Naval Air Station and found a Captain Stuart Chamberlain who had also served on the same aircraft carrier during that time period. What this all meant was beyond me, but it was very interesting that Manning, Potts, and Chamberlain all felt compelled to have a meeting after my visit.

I didn't know exactly what to do with the information I had uncovered about United Recycling. After considering the question for a while, I decided to go take another look at the loan file to see if anything in there might be illuminating. This wasn't an easy task since the federal regulators were now a permanent fixture at Metroplex Savings and Loan. In previous savings and loans seizures that I'd read about all the defaulted loan files had been confiscated by federal regulators or the FBI. Jerry Hartsfield, however, indicated that this hadn't happened yet at Metroplex. He said I could come in any time and view the file. I told him I was on my way.

Hartsfield invited me into his office and we sat around a small conference table. He pushed the file over to me and said, "There you go."

I opened the file and started looking at the contents. There was a promissory note for $2.3 million, a security agreement, UCC-1, loan agreement and corporate resolutions authorizing the transaction. What was absent was any documentation about the business—no financial statements, business plan, or even handwritten notes as to what the loan proceeds were going to be used for. I asked Hartsfield what he knew about the loan.

"Not much. It was Don's baby. He was in pretty thick with Manning and Potts and being that they were pretty powerful politicians, nobody questioned what they were doing."

"What about the loan officer who was indicted. What was her name?"

"Amy Gardner."

"Yes. It sounds like she was doing the same thing Don was doing—loaning money to dummy corporations and then pocketing the proceeds."

"Yes, it appears so."

"I guess I'll have to go visit her in jail and see if she knows anything about United Recycling."

Hartsfield nodded and replied, "It couldn't hurt."

The following day I went to the Dallas County Jail and

visited Amy Gardner. She denied any involvement with United Recycling but did admit she got the embezzlement idea from Don Baker. She had seen him pull it off several times and figured she could do the same thing. She figured if he caught her, she could simply threaten to blow the whistle on him if he tried to bring her down.

Although everything I had learned over the previous few days was very interesting, I still didn't have any direct evidence that Manning, Potts, or Chamberlain had anything to do with Don and Amanda's murder. With Jimmy's trial less than two weeks away, I feared this line of investigation wasn't likely to bear fruit quickly enough and I might have to go back to my original plan of trying to pin the murder on Phil Smart.

40

Blackmail

Now that the media was focusing on Lottie West and her stolen art, I figured I better spend whatever time it took to discover what had happened to it. The obvious place to start was Otto Barringer, but Besch had interrogated him at length and got nothing. The next best source of information had to be his parents, James and Loretta Barringer. They must know more than they had told me during our first visit. They weren't thrilled when I told them I was coming to see them again—particularly when I told them Detective Besch was coming with me. They knew he was the Detective assigned to help the DA prosecute their son Otto Barringer for murdering Lottie West.

Besch picked me up and we drove up to Dennison just south of the Oklahoma border on Highway 75. It was a pleasant forty-five-minute drive and Besch filled me in on the progress of his investigation along the way. When we knocked on the front door, Mrs. Barringer opened it quickly and invited us in. James was standing in the living room near the fire place with a grim look on his face. After making introductions I told them the purpose of our visit.

"We told you everything we know the last time you were here," James said.

I shrugged. "Well, maybe so, but I've learned a lot

since I saw you last. Now maybe I can ask the right questions and get some answers. . . . Detective Besch probably has a few questions too."

James took a deep breath and shook his head. Loretta said, "Well, we'll try to answer them as best we can."

"Good," I said. "Did you know that Otto had a nice stash of cash in his apartment?"

"Why no," Loretta said. "How much cash?"

"Over a quarter-million-dollars."

Loretta and James' mouths dropped. They obviously were not aware of the stash of money, or the amount was more than they expected.

"Do you have any idea where he might have gotten that kind of money?"

James said, "How should I know? That boy had a mind of his own. He didn't consult with us about anything."

"Did you ever see any of William West's art treasures?"

James pondered that question for a moment and then said, "What art treasures?"

James looked like he truly knew nothing about the stolen art, but Loretta looked so tense she was going to explode. Just to humor them, I recited the story of the Ludinburg collection again and how we suspected William West had stolen the art treasures. It was obvious by their reaction that they'd heard the story before. I was sure they could have given me a better rendition of the story had they wanted to.

"I never saw them," James said.

He was a good liar—cool and unemotional. I was sure he'd have no trouble beating a lie detector. Loretta didn't say anything. She suddenly became obsessed with a piece of lint on her skirt.

"How about you Mrs. Barringer? Otto certainly knew about it and even your daughter mentioned it."

"Well. I heard Lottie talk about it once or twice. I've never seen any of the pieces, though?"

"How about pictures?"

"Pictures? Well, yes I think she showed me a picture once."

Detective Besch raised his clinched hand and slammed it hard on the coffee table. Loretta nearly fell out of her rocking chair. He said firmly, "I hope you two understand how serious this matter is. Your son has been accused of murder and may go to jail for the rest of his life. Stan's been trying very nicely to get information out of you but you're not cooperating at all. We're not stupid. We know you know all about William West and his shenanigans. Now you better start coming clean or I'm going to lose my temper."

"Okay, okay," Loretta said. "We'll tell you what we know. We just don't like talking about it. You know. It's just been such an embarrassment to the family."

Besch looked at me and nodded. I continued, "So, how did Otto get a quarter-million-dollars?"

Loretta looked at James and then at Besch. Finally, she replied, "I'm afraid he was blackmailing them."

"Otto was blackmailing William and Lottie?" I asked.

"Yes, it started right after he graduated from college. He couldn't find a job and needed money so he could move out on his own. We told him he could stay with us, but you know kids. He wanted his own place."

"Right. So, how did it work?"

"Well, Otto and Lottie got along pretty well and he had spent some time at their place. On one of those occasions, she had shown him some of the pictures. He was very impressed that Lottie and William owned such valuable treasures. He talked about it all the time when he was here at the house. He took some art classes at Denton County Community College and found out how valuable they were."

"Okay."

"So, at first, he just asked them for a loan since he knew they were so rich, but William refused to give him a dime. Lottie would have, but she didn't have any money of her own. Otto was pretty upset that they wouldn't loan him any money so he got this idea that he could blackmail them. He knew the treasures had been stolen so he threatened to call the police and blow the whistle on them.

"I never knew how much money he had taken from them until you told me just now. I guess that's why they had to sell two of the pieces—to get money to pay Otto."

I looked at Besch and said, "So, that explains how Zimmerman got them."

Loretta said, "Zimmerman. Yes, that's his name. . . . Lottie refused to pay Otto after William died. Otto must have threatened her because that's when she went to the SPCA and adopted all those dogs. Otto hated dogs and Lottie knew it. He had been bitten as a child and was scared to death of them. She figured she was safe, but I guess she was wrong."

On the way back to Dallas, Besch and I discussed what we'd learned. It was obvious both Otto and Zimmerman had been withholding information. They both had lucrative enterprises going that they wanted to protect. Besch said it was time to put some heat on Zimmerman. We agreed he must know where the rest of the collection had gone. In fact, it was likely he had brokered the sale of the ancient manuscripts. Besch said he'd have Zimmerman brought in for questioning and promised to let me know when the interrogation was going to take place so I could listen in.

41

Suspects

With just a few days before Jimmy's trial began, we were all hard at work on our final trial preparations. Jodie was busy sending out subpoenas, organizing our trial notebooks, and getting our evidence ready for submission to the court. Stan and I had spent most of the day with Jimmy and each of our witnesses to make sure they were prepared for the day of reckoning that was rapidly approaching. It was Thursday afternoon and the last witness had just left.

"So, what do you think, Stan?"

"I think you're going to have an uphill battle convincing the jury that Phil Smart is a better suspect than Jimmy Bennett."

"I know. What am I going to do?"

Stan took a deep breath. "I don't know. Maybe the problem is Jimmy *is* guilty."

"Do you really think so?" I asked.

"I don't know and it really doesn't matter. Our job is to keep digging and hope something turns up."

"I agree. But how do you suggest we do that?"

"I don't know. Let's take a look at the other

alternatives. Let's see, there is Congressman Manning and Speaker Potts. I like them for the murder."

"Right, but we don't have an obvious motive and nothing to connect them to the crime scene."

"True. But I'll have Paul Thayer keep digging in that direction. He might get lucky and find us a link."

"Okay," I said. "Who else?"

"Betty. As trustee, she's in control of the company now."Stan said.

"But would she kill her father?" I asked. "That's pretty heartless and she doesn't strike me as being that ambitious. I doubt she wants the responsibility of running a construction company and trying to save a failing thrift."

"I don't know. She's smarter than she looks. I wouldn't be surprised if she was the mastermind behind her father's murder and then tried to make it look like Jimmy did it. And didn't you say she and Jimmy were reconciling?"

"Yes, but that could be just for show," I suggested.

"I doubt she'd be able to do it herself, but she might have hired someone."

"So, you think we should explore that possibility some more?"

"It wouldn't hurt," Stan said. "Let's try to find out if she has anyone in her circle of family and friends who might have been capable of killing Don and Amanda."

"Okay," I said and added that to my to-do list.

"Let's see," Stan mumbled. "What other suspects do we have?

"Margie," I said. "She had good reason to kill her

husband. He was cheating on her and he'd had sex with her sister. That must have pissed her off."

"Right. And, as I recall, Jimmy was the messenger so she probably blamed him as much as Don."

"The problem is we have nothing to connect her to the murder scene and she wouldn't be capable of slitting their throats."

"So, she'd have to have an accomplice," Stan said.

"Right," I said as I added yet another task to my to-do list. "Anybody else? . . . We've eliminated Tex, right?"

Stan laughed. "I don't know, did we?"

I glared at Stan. "Don't even go there."

"I guess that's about it then."

"Okay, I'll do some more digging into Betty and Margie and you work with Paul Thayer on the political angle."

Stan nodded and got up. "Okay, I'll go give Paul a call right now."

Stan left and I looked at my to-do list. There was a lot left to be done and precious little time, so I decided to enlist Jodie's help. I called her on the intercom and asked her to come into my office.

"You want to play detective this weekend," I asked.

"Sure, what did you have in mind."

"I need you to find out as much as you can about Margie Bennett. Find out who her friends are and what she does during the day. You might want to stake out her home and see who comes and goes. If she leaves, follow her."

"You think she might—?"

"She is the sole heir of the Baker fortune now. I just

need to know if she got in that position because of a good plan or good fortune."

"Okay, I'll see what I can find out."

"While you're doing that, I'm going to do the same thing with Betty."

"Good luck."

"You too, and thanks for doing this, Jodie."

"No. Problem," she said with a hint of excitement in her voice. "This will be fun."

42

The Chauffeur

Paula's assignment to prove Congressman Manning and Speaker Potts had conspired to commit murder was pretty daunting. But hopeless causes, according to the press, were my specialty, so I couldn't let the difficulty of the task get me down. I called Paul Thayer and asked him to come to my office for a little brainstorming session. I needed to know everything he'd learned about Manning and Potts and to get some direction as how to proceed from here. He arrived late that afternoon.

"Paula says there were four of them involved in these dummy corporation scams."

"Right. Manning, Potts, Captain Chamberlain, and Don Baker."

"Were you able to track any of the money?"

"Yes, it seems to have ended up in Panama."

"So, our little foursome was borrowing money and then giving it to the Contra Rebels in Nicaragua?"

"That's what it looks like."

"Did they plan to repay the loan?"

"Yes, I think they expected to repay it with proceeds from arms sales to Iran."

"They must have been working with Robert Huntington. He was selling arms to Iran. It couldn't be a coincidence. They must have been working together somehow."

"Something must have gone wrong," Thayer said.

"I guess so. I suspect it was the Congressional investigation and all the controversy over Oliver North's document shredding last November."

"That could be."

"I have an idea how we could find out for sure," I said.

"How's that?" Thayer asked.

"I bet Olivia could help us out."

"Olivia?"

"Yes, the contact we have in Congressman Manning's office."

I called Nicole and asked her to contact Olivia. She said she'd call her and arrange a lunch date. The next day Olivia called me from a pay phone at the Omaha Corral Bar and Grille. I related our theory and asked if she could confirm it. She said she couldn't, but she knew who could.

"Manning's secretary, Christine Bassett just went on maternity leave. She's lives in Red Oak, Texas. I happen to know she's going to be home tonight."

"How do you know that?"

"The Congressman asked me to call her. Her sister answered and told me she'd be out all day, but to call back tonight."

"Do you think she'll talk to me?"

"She might talk to you, if you turn on your Texas charm. Don't go in there like a bulldog detective. She might get spooked."

"Okay," I said. "She's probably our only chance at sorting this thing out in time to help Jimmy Bennett."

"Well, you've got to gain her trust."

"Right. But why *should* she talk to me? She'd be betraying Congressman Manning."

"Let me tell you something about Christine. She's very honest and forthright. I don't think she knows what the Congressman is up to. She probably suspects he's involved in some kind of illegal activity but doesn't want to face that reality."

"I see. She's an unknowing accomplice, so I'm just letting her know what she's involved in for her own good. . . . I'll give it a try."

"Good luck."

That evening I drove my new Nissan 300 ZX south on I35 to Red Oak. After exiting the freeway, I stopped at the light. There had been a lot of air pollution during the day so the sunset that evening was a fiery red. For a moment, I wished I was a worry-free photographer who could spend his days looking for treats like this from mother nature. Wouldn't that be the sweet life? I looked down at the directions to Christine's house that Jodie had prepared. The light changed and I continued on my way. It didn't take long to find it. It was a modest, brick track home, nicely landscaped, with a two-car garage in the front. There was a new Pontiac Firebird in the driveway.

Christine answered the door and looked at me warily. "Yes," she said.

"Hi, I'm Stan Turner. I'm an attorney—"

"Yes, I've seen you on TV. What are you doing here?"

"I need to talk to you. May I come in?"

She squinted and then shrugged. "I guess. What's this about?"

Her stomach was large and it was obvious she was in the last stages of her pregnancy. She showed me into her living room and pointed to a big brown chair.

"So, when are you due?"

"Twenty-one days. I can't wait to have this baby. I feel like a double wide with legs."

I laughed. "Yeah, I bet. I've got four kids so I'm familiar with what you're going through."

"But it's worth it, right?" she moaned as she sat down awkwardly.

"Yes, it is. Soon all this agony will be but a distant memory."

"Thanks for the encouragement. So, how can I help you?"

I guess you know Paula Waters and I are defending Jimmy Bennett. He's accused of killing—"

"Don Baker and his girlfriend. I've read about that in the papers. But what does that have to do with me?"

"Well, Don Baker and Congressman Manning were good friends—actually more than good friends."

"I knew they were friends. The Congressman banks at Metroplex Savings and Loan. I know that, but that's about it."

"Well, Don Baker, Congressman Manning, Speaker Potts, and a Navy captain, Stuart Chamberlain were partners in several corporations."

"Really. I didn't know that."

"United Recycling was one of them. Have you ever heard of it?"

"I've seen the name before, but I never knew much about it."

"What about Continental Exporters?"

"I don't know that one at all."

"I know this may be hard for you to believe, but United Recycling was used to illegally channel money to South America to help the Contra Rebels in Nicaragua."

"I've heard about that happening, but that would be in violation of the Bolan Amendment. Congressman Manning wouldn't have anything to do with that."

"I know it's hard to believe, but you must have known something was going on. He couldn't keep this a total secret."

"He wouldn't do anything illegal," she repeated.

"Think about it. Congressman Manning is a strong conservative who has been warning the American people for years about the Communist threat in Latin America. He's been a longtime advocate of extensive aid to the Contra Rebels. President Reagan has made it known that he wants to help the rebels. Manning probably figured he was doing the right thing and following the unwritten orders of the President."

"I don't want to do anything that might hurt the Congressman. He's a good man."

"I don't either. I just want to uncover the truth. Innocent lives are at stake."

"What do you think the Congressman did exactly?"

"I don't know. Maybe nothing. But with Congress coming down hard on Oliver North and Poindexter and everyone else involved in selling arms to Iran or aiding the Contra Rebels, I'm afraid the business arrangement among the four I mentioned may have become strained."

She thought for a moment and then said, "I did

overhear an argument a week or two before Don was murdered."

"Really? Tell me about it."

"It was late in the afternoon. I was packing up to go home when Don Baker showed up. He insisted on seeing the Congressman immediately."

"Did you overhear anything they had to say?"

"I didn't hear the entire conversation, but they were yelling and I know Don was upset about the federal regulator's demand that the Metroplex shareholders put in another two million dollars in capital."

"What was Manning's response to that?"

"He said he couldn't get involved because he had an obvious conflict of interest. Baker didn't like that answer much. He said the Congressman better figure out how to make the OTS go away."

"Did Manning say he'd do anything?"

"He said he'd find some investors to put up the money. He couldn't risk direct intervention. He didn't say why."

"Did he find any investors?"

"Yes, a week or so later he arranged for several of them to fly to Dallas. In fact, now that I think about it, your client, Jimmy Bennett was supposed to pick them up from DFW Airport and entertain them."

"Really?"

"Yes, I remember the Congressman saying that Jimmy was very good at loosening up potential investors. I guess he really knew how to party."

"I've heard that too. So, did the investors come into

town?"

"No, the weekend got canceled because of the fight between Jimmy and Don."

"Where was the Congressman that weekend?"

"He was in staying at his Virginia house. He stays there while Congress is in session."

"I know this may sound . . . well . . . like I'm impugning the Congressman's integrity, but I'm not really. I've just got to check this thing out from all angles."

"What do you mean?"

"Well, I need to know who handles problems for the Congressman."

Christine squinted. "I don't know what you mean?"

"Well, you know. If things don't go just right, who does he call."

"That depends. If it is a political matter, he'd talk to his administrative assistant. If it was a legal issue, he'd call his attorney."

"What if it was something he wanted handled very discreetly."

She thought a moment. "That would be Skip."

"Skip?"

"Skip Henderson. He's an ex-NFL football player who injured his knee his first year of professional football. Skip's father and the Congressman went to college together at Texas A&M. The Congressman felt really bad about what happened, so he hired Skip to be his chauffeur and to do odd jobs."

"Odd jobs?"

"You know, like picking important people up from the airport, delivering sensitive materials, entertaining constituents, whatever the Congressman needed done Skip was there to accommodate."

We talked at length for some time. Christine assured me she knew of no illegal activity and would never be a party to any such thing. She asked if she needed to get an attorney. I said it was probably premature to worry about that now, but that I would keep her posted on what I found out and advise her if she needed to do anything. I told her I was working with the FBI and the Dallas Police and I'd let them know she would cooperate in any way she could. She thanked me and I left.

When I got back to the office, I called Paul Thayer and briefed him on what I'd learned. I told him to start looking into Skip Henderson. For starters I needed to know if he was with Congressman Manning the weekend of the murder and, if not, where was he? Paul said he'd get right on it and report back as soon as he found out.

43

Jimmy's Trial

When I looked out the window on Monday morning, April 5, 1988, it was foggy and a fine mist was falling. The thermometer was just a tad above fifty degrees and the air was still. It was perfect day for a murder trial. Bart had been extra nice all week and informed me he'd made breakfast. My stomach was in no condition to digest food, but I didn't want to hurt his feelings, so I sat down and dug in. After a few bites, I decided I was hungry after all and ate like it was my last meal.

Bart had appeared before the Walrus several times, so he briefed me on what to expect from him. He also filled me in on the latest scuttlebutt at the DA's office. Wilkerson was very confident he'd get a conviction. So confident, in fact, that he had agreed to give the exclusive inside story of Jimmy Bennett's conviction to a reporter for *Time Magazine.*

The magazine deal was just what I needed to get emotionally prepared for trial. I was ready to shove Wilkerson's magazine deal down his throat. As I was about to give Bart a kiss goodbye the telephone rang. It was Betty.

"He's gone! Jimmy's gone. When I woke up, he wasn't in bed. His truck is gone. Oh, my God. What's going to happen?"

"Okay, calm down. When did you see him last?"

"About ten last night. I was tired and went to bed. He was watching the news."

"Did he go to bed at all?"

"No, his side of the bed is still made. Oh, God. I should have waited for him to go to bed. Damn it!"

"It's not your fault. He's a grown man. Do you have any idea where he went?"

"No. His truck's gone. He could be half way to Biloxi by now."

"Why do say Biloxi?"

"He read an article about those casino cruise ships out of Biloxi. He loves to gamble. He was talking about it last night. He said what if they had his trial and he didn't come? I just thought he was kidding, but I should have realized he'd found some coke. He must have had a stash hidden somewhere."

"Jesus Christ. This is all I need."

"I'm sorry. Should I go after him?"

"No. It's too late. When he doesn't show up for trial, they'll revoke his bond and issue an arrest warrant. We couldn't get him back in time. Now he's going to have to spend some time in jail."

"Oh, God. You can't let that happen."

"I'm sorry. It's out of my hands."

I called Stan and told him the bad news. He said he'd have Paul Thayer get someone in Biloxi to find him and drive him back to Dallas. If Jimmy walked in to court of his own volition, even if he were a day late, it would be better than if he were dragged in kicking and screaming by the police. I hung up the phone feeling like I'd just been hit by a sledge hammer. My head was spinning. I could just see the judge yelling and screaming at me and Wilkerson smiling and laughing at this turn of events.

As I was leaving the house it began to rain hard and I could hear thunder close by. The road between my condo and Preston road began to flood as it often did in heavy rain. I could hardly see the road ahead, so I made my way slowly through the high water. A sudden gust of wind shook my car and sent a road sign flying across the road. I slammed on the brakes to avoid it. Luckily, by the time I made it to the Dallas North Tollway the storm had moved on to the East.

Twenty minutes later I exited on Commerce Street and headed east toward Dealey Plaza. As I came up the hill, I could see the courthouse was encircled with press vehicles and media vans. A mob of reporters was stationed outside the front door to the courthouse. Luckily I was able to park underground and enter the courthouse from the ground floor. I thought I had bypassed most of the reporters but when the elevator door opened on the 7th floor, lights and cameras were flashing.

"Miss Waters. How do you feel about your client's chances?"

I shook my head and replied, "No comment."

There was no way I was talking to the press in the mood I was in. I wasn't sure I could even talk coherently knowing what was about to happen to me. As I made my way through the spectators and reporters, my knees became weak and I felt dizzy. I was about to collapse when I felt a strong arm pull me up.

"Come on, Paula," Stan said. "Don't give out on me before the trial even begins."

"What difference does it make? We don't even have a client," I whispered.

Stan brought me into the courtroom and made me sit right down at the defense table. He brought me some water. I drank a little and took a deep breath. "I don't know what happened. I just suddenly felt faint. This isn't like me."

"It's okay. You'll be all right. Stress can do a number on anybody. You've had enough this morning to last a lifetime."

"What's going to happen, Stan?"

"We'll just have to try the case without Jimmy. He wasn't going to testify anyway."

"I know. But it will look so bad."

"Hey. We can't worry about that. All we can do is put on the best defense we can under the circumstances."

"What about a continuance?"

"Forget it. Let's just try the case and get it over with."

"You sound like you think he's guilty," I said.

"Well, when someone runs it's usually for a reason."

Stan may have been right, but I still believed Jimmy was innocent. Why he ran, I didn't know but I suspected it was out of fear and helplessness rather than guilt.

"Your color is coming back," Stan said.

"I'm fine. Don't worry."

The bailiff stood up and said, "All rise! The 355th Judicial District Court for the County of Dallas is now in session, the Honorable Ernest P. Wingate presiding."

Everyone stood up and the judge entered the courtroom. He went to the bench, took his seat, and nodded at the bailiff.

The bailiff said, "You may be seated."

The judge scanned the courtroom and then looked at the empty chair where Jimmy was supposed to be seated. "Where is the defendant?" he scowled.

I got up and replied, "We're not sure, Your Honor. His wife hasn't seen him since 10:00 p.m. last night."

"Have you talked to him in the last 24 hours?"

"Yes, Your Honor. I talked to him around noon yesterday. He was supposed to meet me here in the courtroom at 8:30 a.m."

"Do you think he is fleeing the jurisdiction of this court?"

"I don't know, Your Honor. I hope not."

"Well, I'm going to delay the start of this case until 1:00 p.m. to give you time to find your client. If he's not here by then I'm going to revoke his bond and issue a warrant for his arrest. Either way jury selection will begin at 1:00 p.m."

"Yes, Your Honor," I said.

When the judge had gone the courtroom erupted in conversation. I looked at Wilkerson and he and his assistant were laughing. I felt Stan take my arm again.

"Come on. Let's get the hell out of here."

I didn't argue. Before I knew it, Stan was leading me

out through the back corridor, down several flights of stairs, and out another door that led into the District Clerks' office. Somehow, we had avoided the crowd of reporters who must have been having a feeding frenzy by this time. We escaped into the parking garage and went directly to my car. Stan said he'd see me back at the office. As I was driving out of the parking garage, the thought occurred to me that maybe I should leave town too.

44

Closing In

When I saw Paula surrounded by the mob of reporters, I was concerned. I rushed over to her and put my arm around her for support. She was pale and obviously shaken by Jimmy's disappearance. It certainly wasn't the way you wanted to begin a high-profile murder trial. She went limp in my arms and I almost had to carry her into the courtroom. She recovered quickly after downing a glass of water. I told myself she would be okay. She'd be fine once the trial began. Later, as she drove out of the parking garage, I began to worry again. She had brought financial stability to my life and a great deal of comfort too. I liked having her around. Practicing law could get lonely and even frightening at times and it was nice to have someone I could trust to talk to. Now that she was part of my life, I didn't want to lose her.

As I walked to my car I wondered how best to make use of the unexpected four hours I now had available. Paul Thayer was researching Skip Henderson's whereabouts on Black Monday. I wondered if he'd found anything out. I'd check on that first thing when I got back to the office. As I approached my car, I spotted Margie Baker and a younger man getting into a red Mazda RX-7. It was a gorgeous car and I had considered buying the same model when I'd been shopping for a new car recently. Margie saw me.

"Mr. Turner. Hi."

"Hello, Mrs. Baker," I said and nodded at the man.

"Oh, this is Earl—Earl Modest, our ranch manager."

We shook hands and I said, "Nice to meet you."

"What happened in there?" Margie asked. "What happened to Jimmy?"

"I don't know. He must have got scared and taken off. I can't say I blame him. A murder trial can be pretty scary, particularly when you're the one on trial."

Earl laughed. "Frankly, I hope they never find him. He did the world a big favor knocking off that little bastard."

"Honey. We can't let him get away with murder. That wouldn't be right. Who will be next? God knows he'd love to have me out of the way so he could get his hands on the Baker money."

"Well, I'm not so sure he killed Don and Amanda," I said. "What do you know about United Recycling and Continental Exporters?"

Margie's eyes widened. "Oh, you mean Captain Chamberlain's fiascos."

"Yes. Captain Chamberlain was a partner along with Congressman Manning and Speaker Potts."

"I told Don he shouldn't be getting Metroplex involved in foreign policy, but he doesn't listen to me."

"What do you mean?"

"Captain Chamberlain came to Don because the President had indirectly asked him to figure out a way to get money to the Contra Rebels in Nicaragua. He said the Communist government had to be ousted or Communism would spread throughout Latin America and be a threat to the United States."

"The President asked him to raise money for the Contra Rebels?"

"Honey," Earl said. "Should you be telling him all about this?"

Margie glared at Earl. "What difference does it make? Don is dead for godsakes."

"Yes, but—"

"Honey. Stan already has figured most of it out. I might as well make sure he gets the story straight. Anyway, I said *indirectly*. He made it clear that despite Congress he would help the people of Nicaragua free themselves of the Marxist regime that had them by the throat. Captain Chamberlain got the message and came to Don for help."

"What exactly did he want Don to do?"

"To help him figure out how to help the President accomplish his goal."

"So, all four of them got together and came up with these dummy corporations?" I asked.

"That's right. Captain Chamberlain knew an ex-CIA operative who had gone into the arms business. They contacted him about a business arrangement. Metroplex would provide funding to buy arms and he'd sell them."

"This man wouldn't by any chance be Robert Huntington?" I asked.

"Why yes. Did you know him? Someone kidnaped him

recently. Did you know about that?"

I nodded. "Yes, I'm familiar with that story. Go on."

"Well, it turns out Iran was in desperate need of weapons so Huntington began supplying them. It worked out very well until Congress got wind of it."

"What happened then?"

"The shipments to Iran stopped and then the money dried up. Don was left with a multimillion dollar loan default."

It all made sense now. Don had gotten himself involved in a very treacherous game—trying to help the President circumvent the express wishes of Congress. He had banked on the President's ability to control the political situation and lost. He was a casualty in the shootout between the President and Congress. But who killed him? Was it the FBI or the CIA? I didn't know whose side they were on. Was the CIA backing the President and the FBI going after the lawbreakers who had defied Congress? Or was Don murdered by his own partners who feared he'd spill his guts to the FBI or the federal regulators?

"The week before Don was murdered, did he have any contact with any of his partners?"

"I don't know. I was at the ranch," Margie said. "Betty told me the other day, though, that Congressman Manning had left several messages for Don on the day he was killed."

"Do you know what the messages were about?"

"No, but I'm sure Betty would."

I thanked Margie and left to get back to the office. I knew Paula would be wondering what happened to me. When I walked into her office, she was on the phone talking to Bart. When she hung up, I told her about running into Margie and getting an earful about Don and his arms dealing.

"So, you met Margie's boyfriend?"

"Right. He's a lot younger than she is."

"What does he look like? Is he as handsome as I've heard?"

"I guess. He's in good shape—must spend a lot of time outdoors judging by his tan. . . . Oh, he's got a Mazda RX 7 kind of like the one I almost bought. His is red, though. I wouldn't get a red one—the cops like to pull over red sports cars."

"Is that right?" Paula said thoughtfully.

"Yeah. Anyway, I'm going to go call Paul Thayer and see if he's found out anything on Skip Henderson. If he was in Dallas on Black Monday, he may be our killer."

When I finally got a hold of Paul Thayer he said he hadn't got his background check back on Skip Henderson, but he had learned that Henderson wasn't with the Congressman in Washington on the day of Don and Amanda's murder. That was great news and I felt certain Henderson was our man.

45

Presumption of Guilt

Paul Thayer called just before noon to tell me he'd located Jimmy Bennett and that he was out on a cruise ship gambling. He said he had someone in Biloxi waiting for him and just as soon as they made contact he'd let me know. I couldn't believe Jimmy was that irresponsible. How could he go out on a cruise ship to gamble when he knew he was about to go on trial for murder?

Stan and I left for court together this time. Stan didn't want me to have to deal with the reporters alone. He led me in the courthouse through the basement entrance and then up the stairs to avoid the reporters who were lurking around the elevators. At 1:00 p.m. the judge made his entrance. After everyone was seated, he looked at me and said, "Miss Waters, I see that your client is still missing."

I stood up and said, "Yes, Your Honor. We've located him but we won't be able to get him here until tomorrow morning?"

The judge just stared at me. Finally, he said, "Is this some kind of joke. Does your client think we're playing games here? Where exactly is he?"

"Ah. Well, he's apparently on a cruise ship out of Biloxi, Mississippi."

"Is he running?"

"No. No. It's a gambling ship."

"What?"

"You know. They go out into international waters so everyone can gamble, then they come back into port."

There was laughter in the gallery.

"Well, I'm going to have a surprise for your client, Miss Waters. There's going to be welcoming party for him when his ship comes into port."

"Yes, Your Honor."

"I'm hereby revoking Mr. Bennett's bail and directing he be arrested forthwith and brought back to this courtroom to stand trial. Now, in the meantime, let's get on with picking the jury."

The bailiff handed us jury information sheets and the judge told us we had thirty minutes to study them before he brought in the jury panel for voir dire. Stan and I went over the list of jurors and discussed those that might be a problem. When the jury panel was brought in, the Judge introduced all of us and explained how the trial would proceed. Wilkerson then gave a short synopsis of the case whereupon we started asking questions of the individual jurors. We worked hard all day but hadn't finished when 5:00 p.m. arrived, so the judge adjourned the case until the following morning.

When we got back to the office a little after six there was a message from Paul Thayer. The local police were at the dock in Biloxi to pick up Jimmy Bennett when the ship docked, but he wasn't aboard or somehow had eluded them. My heart sank at hearing this news as now I knew I'd face another scolding from Judge Wingate and the jury would think Jimmy was running because he was guilty. Depression hit me like a lead pipe. How could everything have gone so wrong? Fortunately, Stan came in to cheer me up and make some suggestions.

"I think we're going to have to adjust our approach a little."

I laughed. "Just a little?"

"Well, a lot actually. Because of Jimmy's little gambling trip, proving reasonable doubt isn't going to be enough to get him acquitted. The jury will be so prejudiced by his absence that only if we prove beyond any reasonable doubt that someone else murdered Don and Amanda, will he walk. That means we'll have to select a suspect and gamble on being able to prove that person is the killer. If we fail, Jimmy will face the death penalty."

"I can't believe he did this," I said. "He seems to be a reasonably intelligent person. What was he thinking?"

"I'm sure he just got scared and went to a bar—one thing led to another."

"So, what suspect are we going to gamble on?"

"I don't know. If we find that Skip Henderson was in town on the day of the murders, I'd vote for him and Don's three partners. If that doesn't pan out, I guess we've got to go with your jealous stalker—what's his name?"

"Phil Smart."

"Right."

"Okay, I'll waive my opening statement until we put on our case. That will give us a little time to make a final decision on our suspect."

"Good idea," Stan said. "It will take Wilkerson two or three days, at least, to put on his case. With a little luck, we'll have the weekend to complete our investigation and make a final decision."

"Yeah, and if we're really lucky, they might find Jimmy and bring his sorry ass back here."

I didn't feel like cooking when I got home so Bart took me out to Carellli's for some good Italian food. I hadn't eaten all day so I was famished. Bart listened attentively as I vented all my frustrations between bites of lasagna and garlic bread. He didn't complain about my tirade, but just listened and smiled. After eating my fill and having a few glasses of Chardonnay, I was starting to feel better.

When we got back to my condo Bart wanted to make love. I didn't really feel like it, but he had been so nice to me all evening I could hardly say no. When we finally made it to bed, it was after midnight and I was so exhausted I fell asleep almost immediately. It had been the worst day of my career and the only positive thing I could think of was that it couldn't get any worse.

I had been sleeping for some time when the telephone rang. Bart rolled over and tried to answer it but only managed to knock it on the floor. I got up, went around the bed and picked the phone off the floor.

I sat down on the side of the bed and said, "Hello."

There was music in the background like the radio was on or the caller was having a party. After an awkward moment of silence, I said, "Who is this?"

"Who do you think?"

"Jimmy?"

"I have to whisper. I'm being watched. Every damn cop in the state of Mississippi is looking for me."

"What did you expect? You shouldn't have left?"

"Right, and face a certain death sentence."

"It's not certain. We've got a good shot at proving reasonable doubt."

"It doesn't matter. They'll buy the jury."

"Who's they?"

"The same people who killed Don. The hit men from the Agency."

"We're not certain they did it. It's just a theory."

"It all makes sense though. Don knew too much, so they had to kill him but make it look like someone else did it. I was the perfect fall guy. So, now they can't afford to let me get off."

I suddenly regretted having told Jimmy our United Recycling theory. That was the problem with keeping clients fully informed, they sometimes couldn't differentiate between fact and theory. Now Jimmy was sure the CIA was out to get him convicted even though we couldn't prove it. We certainly hadn't intended to spook him so much that he'd start running.

"You need to come back to Dallas. Tell me where you are and I'll send someone to pick you up. They'll bring you to the courthouse and you can walk in and apologize to the judge and jury for leaving."

"But they'll put me in jail."

"I know. But running isn't the answer. If you believe the CIA is out to frame you, maybe we can sell that scenario to the jury."

"I can't take that chance. I'm sorry."

The phone went dead. "Jimmy! Jimmy! Damn it!" I said and slammed down the telephone.

46

Tough as Titanium

As I was leaving the house, I got a call from Paula. She said she was running late because Jimmy had called her. She wanted me to pick her up at her condo to save time. Fortunately, I had packed up everything I needed for day two of the trial, so I didn't need to go by the office. When I got to Paula's place she wasn't anywhere to be seen, so I went up to her front door and knocked.

"Come on in," she said. "I'm almost dressed."

I opened the door, stepped inside and looked at my watch. It was 8:35 a.m. We had to be in court at 9:00 and it was a thirty to forty-five-minute drive, depending on traffic and weather conditions. Fortunately, the skies were clear and traffic usually subsided quickly after 8:30.

Paula walked in the living room with a tube of lipstick in her hand. She was dressed in a white textured tank dress that clung to her shapely body. She sat up against me, and put her hand on my leg to steady herself while she put on a pair of white heels. My eyes were drawn to her luscious legs which she extended before me. She looked at me, shook her head, and said, "Do you like this color of lipstick?"

I looked at her burnt orange lips and nodded. "Yeah, it looks great. . . .You look great."

I don't know why I said that but she perked up immediately. She tilted her head slightly and smiled seductively. "Thanks. If we had more time—"

"Right. But we don't," I said and stood up.

"Yeah, well I'm sorry I'm running late but Jimmy called. He's not coming back voluntarily."

"Oh, wonderful. Couldn't you talk some sense into him?"

"No. He's convinced the CIA is going to make sure he's convicted—buy the jury if they have to."

"Buy the jury? That's a little farfetched."

"Not really. If they killed Don Baker, jury tampering would be nothing to them."

I took a deep breath. "Well, we better go. If we're lucky, we won't be more than five or ten minutes late."

"They'll wait for us," Paula said. "What choice do they have?"

Paula seemed to have recovered from the disastrous first day of trial. She was even flirting with me which made me feel like things were back to normal. At least as normal as they got at Turner and Waters. It was a good thing Paula was back on her game because the next few days, while Wilkerson put on his case in chief, wouldn't be pleasant. He would be laying out a very convincing case against Jimmy Bennett and Paula would have to be in top form to discredit it.

As we drove south on the Dallas North Tollway, I

wondered if Paul Thayer had found out anything yet on Skip Henderson. I made a mental note to call him during the morning break to find out. As we approached the courthouse, I could see the press corps had grown considerably from the previous day. No doubt Jimmy going AWOL and the issuance of an arrest warrant had increased the entertainment value of his murder trial. As we walked through the basement entrance to the courthouse, we were met by some reporters.

"Miss Waters? Have they arrested Jimmy Bennett yet?" the first reporter asked.

Paula shrugged. "Not unless they got him in the last twenty minutes. He just called me."

"Where is he?" the second reporter asked.

"Somewhere in Mississippi. He didn't say exactly where."

"Is he going to turn himself in?" the first reporter asked.

Paula shook her head and replied, "No, I don't think so."

"How do you think his absence will affect his trial?" the second reporter asked.

"It will make our job more difficult, but it shouldn't affect the eventual outcome. Jimmy's guilt or innocence doesn't have anything to do with his presence during the trial. The facts themselves will determine whether he is convicted or acquitted."

I was amazed at Paula's impromptu news conference. She was already laying the foundation for her defense strategy and practicing her opening statement. She was right, it didn't really matter if Jimmy was present or not. He wasn't going to testify so we didn't need him. It was only the jury's reaction to his absence that could hurt us. As I watched Paula, I could see her mind working hard to conceive some compelling reason why Jimmy had fled. I couldn't wait to hear what it would be.

When we arrived in the courtroom the judge was on the bench and Wilkerson was talking to the bailiff. The judge watched us while we took our places at the defense table. The judge shook his head and said, "Well. Glad you two could join us."

Paula replied, "I'm sorry, Your Honor, but I was on the phone with my client trying to persuade him to turn himself in."

"Is that right?" the Judge said. "And were you successful?"

"No, I'm sorry to report that I was not. He's concerned for his safety. He's received threats on his life."

"Who has threatened him?"

"He didn't say."

The judge snorted and said, "Well, he'll be perfectly safe in jail when the local authorities catch up with him."

"Yes, sir," Paula said.

"Okay. Let's get on with it. I'll deal with Mr. Bennett later."

"Yes, Your Honor," Paula said.

"You have twenty minutes to make your strikes, then we'll seat the jury," the Judge said.

It was nearly eleven when the Judge read the names of the jurors and they took their places in the jury box. When they were all in their places, he instructed them on their role as jurors and outlined the rules they must follow. When he was finished, he gave us a ten-minute break and told Wilkerson he could make his opening statement just as soon as the break was over.

During the break, I called Paul Thayer. He told me that he had finally been able to confirm that indeed Skip Henderson had been in Dallas on October 19. He said his information had been obtained from one of his contacts at Checker Cab. Apparently, one of their drivers drove him to the airport and remembered that he checked his bags to Dallas. He said he was on his way to Dallas to try to track Henderson's movements while he was in town. I thanked him and hung up. This was good news, but not quite enough to prove our alternate scenario. I went back to the courtroom and told Paula what I'd learned. While we were talking the judge returned.

Wilkerson stood up, strolled over to the jury box, and began. "Ladies and Gentlemen of the jury. We are here today because of events that occurred on Monday, October 19, 1987. This day, known as Black Monday, was indeed dark for Don Baker and Amanda Black, who were brutally murdered while they slept after a night on the town.

"We will show that Don Baker was a prominent citizen of the community, a businessman who owned the largest construction company in North Texas but also was the majority owner of Metroplex Savings & Loan.

"In the course of the trial of this case you will come to find out that the defendant, Jimmy Bennett, was the son-in-law of the decedent, Don Baker, and that they had a very close relationship—both business and social. It will become clear after hearing the testimony of the witnesses that Don Baker and Jimmy Bennett began to have a falling out in the late summer and fall of last year. The cause of this rift is unclear but what we will show is that on the Saturday before Don Baker was murdered, Jimmy Bennett and Don Baker had an argument that nearly came to blows.

"The immediate cause of the argument was Jimmy Bennett's wife's announcement that she had filed for divorce. This news was unexpected and outraged Jimmy Bennett who blamed his wife's unhappiness on her father's insistence that Bennett work long hours and entertain guests in the evenings.

"We will also show that Jimmy Bennett drank too much, took drugs, and had a hot temper. We will show that all of this contributed to the rampage he went on that resulted in the murder of Don Baker and Amanda Black.

"As the judge explained the state has the burden of proof in this case and we intend to meet that burden by establishing beyond any reasonable doubt that Jimmy Bennett carefully planned and carried out the murder of his father-in-law and ex-lover. We will show that there was no evidence of a forced entry at the crime scene which is consistent with the fact that Jimmy Bennett had a key to the condominium apartment. We will show that the killer used a six-inch hunting knife to slit the throats of his victims while they slept. We will show that Jimmy Bennett was the owner of that knife and that his fingerprints were found on the knife and as well as numerous other places around the bedroom where the murder took place.

Finally, we will show that Jimmy Bennett stood to gain substantial financial advantage from Don Baker's death—namely his wife would immediately become trustee of the trust that controlled the Baker fortune. When all is said and done it will be clear to all of you that Jimmy Bennett is guilty of capital murder and should be sentenced to die by lethal injection. Thank you."

Texas had recently adopted lethal injection as its official method of conducting executions. The first execution by this method occurred on December 7, 1982 when Charles Brooks was put to death for the murder of second hand car salesman David Gregory in Huntsville Texas in 1976. It was supposed to be a more humane way to put people to death, but the words still sent a chill through me.

The judge looked at Paula and asked, "Do you wish to make an opening statement?"

Paula stood up and replied, "No, Your Honor. The defense will make its opening statement after the state puts on its case."

"Very well," the Judge said. "We'll break for lunch and start testimony at 1:30 p.m."

Everyone rose and watched the judge exit out the rear door. Reporters mobbed Wilkerson as he was leaving the courtroom. Paula and I left by the rear door and went down the back stairway as usual, slipping away without encountering any reporters. We walked through the underground parking lot and up a stairway to the street in front of the Old Red Courthouse.

The throng of reporters was across the street so we dashed across Kennedy Square and into the West End. Paula felt like Italian food so we went into the Spaghetti Warehouse. Paula ordered a pasta salad and I got a meatball sandwich. While we were waiting for our orders, we discussed strategy.

"We're going to have to decide pretty quickly which scenario to use to create reasonable doubt," Paula said.

"You've already decided, haven't you?"

Paula frowned. "What makes you say that?"

"Well, when you were talking to the reporters this morning it seemed like you were leaning toward blaming the murders on Manning and his gang."

"That would be my preference but it's probably not an option."

"Why not?"

"It would be too dangerous considering the threats on your life. I don't want Mr. Z coming after you again."

"We can't worry about that. We have to do what's best for our client. Anyway, I think Mr. Z is long gone by now."

Paula sighed. "Well, we're a little short on proof anyway. To a jury this whole Iran-Contra connection might seem a bit farfetched. They could easily see it as just an act of desperation."

"Well, Margie's account of the whole affair seems pretty credible."

"But it's all hearsay," Paula said. "She doesn't have any direct knowledge of the arms dealing and how the whole operation worked. . . . Even if we could overcome the hearsay objection, she may not be willing to testify."

"Why wouldn't she?"

"Because she wouldn't want to blemish her husband's memory. I think she'll be very reluctant to do it and if she does agree, her testimony won't come off nearly as convincing as when she was talking to you."

"Hmm. Well, hopefully Paul will come through with the missing link."

"I hope so. We need a break here pretty soon or Jimmy is going to get convicted."

When we got back to the courthouse, Wilkerson began parading witnesses through the courtroom. He started with the detective who handled the crime scene, then the medical examiner, a crime scene investigator, and finally a neighbor who talked to Don and Amanda just before they retired to the condo for the evening. At 5:00 p.m. the judge adjourned the trial until the next morning at 10:00 a.m.

When we got back to the office, Jodie was back from West Texas where she had been investigating Margie Baker. She said she had a lot of interesting information to give us. We all went into the conference room and she began to tell us what she had learned.

"Well, let me tell you it's a long drive to Abilene. I got into the worst thunderstorm I've ever driven in."

I laughed. "Yes, I've made that trip many times. I'm sorry the weather was bad, but that's not unusual out there."

"Well, at least it was worth the trip. Buffalo Ridge is a beautiful place."

"Where is it exactly?" I asked.

"About ten miles northeast of Abilene. It takes about fifteen minutes to get from the road to the main house."

"I bet the house is nice."

"Oh, my God. It's gotta be five thousand square feet and there's a detached servant's quarters."

"That figures."

"It appears to be primarily a cattle ranch, but there are a lot of horses too. I saw twenty ranch hands easy. There are three big barns, an Olympic size swimming pool, and lighted tennis courts. Everything is first class."

"So, how were you received?"

"Fine. I told them you wanted me to talk to all the hands to see if any of them knew anything that might help us defend Jimmy. They thought I was wasting my time, but pretty much gave me the run of the ranch anyway. A cowboy named Roy Olsen drove me around in his pickup truck and introduced me to everyone."

"Did you talk to Earl?"

"Yes, but he's a very quiet man. I think he was suspicious of my intentions. He didn't tell me much, but he did say that Don Baker had been unfaithful to Margie from day one and that he treated her like she was one of his cattle. I think he really loves Margie to hear him talk. They've been together going on three years now."

"Where were they on Black Monday?" Paul asked.

"They were a little vague on that point. Apparently,

they were at some kind of cutting horse competition in Gainesville. They were staying at a friend's ranch just south of the city. The competition began on Thursday and ended at 5:00 p.m. on Saturday. I called the sponsors of the competition and they told me that Earl competed on Friday morning at 9:30 a.m. and on Saturday at 11:00 a.m. but that other than those times they would have no way of knowing their whereabouts."

"Were you able to find out whose ranch they were staying at?"

"No, I couldn't get that information out of them without pushing harder than I thought was wise."

"So, Margie and Earl could have easily made it to Dallas in time to kill Don and Margie."

"Sure, it's less than two hours from the ranch to Don's condo."

"Did anyone know anything about Continental Exporters or United Recycling?" I asked.

"Yes, Roy Olsen, the man who drove me around, used to work for United Recycling. He said he did security for a while and handled some shipping and receiving."

"Did he see any recycling done?"

"No, it was apparently contracted out."

"Contracted out?"

"Yes, he was told that the Dallas office was just an administrative office. The actual recycling was done elsewhere."

"Someone else mentioned that," I said. "They had to tell their employees something so they wouldn't wonder what was really going on. Are there any company records around?"

"No, he said when the company moved out of their space he was directed to shred everything."

"That sounds familiar," I said. "Ollie North did the same thing when the heat from Congress got too intense."

"So, do we have enough to pin the murder on our threesome yet?" Paula asked.

"We still need to somehow put Skip Henderson at the scene of the crime," I said. "We do that and we've got them nailed."

"Did the crime scene investigators find any unidentified fingerprints?" Jodie asked.

"Yes, I think there were several, if I remember the forensic report correctly," Paula said.

"We need to get access to them and compare each to Skip Henderson's," I said.

"How do we get Skip Henderson's fingerprints?"

"That will be Jodie's job."

"My job?" Jodie asked.

"Yes, if Skip Henderson is the killer, you can bet he'll be at the trial tomorrow," I said. "If he is, you can pretend to be a fan and buy him a coke or something. Then just leave the can somewhere where we can retrieve it later. Then we'll have his fingerprint."

"Oh, cool. That will be fun." Jodie exclaimed.

"While you're talking to him, see what else you can find out."

"Of course. No problem."

"Keep in mind he may be a killer. Be careful and don't leave the courthouse."

"Right."

When I got home that night I pulled out some old Dallas Cowboy programs and found a picture of Skip Henderson. He had been a tackle for the Minnesota Vikings and he looked as tough as titanium. I could see where he could be a very valuable errand boy for a Congressman. I just hoped he liked Jodie. If he did, we might just nail him.

47

The Note

Jodie and I got to the courthouse early to take a look at the visitor's log and see if Skip Henderson had been attending the trial. The log showed that he had signed in but didn't get a seat. Since there weren't enough seats to accommodate everyone who wanted to watch the trial, the bailiff had drawn names out of a hat. We asked the bailiff if he drew new names each day and he said he did. I gave Jodie Skip's picture and told her to hang around and hopefully she'd see him.

When I went back into the courtroom, Stan was unpacking his briefcase and the court reporter was organizing the exhibits from the previous day. I went into the jury room, got two cups of coffee and brought them to the counsel table. I handed one to Stan and said, "I don't know about you, but I need a little caffeine boost."

"Didn't sleep well?" Stan asked.

"Are you kidding? Sleep?"

"Well, it will all be over soon."

"One way or another," I replied

"Come on. It always looks bad when the prosecution is putting on its case. The situation will change quickly when you start pointing out other suspects with better motives to kill Don Baker."

As we were talking Wilkerson walked in and set his briefcase next to the prosecution table. He came over to us and said, "Well, you find your client yet?"

"No, he's still MIA," Stan said.

Wilkerson said, "If he's smart he'll stay away. If he comes back, he'll die."

I raised my eyebrows and frowned. Wilkerson smiled and went back to the prosecution table. The bailiff stood up and said, "All rise."

The back door of the courtroom opened and Judge Wingate waddled in and took his seat. After sorting through some files, he told Wilkerson to proceed. Wilkerson stood up and was about to say something when the judge's administrative assistant walked in and handed Judge Wingate a note. He opened the note quickly, read it, and shook his head. His face was grim as he looked up at us.

"Ladies and gentlemen, I've just been given some rather startling news that will affect the continuation of this trial. Due to the sensitive nature of this information, I'll need to meet with counsel in chambers before I explain to all of you what has happened. This court will be in recess for thirty minutes," he said and stood up.

Stan looked at me and I shrugged. I didn't know what could have happened but it had obviously shaken up the judge. I followed Stan into the judge's chambers. Wilkerson and his assistant joined us.

The judge said, "I'm sorry to have to tell you this, Miss

Waters, but the Mississippi state police have found Jimmy Bennett.

"Is he in custody?" I asked.

"Well, not exactly. They found him unconscious in a motel room in Jackson. By the time they got him to a hospital, he was dead. The coroner has made a preliminary determination that the cause of death was a lethal combination of cocaine and alcohol."

"Oh, my God!" Paula exclaimed.

"Has anyone told Betty," I asked.

"No," the judge said. "You're the first to find out about this. Is Mrs. Bennett in the courtroom?"

"Yes," I said. "I believe I saw her."

The judge looked over at the bailiff and said, "You better go get her and bring her in here. She should hear this from us rather than the media."

A few moments later the bailiff bought Betty in and the Judge gave her the bad news. She was visibly shaken and nearly collapsed. Stan grabbed her and helped her sit down. The judge's assistant brought her some water. Tears were flooding from her eyes. We all watched her, not knowing what to say. After a few minutes, she wiped away the tears with her sleeve, got up, and rushed out of the room."

"So, now what happens?" I asked.

The judge scratched his head and said, "Well, without a defendant we don't have much reason to continue the trial. I'll just recess the trial for now, but I will entertain motions from either side tomorrow morning at 9:30 a.m."

"Thank you, Your Honor," Paula said.

Wilkerson turned and left the room with a look of relief on his face. Stan and I looked at each other in disbelief. When we made it back into the courtroom John Bennett and Margie Baker were consoling Betty. I went over to them.

"I'm so sorry, Betty. This is such terrible news. I thought for sure we'd get a favorable verdict and you two could get on with your lives."

"Thank you," Betty said. "I've feared this day for a long time. When someone you love is on drugs, you know this can happen at any time."

"We'll take her home," Margie said. "Don't worry about her."

"When I get more details on what happened in Mississippi, I'll give you a call," I said.

"Thank you," John said. "We really appreciate what you tried to do. I just wish Jimmy had been a stronger person. But who are we to question the Lord's will."

The judge entered the courtroom and advised the jury and the spectators of Jimmy's death. Then he announced a recess until the following morning and returned to his chambers. Margie and John left the courtroom amidst a mob of reporters screaming questions at them. John led the way pushing them aside and saying, "We have no comment. Please just let us through."

I turned around and saw Stan talking to Wilkerson. I walked over to them. Stan was telling him about Skip Henderson and our theory that he was hired to kill Don Baker. Wilkerson was looking at him like he was a lunatic.

"So, I know you think this wraps up the Don Baker

case, but I'm convinced Jimmy was innocent."

"Well, I seriously doubt Congressman Manning and Speaker Potts had anything to do with Don Baker's murder and I don't intend to waste the taxpayer's money on a wild goose chase."

"Suit yourself. I just wanted to point out what we'd discovered in case you thought it warranted further investigation."

"I don't," Wilkerson said sharply. He turned and when he saw me he said, "Miss Waters. Sorry about your client."

I smiled and replied, "Thanks."

Looking at Stan, I said, "So, what was that all about?"

"Well, we have a duty to report any new information about this case to opposing counsel. Since the trial was prematurely terminated, I figured I better tell Wilkerson what we had found out about the Congressman and Speaker Potts in case he wanted to act on it. I didn't figure he would, but at least I've done my civic duty."

I laughed. "He looked like he thought you were nuts."

Stan shrugged and said, "I suppose it does sound a bit bizarre."

"So, have you talked to Jodie? Did she ever hook up with Skip Henderson?"

"I don't know. I'll go see if I can find her."

I went to the door and peeked outside. There were several reporters still lurking about so I didn't want to venture out in the hall needlessly. I saw Jodie talking to a man I figured to be Skip Henderson. He was a white male, tall, muscular and wore his hair in a flat top. I waited until she saw me and then went back to see Stan. A few moments later Jodie walked in the courtroom and joined us.

"He's a nice guy. He invited me to dinner."

"That figures," Stan said smiling.

"Did you learn anything so far?" I asked.

"Well, he told me all about his job working for the Congressman."

"Did he say why he was attending the trial?"

"Yes, the Congressman asked him to monitor the case since Don had been a good friend. He said the Congressman wanted to make sure Don's killer was convicted."

"Yeah, I bet," Stan said. "Did you find out what he was doing Sunday night?"

"No, I had to take it slow. I'll find that out tonight. I didn't want him to think I was interrogating him."

"That's all right Jodie," I said. "I'd milk the job for a dinner with an NFL football player too, if I were in your shoes."

Jodie blushed, "Well, he is kind of cute. How far should I go to get this information?"

"Dinner is all," Stan said. "You don't have to sleep with him."

I laughed and added, "Unless you want to."

You'd think I'd be relieved that I was spared having to try a murder case that I had little hope of winning, but instead I felt angry. This was my first death penalty trial where I was first chair and fate had snatched it away from me. I felt bad for Jimmy Bennett and ever more so for Betty, but I must confess I was feeling sorry for myself as well. I knew Jimmy had an addiction, but it never crossed my mind that it might be life threatening. The only positive note was that I could now put all this mess out of my mind and concentrate on my wedding.

48

RX7

The next morning Detective Besch called to offer his condolences over Jimmy's death and ask me about my conversation with Wilkerson. Apparently Wilkerson had told his assistant about it and the story spread from there.

"You think Huntington was working with Congressman Manning and Speaker Potts?" Detective Besch asked.

"Yes, you can confirm that with Margie Baker. We also found a ranch hand at Buffalo Ridge who worked for United Recycling."

I filled Besch in on everything else we'd learned. I told him Jodie was due in shortly and we'd hopefully find out whether or not Skip Henderson could be the killer. He said he was on his way over. He wanted to hear what Jodie had to say and talk to us some more about Congressman Manning, Speaker Potts, and Captain Chamberlain.

Paula and I were already talking to her when Besch walked into the break room. Jodie poured him a cup of coffee and he sat down to hear her story.

"Skips a cool guy. We had a great time last night?"

"Where did you go?" Paula asked.

"To Anthony's."

"Oh, I love that place," Paula said.

"So, what did you find out?" Besch asked.

"I've got bad news, I'm afraid," Jodie replied.

"No. Don't tell me that," I said.

"Yes, Skip's got an alibi."

"Come on. You're not saying that just because you like the guy, are you?" I asked.

"No. He spent that Sunday evening at Texas Stadium watching the Cowboy game. He's got three witnesses."

"Damn it," I said. "Now we're back to square one?"

"Not necessarily," Paula mumbled.

We all looked at her. "What did you say?" I asked.

"Well, think about it. Who benefits if both Don and Jimmy are dead?"

"You think Jimmy was murdered?" Besch asked.

"I don't know but, let's assume he was."

I thought for a moment and said, "Margie would get control of the Baker fortune, but Don gave her everything she wanted. I can't see why she'd want him dead."

"I know it doesn't make sense with what we know, but let's think about this some more. Do you remember when we went back to the courtroom yesterday?"

"Sure."

"Margie was alone. Earl was nowhere to be seen."

"He could have been in the bathroom," Besch said.

"No, I didn't see him at all yesterday. What if he was in Mississippi? What if he tracked Jimmy down, killed him, and made it look like a drug overdose?"

"It's possible, I guess, but we have no proof," I said.

"You know I didn't connect these two dots until now,

but Earl drives a red Mazda RX7," Paula said.

"So?"

"Remember the pool maintenance man who was hanging around all day at the condo pool but didn't actually work for the pool service?"

"Yeah," I replied

"Well, he was seen driving a red Mazda RX7 the day of Don's murder. Earl matches the description of the pool contractor," Paula said.

"Oh, my God, you're right," I said. "We need to get a picture of Earl and show it to the manager and your other witnesses at Don's condo."

"I'll do that," Jodie said.

I looked at Jodie and replied, "Great. Where can we get a picture of Earl?"

"Betty probably has one. I'll call her and see."

"Don't tell her why you need it," I said. "We need to be sure about this before we start pointing fingers."

"We should have someone show Earl's picture around the motel where they found Jimmy's body."

"I can arrange that," Besch said. "I'll also see if anyone saw Earl's RX 7 in Mississippi or if he used a credit card along the way."

"I think I'm going to take a trip out to the ranch and talk to some of the hands while Earl and Margie are busy with Jimmy's funeral," I said.

"I'll tag along, if you don't mind," Besch said.

"Sure," I replied. "It's always easier to get people to talk when you have a badge to flash in their face."

"It will be safer, too," Paula noted. "If Earl is the killer, he wouldn't hesitate to kill again to protect him and Margie. I'll hang around the office and look back through my notes to see if there is anything else that links Earl to the murders."

Detective Besch went back to his office to get some of his staff working on the case. He told me he'd be back at noon and we could head out to Abilene. Jodie left to call Betty and see if she had a picture of Earl and Paula went back to her office. As I was sitting at my desk it occurred to me a man like Don Baker would have a lot of insurance. I wondered how much he had and who were the beneficiaries. That information would no doubt tell us a lot.

49

Insurance

After Stan and Detective Besch left, I went back over my notes and decided it would be useful to talk to Betty Bennett and Margie Baker to see how the funeral arrangements were going and also to pry into Don Baker's finances a little. Betty had confirmed to Jodie that she had a picture of Earl, so I'd use that as an excuse to go over there. Everyone was gathering at Betty's place in preparation of the wake and funeral so I was hopeful I'd get a chance to talk to other friends and family about Don and Jimmy. Jodie wanted to come to but I had to say no since someone had to hold the fort down.

When I got there, the driveway was lined with cars and pickups of every make and model. There was even a limousine. I wondered if Congressman Manning or Speaker Potts had stopped by. As I approached the front door it opened and Betty Bennett and a distinguished looking man in his late fifties stepped out. Betty saw me and introduced me to Winston Rutlege, M.D.

"This is the doctor I told you Jimmy was seeing about his addiction."

"Oh, yes. I'm so glad I bumped into you. I need to talk to you here in a minute. It's very important."

"Well, I usually can't talk about my patients—"

"Since Jimmy is dead, I'm sure it would be okay, wouldn't it Betty?"

"Yes, I guess. If the doctor can help you in any way, he should."

I smiled at Dr. Rutlege and said, "Good, then. Let me speak to Betty a minute and then I'll come find you."

He nodded and went back inside. I turned to Betty and said, "I'm sorry to intrude at a time like this, but there's been some new developments I need to talk to you and some of your guests about."

"Well, it's not a good time. We're expecting the body back anytime. The wake is tonight."

I took Betty down the front walkway a few yards so nobody could overhear us.

"I know, but Stan and I have been talking and we think Jimmy may have been murdered."

"Murdered?"

"Yes, his drug overdose was a little too convenient. That's what I want to talk to Dr. Rutledge about."

Betty looked genuinely shaken. "Okay, but—"

"Can we go somewhere private?"

"Sure. We can go upstairs to my study."

We went inside through the entryway and up a winding staircase. People were milling around, talking, drinking, and grazing off dozens of trays of meats, cheeses, fruits and vegetables lined up on the dining room table. I followed Betty into her study. She pointed to a finely decorated chair in front of her small desk. I took a seat and she sat down at the desk.

"Okay, you think Jimmy was murdered? But why?"

"How is your relationship with your mother?"

Betty turned a little pale. "My mother? What do you mean?"

"We have to look at everyone who stood to gain by Don and Jimmy's death. We know you didn't kill Jimmy so that leaves your Mother."

"My mother didn't like Jimmy, but so what. A lot of mothers don't like their sons-in-law. My mother isn't capable of killing anyone."

"I know, but what about Earl?"

"Earl. Well, he is an ex-Marine," Betty said thoughtfully, "but why would he want to kill Daddy or Jimmy? They had the ranch and mom had an allowance that would fund a small country."

"What about Metroplex? Wasn't your Dad in a cash crunch? Is there a chance that the money was going to be cut off?"

"No, the construction company was doing well. Mom was paid from Baker Construction."

"Is there a loan on the ranch?"

Betty's eyes widened. "Yes, a very large one—about two and a half million."

"What would have happened if that loan were called?"

"But Daddy wouldn't call his own loan."

"What if the OTS demanded it?"

"Oh, my God! Do you think that happened?"

"I don't know. How can we find out?"

"Jerry Hartfield is downstairs. He'd know."

"Okay, let me talk to Dr. Rutledge first, then I'll talk to Hartfield."

Betty went downstairs and brought up Dr. Rutledge. I thanked him again and then got right to the point.

"Dr. Rutledge, I guess you heard Jimmy Bennett supposedly died from a lethal combination of drugs and alcohol."

"Yes, that's what I heard."

"Does that surprise you?"

"Nothing surprises me when it comes to cocaine. It affects people differently. People die from cocaine every day."

"How long have you been treating Jimmy?"

"About five years now."

"So, you'd gotten to know him pretty well, right?"

"Yes."

"Knowing Jimmy the way you do, would you have expected him to die the way he did?"

He shrugged. "Probably not. Jimmy had been using drugs for a long time and has built up a pretty high tolerance for them. It would take a lot to kill him. I can't remember his life ever being in danger in the past."

"So, it's possible that someone drugged him and made it look like he'd overdosed himself."

"That wouldn't be hard to do."

"Is there any way you could find out whether that happened or not?"

"An autopsy might provide evidence of it, but it would

be hard to prove it conclusively."

"I see. Well, you've been a big help. Sorry I had to bother you at a time like this."

"It's all right. I'm glad I could help."

Dr. Ruthledge left and Betty ushered in Jerry Hartfield. As I recalled, Don and he didn't get along too well, so I felt certain he would level with us about the ranch. Betty brought him in and he sat in a chair next to me.

"Sorry, to bother you at a time like this, Mr. Hartfield, but we have a question about Metroplex that needs answering."

"It's okay. How can I help you?"

"Betty tells me Metroplex Savings and Loan has the mortgagee on Don's ranch."

"No. Not Metroplex. Don borrowed $2.7 million to purchase it several years ago, but it would be improper for him to borrow the money from Metroplex. He got the mortgage from Advantage Savings & Loan. You know, the one that Simon Trueblood owns."

Simon Trueblood's name sounded familiar but I couldn't place who he was. I knew it was a common practice of bankers to strike up relationships with other bankers so that the insiders of one bank could borrow from the others and thus avoid problems with regulators.

"So, Metroplex had some loans out to Trueblood?"

"Oh, yes, several."

"And were there any problems with those loans?"

Jerry nodded. "Oh, yes. They all were in default. It was a big problem for Don. The regulators finally made him call one of them."

"And how did Trueblood react to that?"

"He threatened to call the note on the ranch."

"Did Trueblood require Don to have a mortgage insurance policy on the ranch in case he died?"

"Yes, that's standard practice."

"Did the policy pay when Don died?"

"Not yet. The insurance company was waiting on the outcome of Jimmy's trial. If Jimmy was found guilty they were prepared to pay off the mortgage.

I looked at Betty who I could tell instantly understood the situation. If Margie knew the ranch note was about to be called, she would have been devastated. Her wonderful little life would have been ruined, but if Don were to die the ranch would be saved. I thanked Mr. Hartfield and told him he could rejoin the guests downstairs.

After Hartfield had left, I said, "So, do you think your mother could have conspired with Earl to kill your father?"

The look on Betty's face told me the answer. She excused herself and I went downstairs to mingle awhile and see if Margie and Earl were there. I saw them in the corner with John Bennett. I approached.

"Hello, Mrs. Bennett, Earl."

"Miss Waters, it is so nice of you to come," Margie said.

"Well, it's the least I could. This has all been such a shock."

Margie nodded, "Indeed. Pour Betty losing a father and then a husband in such a short time. It's much worse for her than for me. It was no secret that the love between Don and I was over years ago."

"Yes, but I'm sure it must be difficult for you too. You must have had some feelings for Don. After all, you were together a long time."

She shrugged. "Yes, I suppose so. Luckily I have Earl to comfort me now."

I looked at Earl. "Yes, Earl. I didn't see you at the trial yesterday."

"Oh, yeah. . . . Well, there was an emergency back at the ranch I had to deal with . . . you know how that goes."

"Sure," I said. "You've got to mind your business."

Earl nodded and replied, "That's right or you'll find yourself in bankruptcy."

"So, what are you going to do with Metroplex Savings and Loan now? Are you going to be able to save it?"

"I don't know. We haven't met with the lawyers and the board of directors yet. But we know it will take a lot of money to keep it afloat."

"Is the ranch okay? You won't lose it, will you?"

"No, no. It's . . . it's insured."

Her voice trailed off and she turned a little pale.

"Good. That would be horrible if you lost the ranch."

Margie stiffened up and replied." Yes, it would have been, but luckily Don was a good businessman and thought ahead."

"You're lucky to have married such a smart man," I said.

Earl frowned. "If he was so smart, why did he let the

bank become insolvent."

Margie elbowed Earl. He glared at her and said, "What? It's true. Your ex was a greedy son of a bitch and that was his downfall."

Margie turned red this time and glared back at Earl. "Well, you've lived pretty well off his money!"

Earl took a deep breath. "Yeah, you're right, I have. But what I meant was he had all the money a man could ever use, yet he wasn't satisfied. He had to have more and it cost him everything."

"That's what greed will do to a man," I said looking directly at Margie, "or a woman."

Margie gave me a look that made it clear it was time to go home. I'd got the answers I'd come for and if I stayed any longer I was liable to talk too much and perhaps cause Margie and Earl to realize I was on to them. As I was leaving, Betty announced that Jimmy's body was at the funeral home and would be available for viewing at 7:00 p.m. that evening. I'd skip the viewing. I didn't like seeing dead bodies. I preferred remembering people as they were when they were breathing. Besides, I was hoping to get a call from Stan. I couldn't wait to tell him what I'd learned and find out if he and Detective Besch had come up with anything new at Buffalo Ridge.

50

Back to the Ranch

On the long drive to Abilene Detective Besch and I had lots of time to talk and discuss the cases we were working on. I was a little surprised that Detective Besch wanted to go to Abilene with me since he hadn't been assigned to the Jimmy Bennett case. I knew he said the Huntington case and Bennett case were now related, but Wilkerson made it pretty clear he didn't want anything to do with dirty politicians and illegal arms dealing.

"Isn't Wilkerson going to be pissed at you for getting involved in this case?"

"He'll get over it. Anyway, he's not my boss. I've got the discretion to take my investigation wherever it legitimately should go. Fortunately, you found out Huntington and Baker were working together. That interests me and raises a lot of questions."

"Like what?"

"Like who really killed Don Baker and now, possibly, Jimmy Bennett? Was it the same people who kidnapped Huntington and tried to kill you?"

"Listen, I didn't get a chance to tell you this and, I was told not to tell you, but you need to know."

Besch looked over at me intently. "What wasn't I supposed to know?"

"My old contact at the CIA I told you about. He contacted me and said Huntington and his partner were alive. He said they were going into hiding because the CIA had disavowed knowledge of them and their activities. He said that I should quit looking for them."

"That makes some sense actually. The FBI wants to prosecute anyone involved in illegal arms dealing with Iran. If the CIA disavowed knowledge of them, they'd just look like a bunch of greedy gunrunners."

"And if they had information that might link the illegal arms dealing to other politicians and prominent businessmen, their lives wouldn't be worth a bucket of spit."

Besch frowned. "So, you're telling me you want me to quit looking for Huntington?"

"If he's alive then why should you keep looking for him"

"But do you trust this contact at the CIA?"

"I don't have any concrete reason to trust him, but my gut tells me he's telling me the truth."

The problem is the FBI won't quit looking for them even if I did."

"Yeah, but for some reason they're worried about you and I looking for them more than the FBI."

"Why would that be?" Detective Besch asked. "Unless . . . They knew the FBI really wasn't looking for them."

"Exactly, nobody in Washington really wants the truth to come out. They just want the entire mess to go away."

It was nearly 4:00 p.m. when we arrived at the ranch. We asked the first person we talked to if Roy Olsen was around. He said he was and pointed to a small house down the road. We drove down and parked behind a big Ford F250. We knocked at the door and Roy answered. We introduced ourselves and Roy invited us in.

"It was a shame about Jimmy. I liked him a lot. He was kind of a hot head, but Don loved him like he was his own son."

"I think Jodie talked to you a few days ago," I said.

"Yes, Jodie. She's a nice girl. Very intense though, all business."

"Yes, Jodie is very focused. It's hard to distract her."

"I just wanted to buy her some dinner before she drove back to Dallas, but she wouldn't hear of it."

I laughed. "She's had a tough breakup a year or so ago. I think she's sworn off men and is concentrating on her career. She wants to be a lawyer."

"Wants to be. I thought she was."

"Anyway, Detective Besch and I had a few more questions that we hoped you might help us with."

"Sure, fire away."

"How close are you to Earl Modest?"

He shrugged. "I've worked for Earl now for a couple years. He's okay. We don't socialize or anything. Margie keeps him pretty busy."

"How about Margie? Do you like her?"

Roy shrugged again. "Well, to be honest. She's a difficult woman to work for, if you know what I mean."

"Not exactly. Elaborate, would you?" I asked.

"Well, she's pushy, demanding, self-centered, and half drunk most of the time."

"I see."

"But worst of all she's got Earl so pussy whipped that he'd do anything she asked."

"Anything?"

He nodded. "Trust me. Anything."

Besch said, "Would it surprise you if Margie and Earl were involved in Don's death?"

Roy looked at Besch without expression. He thought for a moment and said, "No. That makes more sense than Jimmy's involvement."

"That's why we're here," Besch said. "To find out if perhaps Margie and Earl were responsible for Don's death. We also are looking into the possibility that they had something to do with Jimmy's death."

"You think Jimmy was murdered?"

"We don't know. But it is a possibility. Was Earl here yesterday?"

"No. He hasn't been here all week. I thought he was in Dallas at Jimmy's trial."

"Has he called here this week at all?"

"No," Roy said. "We didn't hear from them until yesterday afternoon. They called to tell us about Jimmy's overdose and to say they'd be delayed awhile until the funeral was over."

"You told Jodie you used to work for United Recycling, right?"

"Un huh. I worked for them about thirteen months until they shut down last December."

"Did Jimmy know anything about United Recycling?"

"He knew it existed. I don't think he knew all that was going on or exactly how it worked. Don kept everything pretty close to the vest."

"Do you know anything about the fight Don had with Jimmy just before the murder?"

"Just what Luther told me?"

"Luther?"

"Luther Palmer. He ran the operation here for Continental Exporters. Don called him right after the fight. He told him Jimmy was not cooperating and it didn't look like he'd be able to raise the two million to save Metroplex. Bottom line—the party was over and it was time to clean up the house."

This confirmed my suspicions that Luther Palmer wasn't in Beijing but was actually commuting between Tehran and Abilene running the arms sales to Iran. Huntington had used the threat of his imminent death to motivate me to get his money out of the clutches of the IRS. Huntington had fed me a pack of lies to get me to do what he wanted.

"Earl was involved in all this too?" I asked.

"No," Roy replied. "Don just let them use one of the barns as a warehouse. They had a warehouse in Washington, D.C. too."

"In DC?"

"Right."

Roy told me about the DC warehouse and how he had helped locate the facility and hire crews to handle the guns and military hardware that went through there.

So, what did Don want Palmer to do?"

"Shut down the operation and clear out the barn. If the feds came to Buffalo Ridge, he wanted the barn full of straw and horses with no evidence of weapons ever having been stored there."

"So, the weapons are all gone?" I asked.

"Yes. You'd never know they'd ever been there."

On the way back to Dallas, Besch and I discussed what we'd learned and tried to put all the pieces of this very complex puzzle together. It appeared the big fight between Jimmy and Don wasn't just about Betty but also over illegal arms trading. With Metroplex Savings & Loan near collapse and Congress coming down hard on anyone involved in selling arms to Iran, Jimmy must have got spooked and tried to distance himself from his father-in-law. He had mentioned the feds had been snooping around but I had thought he meant the bank examiners. He must have been questioned by the FBI about Continental Exporters or United Recycling. Now it all made sense.

51

The Final Pieces

Stan called me when he and Besch stopped to get gas on the way back to Dallas. He said they'd learned a lot and were anxious to tell me about it. I told them I had lots to share too. We agreed to meet for coffee at Denny's at Park Central that evening at 8:30 p.m. I looked at my watch and saw it was almost five o'clock. There would be plenty of time to get home, change and have dinner with Bart before the meeting.

When I got to Denny's Stan and Detective Besch were just being seated. They both looked tired and disheveled from their ten-hour excursion to the ranch. I was glad I hadn't gone with them. They told me about their meeting with Roy Olsen and the arms stash kept at the ranch. I told them about the loan on the ranch being called and the mortgage cancellation insurance that paid off the loan on the ranch upon Don Baker's death.

"Just before you got here, Paula," Detective Besch explained, "I called my office and they reported that the manager of the motel where Jimmy's body was found remembers seeing Earl at the hotel. Apparently, someone's

TV wasn't working and the manager went to check it out and saw Earl loitering in the hallway. The manager asked him if he could help him and Earl said no and then made a hasty exit."

"Is that enough to arrest him," I asked.

Besch shrugged. "Along with everything else we have, I would think so. I'll call the DA's office here in a minute and set up a meeting to review the evidence with them. Maybe we can get a search warrant for the ranch. In the meantime, I've got someone going out to Betty's place to keep an eye on Earl and Margie in case they decide to run."

"What about Congressman Manning and Speaker Potts?" I asked.

"I'm going to leave that to the FBI. I'll share with them everything you've told me and then leave it up to them whether they want to do any further investigation of Manning, Potts, and Chamberlain. I suspect they'll do nothing."

"So, we just forget about Huntington and Palmer?" Stan asked.

"You said they left of their own free will, right?" Besch said. "If that's the case, there's no kidnaping and no reason to keep the file open. I know it seems a little sloppy, but the powers that be won't let me pursue the investigation any further under the circumstances."

"Okay, then," Stan said. "I guess we've done all we can. It's been a pleasure working with you Detective."

"Likewise. Maybe we'll get to do this again sometime."

"I hope so," Stan said.

We all got up and Paula extended her hand, "Thank you, Detective. Will we see you tomorrow at Jimmy's funeral?"

"Oh, yes," Detective Besch said. "I suspect you will."

52

The Funeral

Rebekah wanted to go to Jimmy's funeral so we arranged for the kids to spend the day with their grandparents. It was a cold, windy day and thick cumulus clouds were rolling in from the west. Just as we arrived at St. Paul the Apostle Catholic Church the skies let loose. I fumbled with my umbrella and finally got it opened. I ran around the car and Rebekah and I dashed inside the church.

The church was filled with Jimmy's friends and family. We found a seat near the back of the church and waited. I noticed Margie and Earl seated up at the front with the rest of the family. Betty, her children, and John were standing around the casket. Precisely at 9:00 a.m. the funeral mass began.

The mass lasted over an hour. The priest as well as many of his family and friends talked about Jimmy's life, how much they loved Jimmy and would miss him. The ceremony was so moving that even Margie was in tears. When she and Earl got up to leave, they were met with a stone-faced detective, Bingo Besch.

"Margie Baker and Earl Modest, you are under arrest

for the murders of Jimmy Bennett, Don Baker, and Amanda Black."

Margie let out a shriek of despair and then mumbled a few obscenities. Besch yanked her around and cuffed her. When a second officer tried to handcuff Earl, he pulled out a big knife and sliced the officer's wrist. Blood spurted out of the wound and several women screamed. Earl took off running toward the back of the church, tossing aside several bystanders in his path. Another officer went after him. I flew out a side door hoping to get a good view of the action. As I ran toward the front of the church, Earl suddenly appeared and charged straight at me. In my mind's eye, I saw the big blade slice through my stomach and could almost feel the unbearable pain. I dove to the right to avoid a collision but Earl tripped over my foot and went sprawling head over heels. After righting himself, he came at me with his knife.

A helpless feeling shot through me. Then I remembered the gun around my ankle. I reached down and pulled it out. He lunged at me with the knife narrowly missing my abdomen. When he came at me again, I aimed the gun and fired. He grabbed his side where the bullet had hit him and fell to the ground still wielding the knife. The other officer yelled for him to drop it. He finally obeyed and the officer cuffed him.

Paula, who had followed me out the side door, rushed over to me. "Are you okay? You could have been killed."

"I'm fine," I said trembling. "I didn't expect him to come back this way."

Sirens could be heard in the distance. I thought of the poor officer who'd had his wrist sliced open. We rushed inside where Rebekah was tending to the injured officer. Detective Besch was holding a bandage over the wound struggling to stop the bleeding. Rebekah had taken her scarf and tied it tightly around the officer's upper arm. She was telling Besch to raise the arm up to slow the blood flow. A few minutes later the paramedics arrived and took over. They put the injured officer on a gurney and rolled him out to the waiting ambulance.

"I forgot your wife was a nurse," Besch said.

I looked at Rebekah and smiled, "Yes, it comes in handy sometimes, particularly with kids."

"I bet."

"Thank you, Rebekah," Besch said.

She shrugged. "It was nothing. All in a day's work. I hope he'll be all right."

"I'm sure he will, thanks to you."

After the paramedics and police had left, the funeral continued. We followed the limousine to the grave site to pay our last respects. As the ceremony was coming to an end, I felt great satisfaction that we had found Jimmy's killer and cleared his name. Now, at least, his family would be able to honor and cherish his memory.

53

A Cruel Twist of Fate

After Jimmy's death, I decided not to take on any more serious cases until after the wedding. June 24 came quickly. Fortunately, Monique proved to be an excellent wedding planner and had everything arranged for the perfect affair. Bart and I spent a lot of time together those last few months before the wedding and became best friends as well as lovers. We decided to spend our honeymoon in Tahiti as we heard it hadn't become a tourist trap like most of the exotic places in the world.

On Friday night, we had the rehearsal dinner at Baby Doe's as we had planned. It started out to be a small affair with just family, the wedding party, and a few friends, but as time went on more and more people somehow made the invitation list. By the last count there were 42 attendees sitting down for various salads, cheeses, cheese soup, filet mignon, shrimp, numerous vegetables, and strawberry cheesecake for dessert.

There were many toasts, a few speeches, and lots of laughter as the evening progressed. By 10:00 p.m. many of us had made more trips to the open bar than we cared to count. I was feeling a little light headed and decided to go the ladies' room and throw some water on my face. As I approached the restrooms, I saw Stan go into the men's room. I know it was a stupid thing to do on the eve of my wedding, but I suddenly got the urge to tease Stan one last time.

I looked around and spotted a small storage room. I opened the door and saw there was just enough room for two people to go inside and close the door. When Stan emerged from the men's room, I stepped in front of him and put my hands on his shoulders. He looked a little startled, but didn't resist.

"This is your last chance," Stan.

He looked at me thoughtfully but said nothing, so I took his hand, led him into the closet, and closed the door. Before he could say anything, I placed my lips over his and pulled him close. There was no response for a moment, then his lips opened and let me in. A rush of excitement resonated through my body as I pushed my tongue deep into his mouth.

We made out for several minutes until he finally pulled away and said, "Okay, you proved your point."

"My point?" I said.

"Yes, isn't that what this is about—that you could seduce me? That I couldn't resist you?"

I didn't know what to say. Was that it? Did I want him only because I couldn't have him? No, I loved Stan. I tried to remember when I fell in love. It was in law school when we used to hang out together between classes. But he was married and wasn't interested in anything but friendship.

"Well, you win," he said and started unbuttoning my blouse. My pulse quickened and I could feel my body temperature rising as I anticipated his next move. He slid his hand around my back and started to unlatch my bra. My nipples felt like they were going to explode."

There was laughter in the hallway outside the door. Stan stopped and we both quit breathing. I knew that laugh. It was Bart and one of his friends. Stan pulled me up close and held me so tightly I thought I'd pass out. When the voices faded, he let me go and without a word opened the closet door and left.

For a moment, I stood there in the dark trying to regain my composure, then the tears began to pour from my eyes. As much as I tried, I couldn't keep from sobbing. My legs felt weak. I fell to my knees. It was over between Stan and me. I knew that now. He'd never be mine. It wasn't right. It wasn't fair. It was a cruel twist of fate to have the man you loved dangled before your eyes, just out of reach.

54

The Wedding

The next morning sharp rays of light from the rising sun awakened me. I moaned as I rolled over. My head was killing me. I couldn't remember ever having such a bad hangover. I wondered how many bourbon and sevens I'd consumed. My memory of the previous evening was a little dim, but I had a sick feeling in my stomach that something bad had happened. I thought I remembered kissing Paula, but did it really happen or had I been dreaming? I wondered.

Rebekah wasn't next to me, so I figured she must be making breakfast or reading the paper. I got up, pulled a T-shirt on and walked into the kitchen. Reggie was eating a bowl of cereal and reading the sports section. Rebekah was drinking a cup of coffee and flipping through the entertainment section.

"Good morning," I mumbled. "I need some of that coffee."

Rebekah got up and poured me a cup of coffee. "I told you that you were drinking too much."

"I know. I should have listened."

"You're lucky I was sober enough to drive us home."

"I don't remember that."

"Did you get drunk, Dad?" Reggie asked.

"No. No. Just a little light headed."

Rebekah laughed. "Yeah, right. You were so drunk you tried to piss in the broom closet."

"What?"

Reggie started laughing. He got up and ran out of the room. "Dad pissed in the broom closet?"

"I did not," I protested.

"Jodie said she saw you come out of the broom closet. Obviously, you were too drunk to find the men's room."

The sick feeling I had in my stomach suddenly got much worse. I started to gag.

"Oh, God! Don't throw up here," Rebekah screamed. "Go to the bathroom."

I walked quickly to the guests' bathroom, taking deep breaths hoping I might avoid vomiting. I stood over the sink a moment trying to remember the broom closet. Paula's face flashed through my mind. I remembered being led into the closet but it was a blur after that. What had happened in there?"

Rebekah came up behind me and put her hand on my shoulder. I jumped.

"Whoa! Steady cowboy. It's just me."

"Oh, you startled me," I said.

"I've been waiting for you to wake up."

"I'm sorry. I guess the booze knocked me out."

"I've been dying to ask you something."

"What?"

"How did you get lipstick all over your collar?"

A chill darted through me. How had I got lipstick on my

collar? I didn't remember. Did Rebekah know what had happened? She wouldn't tolerate infidelity. My mind was in such a haze I struggled to conjure up a plausible explanation.

"Ah. Well, you can blame that on the drunken bride. While we were dancing, she stumbled and fell into my arms. Didn't you see that? We both almost landed on the floor."

"Hmm. I must have missed that," Rebekah said warily.

"I bet she's got a really bad hangover too," I said. "I've never seen her drink like she did last night."

Rebekah's eyes narrowed. "Do you two do a lot of drinking at work?"

"No. Of course not. Sometimes we have a drink at lunch, but that's rare."

"Hopefully she'll recover before the ceremony at four o'clock," Rebekah said.

"I'm sure she will. A little coffee, a couple aspirin, and a hot shower do wonders for a hangover. Speaking of which, that was my plan of attack."

Rebekah nodded. "The aspirin is in the cupboard.

Marcia and Mark walked in the kitchen. Mark said, "Dad, did you really get drunk last night?"

I shook my head no and said, "I'm going to take a shower."

While taking my shower, I wondered if Rebekah knew more than she was letting on about the broom closet. I didn't think so because she was not good at controlling her anger. Had she suspected anything serious, she'd be all over me. I prayed nothing had happened with Paula.

At 3:30 we arrived at All Saints Catholic Church. People were already starting to gather. As we walked in the foyer, I noticed the groomsmen, dressed in white cutaways, escorting guests down the aisle. I saw Bart standing amongst several groomsmen and a bridesmaid. Despite feeling a little envious, I walked over to wish him well. He looked at me suspiciously.

"Well, the big day has finally arrived," I said. "How are you feeling?"

"Good, " Bart said.

"Well, you're a lucky guy. Paula's a wonderful woman."

"I know," he said.

"Anyway, I wish you the best."

He nodded and said, "Thanks."

I turned and rejoined Rebekah who was talking to Paula's father. I felt sick.

"I bet you're so proud," Rebekah said.

"That I am," he said. "She's had a tough life growing up without her mother. I'm just so glad she finally found someone."

I took a deep breath and said, "Bart's a good man. I'm sure they'll be very happy."

"I hope so," he said.

Several minutes later we were seated and the wedding began. The altar was decorated with several large bouquets of white and pink roses. A unity candle was set off to the right side and the podium was set to the left. The pianist played softly while the families were seated.

As Bart, the groomsmen, and bridesmaids took their places I prayed Paula and Bart would be happy together. They both certainly deserved it. Lurking in the back of mind, however, was a fear that what had happened between Paula and me the previous night, might spoil this day. I hoped that wouldn't be the case, but I couldn't shake the ominous feeling that had overcome me.

Finally, the music picked up and I saw Paula in the back of the church getting ready to make her entrance. She looked magnificent in her long-sleeved, silk wedding dress with the traditional long train. I felt a rush of excitement as she made her way toward me. Our eyes met for an instant as she passed by. A tingling sensation like I'd been pricked by a thousand needles made me squirm. Rebekah gave me a dirty look. I closed my eyes and took a deep breath. When I opened them Paula and Bart were at the altar.

The ceremony went quickly and before long Bart and Paula were man and wife. I didn't feel particularly happy at that moment but I was relieved. At least now it would be easier for Paula and me to work side by side without the sexual tension that had pervaded our past relationship. Perhaps now we could focus better on our work and become even more effective. At least that's what I kept telling myself.

That Sunday in church Father Bob was in great spirits. He gave a great homily and after the service he said he wanted to say a special prayer of thanks.

"This prayer is for the person who left the black sports bag at the rectory on Saturday. A note in the bag said it was a contribution for the new women's center. The bag contained $100,000 in large bills.

There was a gasp from several women at the front of the church. The crowd erupted into excited chatter.

Father Bob continued, "I'll confess, with the economy so bad, I had almost given up hope of raising this money. But the Lord works in mysterious ways that mere mortals will never understand."

Rebekah turned and gave me a hard look. I looked into her big brown eyes and smiled. She shook her head and looked back toward the altar. A moment later she smiled and took my hand. She whispered. "I knew you'd never keep the money."

I shrugged and replied, "What money?"

Epilogue

When Paula returned from her Tahitian honeymoon she seemed like a new woman. She was happy, confident, and relaxed. Married life was obviously agreeing with her. But it wasn't long before she was ready for her next big case and started complaining about the DUIs and possession cases that always seemed abundant. I told her to be patient. With the reputation she now enjoyed, it wouldn't be long before someone in a dire peril would be walking through the door looking for the best criminal defense lawyer in town.

By fall 1987 I was winding down my administration of Lottie West's estate. With the money we'd found we had nearly a quarter-million-dollars to give the SPCA after expenses of administration. But there was another $288,000 that Otto had extorted from Lottie that I wanted to collect. Unfortunately, it was evidence in Otto Barringer's murder trial set for September 22, 1987. Fortunately, just before trial, Otto got cold feet and struck a deal with the DA that guaranteed he wouldn't be executed for his crimes and would be eligible for parole in 20 years. As part of the deal he agreed to cooperate in finding the rest of the Ludinburg Art Collection.

It was late one morning that I got a call from Detective Besch. He said they were going to be taking Otto to

Huntsville in the morning and if I wanted to talk to him one more time before he left, I needed to go over to the Johnson County Detention Center that afternoon. It was a dark, stormy day so I wasn't thrilled with the idea of driving sixty miles in that weather, but I couldn't pass up this last opportunity to talk to Barringer.

When I got to Fort Worth and turned south, the rain became so intense I could hardly see the road. The radio said the rain was coming down at the rate of three inches per hour and that considerable flooding was expected. Not ten minutes later traffic came to a standstill when a small creek overflowed and submerged the bridge that usually traversed it. I looked at my watch and saw it was nearly 2:30 p.m. I knew I only had until 4:30 p.m. to talk to Otto so I had to find another route to the detention facility.

Up ahead I saw some cars turning left. I figured they were locals who knew an alternative route so I followed them. Sure enough, they went down a residential street and over another bridge. This bridge was a little higher and the water had just started to flood onto the roadway. Several cars tried to pass anyway and succeeded. The water was only a foot deep on the bridge, so I carefully followed several other fools over the bridge holding my breath that I wouldn't be swept away down the water.

Fortunately, I made it across and eventually made it back to the main highway. At 3:45 I arrived at the Johnson County Detention Center and asked to see Otto Barringer. They put me in a small room with a chair facing a thick glass screen with a small hole so we could talk. A minute later

Otto was let in and the door locked behind him.

"Otto. Thanks for agreeing to meet with me."

He shrugged. "Why not. What else do I have to do?"

"Are they treating you okay?"

"Yeah. It's just so boring in this place. I don't have anything to do."

"I bet. Listen, we don't have much time so I'll get started. There are a lot of unanswered questions I'd like you to address, if you don't mind."

"Fire away," he said. "I'll tell you what I know."

"After you killed Lottie and the dogs, what exactly were you looking for when you searched Lottie's place? The art treasures?"

"No. I knew they weren't there. Lottie wouldn't keep them at her house. They were much too valuable. I was looking for a safety deposit box key. Lottie told me Uncle Bill kept the treasures in a safety deposit box. She wouldn't say where, but I figured if I had the key I'd be half way to finding the treasures."

"I see. So, is that why you were following me?"

He nodded and smiled. "And that's why I broke into your office. I figured you must have the key. Did you?"

"Yes. I did. But I haven't been able to find a bank that uses keys like that. Do you have any idea where the safety deposit box might be?"

"No, I'd check up around where my parents live, though. I know they used to bank up there before they moved to Dallas. One of those small local banks. That would be my guess."

Otto and I talked until 4:25 p.m. when a guard came in and warned us to wrap it up. I thanked Otto, wished him well, and started to leave, but he looked at me like he had something to say. I waited.

"You know, Mr. Turner. I didn't mean to kill Lottie, I just thought she'd pass out for a while and then wake up. I just had to get rid of those damn dogs so I could search for the key. I tried to revive her, I did. But she wouldn't wake up."

I smiled and said, "I believe you, Otto. You never struck me as a killer. If we find these art treasures, I'll be sure to tell everyone that you were instrumental in their recovery. Maybe that will help when it comes time for your parole."

He nodded and I turned and left. The rain had subsided considerably by the time I left, so my journey home was much easier. When I got back to the office I pulled out the Texas map and wrote down all the small towns in the area of North Central Texas that Otto had suggested. There were forty-five that showed up on the map and I knew each one probably had a First National Bank or a First State Bank. Unfortunately, they all were independent so I'd have to contact each one.

Contacting them by telephone wouldn't work because I'd end up on hold or playing telephone tag for weeks. Mail would have been another option but that would have a slow process as well. I finally decided a sightseeing trip was in order. The next day was State Fair Day and the kids had the day off, so I suggested to Rebekah and the kids that we go up to Lake Texoma for the weekend. I didn't mention, however, that we were taking the scenic route.

After stopping at eleven banks the kids started to complain about the delay at getting to Lake Texoma, so I told them we were on a treasure hunt. I told them about the Ludinburg Art Treasures that were stolen after World War II and that there was a good chance they were at one of these banks. I showed them the key and said that this key would open the box that held the treasures worth millions of dollars.

After that there were no more complaints. In fact, the kids started fighting over the map and arguing how to get to the next bank. When we arrived at each bank, they all rushed inside with me and listened attentively as I quizzed the first bank officer who would talk to me.

We stopped at a Dairy Queen for lunch and I showed the kids pictures of the art treasures and explained the history behind them. They were amazed that an American would have stolen these treasures and then hidden them for over forty years. It was around two-thirty when we rolled up to the First National Bank of Pottsboro. It was located in an old brick building downtown. There were only a few customers and everyone looked up when all six of us walked in. An elderly lady spoke up.

"Can I help you?" she said.

I walked over to her and said, "Yes, I'm Stan Turner. I'm an attorney in Dallas and have been appointed the executor of the Estate of Lottie West."

The ladies' face showed a hint of recognition. "Lottie died?" she said.

A rush of excitement hit me like a brick. "Yes, I'm afraid so," I said, trying to restrain my joy which I knew she'd misunderstand. "Several months ago."

"Oh, what a shame. I really liked Lottie. I didn't know her that well, but she seemed like a nice person. Are you here to close out her account?"

"Yes, and clean out her safety deposit box."

"Of course. Do you have the key?"

I nodded and pulled the key out of my pocket.

"All right. I suppose you have your letters testamentary?"

I opened my briefcase and pulled out the document she wanted and showed it to her. She looked it over and then asked for my ID. I showed her my driver's license and she compared my face to the photo.

"You can't be too careful these days," She said. "There are so many thieves out there these days."

"Boy, ain't that the truth," I said.

She turned and walked toward the vault. "This way," She said.

We all followed her into the vault and into a room containing hundreds of boxes. The kids looked around in amazement. She went over to a large box and slipped in the key. Then she produced her master key and put it in the lock. She opened the door and then motioned for me to help her pull out the large box. After we'd put it on a table, she left.

Everyone gathered around as I opened the box slowly. We all peered inside. A gold and silver jeweled goblet glistened in the dim light of the vault. It was lying on its side partially hiding a large book of immeasurable beauty. I looked up at Rebekah, tears welling in my eyes.

"We found them! We found the Ludinburg treasures."

The kids started yelling and screaming with joy. Everyone in the bank heard the commotion and came running in. I had embraced Rebekah and we were laughing and hugging each other. They all looked at us like we were crazy. I told the kids to quiet down and then began to explain to them that they were to bear witness to a great moment in art history. I went up to the box and pulled out the golden goblet and held it up. They all gasped at its beauty. Then I carefully pulled out the other treasures, one by one, until they were all on the table.

"Ladies and Gentlemen, behold the Ludinburg Collection!"

THE STAN TURNER MYSTERIES
by William Manchee

Undaunted (1997)
Disillusioned (2010)
Brash Endeavor (1998)
Second Chair (2000)
Cash Call (2002)
Deadly Distractions (2004)
Black Monday (2005)
Cactus Island (2006)
Act Normal (2007)
Deadly Defiance (2011)
Deadly Dining (2014)

"...appealing characters and lively dialogue, especially in the courtroom . . . " (*Publisher's Weekly*)

"...plenty of action and adventure . . . " (*Library Journal*)

"...each plot line, in and of itself, can be riveting . . . " (*Foreword Magazine*)

"...a courtroom climax that would make the venerable Perry Mason stand and applaud . . . "(Crescent Blue)

"...Richly textured with wonderful atmosphere, the novel shows Manchee as a smooth, polished master of the mystery form . . . " (*The Book Reader*)

"...Manchee's stories are suspenseful and most involve lawyers. And he's as proficient as Grisham . . . (*Dallas Observer*)

"...fabulous-a real page turner-I didn't want it to end!" (Allison Robson, CBS Affiliate, *KLBK TV, Ch 13*)